Winchinchala

Winchinchala is the daughter of Seawolfe, Sagamore of a Wôpanâak (Wampanoag) Indian tribe of Massachusetts and Joy of Austrian descent. Studies, work and curiosity have taken her around the world. Its history, peoples, their myths and her life experiences inspire her stories. Many of her characters' psyches have been affected by familial dysfunction and trauma, areas she confesses she is "sadly too familiar with."

Winchinchala is a graduate of Columbia University in the City of New York where she earned her MFA in Film/Writing and B.A. in social anthropology. She won the Warner Brothers' Award for *The Tea Party*, a screenplay. Prior to a decade as a professor at Berklee College of Music in Boston, she spent one teaching at Boston University. Currently she writes full time.

iv

The Life & Loves of Mariner JACKIE VIK

A Sexy Paranormal Historical work packed with ACTION, MYTH & a SECRET Shhh! Don't tell.

dozens of period photos

by
Winchinchala

Also by Winchinchala

FICTION/ NON-FICTION

Sexy Solitary Suicide & That Beat-Hippie Indian Chick, a trip
thru the Racism & Changes of the 50's & 60's
to Overcome Depression (2011)
Hope, an Unfinished Diary (2012)
Only Human Short Stories (2011)
Seinfeld & Neeneemoosha Sweetheart (2012)
A Little City Indian in the 1950s (1997/2013)
Derriere: Premiere Seat to Writing (2012)

POETRY

Sexy Solitary Suicide & That Beat-Hippie Indian Chick, a trip
thru the Racism & Changes of the 50's & 60's
to Overcome Depression (2011)
Series: Sexy Red/Crazy Yellow/Bohemian Blue (1992)

TV /SCREENPLAYS

SEINFELD Episode: "Schleppen Feathers" (1997)
Remote Man, a play ©1990/publication 2002
SAVING GRACE (1982)
THE TEA PARTY (1979) Winner of Warner Bros. Award

SELECTED VIDEOS (writer/producer/director: Winchinchala)

The Empress Dowager's Robe (2001)
Reflections of An Evening (1999)
Young Lovers' Christmas Cowboy Caviar (1998)

The Life & Loves

of

Mariner

JACKIE VIK

People With Wings Illustrated Books
Since 1992
Boston -- Denver -- Amsterdam - Paris

People With Wings Illustrated Books, 2013 Edition

Copyright © 2011/2013   Winchinchala & People With Wings

Printed in the United States of America.

Library of Congress Cataloging-in-Publication Data
ISBN 9781889768311
The Life & Loves of Mariner JACKIE VIK, /Winchinchala 1st ed.
Cover design by Winchinchala /Cover:
First Edition: People With Wings Edition

10 9 8 7 6 5 4 3 2 1

With Gratitude to the Great Spirit.

Dedicated to:

Seawolfe, my Father
&
F. T. Tabata

Contents

Acknowledgements

Jackie Vik nagged me to get him into the world for over a decade. I could not have created him, a Norwegian-American man, a Merchant Marine or his 1940's world without inside information. I owe heartfelt thanks to the many who took time out of their days to share their knowledge and experience on the following:

* United States Merchant Marine:
Seawolfe, Sagamore of the Chappaquiddick Wampanoag Nation. Seawolfe is always a fascinating man to speak with. Not only have I been told that by hundreds of people over the years, but I know that as his daughter. Through his magnificent, innate storyteller's ways, he conveyed first hand accounts regarding the culture, language, customs & rules of mariners ashore & aboard ship. Seawolfe also generously shared recollections on how things were in society in the 1930's, 40's & 50's

Professor Joshua Smith, Professor of History at the Merchant Marine Academy, Kingsport, NY

Christopher B. Havern, historian at the United States Coast Guard Office –

* United States WWII Policy in historical context.
Anders Stephanson, Rudd Professor of History at Columbia University in the City of New York

* Military Training & Combat Consultant:
Jon Tripp, AIG T&E CASS -Agent-In-Charge of Training and Evaluation, the Center for Advanced Security Studies & Para Military & Security Consultant

* Women in Academia in the 40's:
Barbara Sykes-Austin, Librarian, Avery Library

Susan Hamson, Columbia University Archivist, New York.

*Norwegian Language & Culture:
Kristin Sevaldsen of Lillehammer, Norway, founder of Musiko-
logen Productions an International Jazz Saxophonist, Music
Producer, Composer – Norwegian idiomatic expression; Nils
Velle Espeland, Director of the Norwegian Visarchiv (Norwegian
Song Archive) in Oslo, Norway – Shanty Translation and history.

*Greek Language Translator:
Yianni (John) Courduvelis of Lexington, Massachusetts & Ne-
mea, Greece.

*New York residences for servicemen in the 40's & 50's
General David Ramsay and Hazel Cathers, Executive Director of
the Soldiers', Sailors', Coastguard & Airmen's Club in New York
City. The club is located in the Murray Hill section of New York.
It was founded in 1919 by General John J. Pershing, Mrs. Corne-
lia Barnes Rogers & Mrs. Theodore Roosevelt, Jr. Its mission is,
until this day, "To promote the general welfare of men and
women of the Armed Forces of the United States and its Allies,
and their families, by maintaining and offering club and lodging
rooms."

Thank you's & love to my family and the precious few friends
who have been so incredibly supportive, in particular crooner,
Frank Tabata. CD Take One http://www.cdbaby.com/cd/tabata
"Thoroughly enjoyable renditions of great jazz standards interpreted by the best jazz musicians in Hawaii and a fresh new voice
that brings to mind some of the greats of the past."

Notes to the Reader:

Images: Readers have often commented that Winchinchala's descriptions create images in their minds, that they can "see what is happening." Despite her descriptive skills, she enjoys including actual images in her writing for various reasons. "In the case of *Jackie Vik,* I wanted to show the readers the ration stamps and letters from the government. I felt as if I was sharing paintings from the caves in which the U.S. WWII society is cached. I also added photos of a few key historical people with whom all readers might not be familiar.

Each was created or chosen with great care by the author herself. Almost 90% of them are period specific photographs, government posters and military documents from the Library of Congress or the National Archives administration, and most are in Public Domain. For the purposes of formatting, liberties were taken in adjusting the quality, size and appearance of the media, and changes in content were made so they would fit into the story.

Language: *The Life and Loves of Mariner JACKIE VIK* takes place during the pre-Civil Rights era in the 40's, 50's. Obviously in writing from that distant time words from that era used for homosexuals, women or minorities were used.

Inner Monologue: Inner monologue, meaning dialogue for a character speaking to him/herself can be done with quotes, with nothing or with italics. People With Wings uses italics.

Our readers are smart; they will get it.

Font/Spacing/Layout: People With Wings Publishing wanted readers to have an easy reading experience. For this reason, we have chosen fonts whose size and shape are reportedly easy on eyes. To that end, we have also provided additional centimeters of space between the lines of text.

Preface

The character of Jackie Vik, a merchant mariner from the 1940's came to me, as most characters in my writing and people in my life, out of the blue. While he was a handsome, respected, well-liked and financially secure man, who lived an adventurous life filled with travel and women, he was not to be envied. He was missing, what he though, the most important aspect of happiness, love. I brought him to life sixteen years ago in the short story "Aeschylus on Ocean Avenue." While a professor at Berklee College, many students read it as well as friends, and among that broad and varied audience, it passed muster. Feedback reassured me: "It's a sexy and romantic mystery." It would fit in *Only Human Short Stories*, perfectly. Upon another rereading, Jackie asked if I could add more of his life, particular people and events in the 40's. I had promised myself after writing *A Little City Indian in the* 1950's, that I would not write an historical work, but Jackie wouldn't leave me alone.

I had to dip back into my research. It brought me not only to a time but to a country with its own culture, dress, language, rituals, values, etc. Men wanted good jobs to support their families; women wanted good husbands to provide for their children, and they all wanted the "American Dream," a family and a nice house in which to protect it. A college education was not on the list, but the country had low unemployment rates, perhaps due to arms production. A huge shift from working on farms and in agriculture to the city and business was underway. Racial and gender issues were shamefully obvious; nevertheless, our citizens were unified. We recycled and grew Victory gardens, even in New York City, encouraged by our government. More than 20 million citizens in urban areas planted Victory Gardens. Foods were prepared at home and an attitude of community prevailed. Daily life involved recycling. Dry goods were sold in feed cloth bags whose fabric was repurposed into dish towels, pillow cases and clothing. Plastics had not entered the market place or our homes. Styrofoam and aerosol were not invented until the middle of the forties. Trash was almost non-existent because everything was saved, used or reused at home or given to the government for the war effort. Strange how we now struggle to be thoughtfully economical and recycle when it was once a way of life. Being community-minded, self-sufficient, environmentally conscious and economical was a way of life, as patriotic as joining the military as every man was compelled to do.

Victory Garden Poster[1]

---

[1] Victory Garden posters Office of War 1940s. [Image from digital collection, US Library of Congress.]

Looking at photographs from the time, hats are noticeably ubiquitous and jeans missing. Everyone is smoking and drinking, though not women, at least not publicly. Bars hung out "Ladies Invited," "signs, but women who accepted wouldn't be viewed as decent. Radio, though not everyone had one, was the major source of entertainment; thus, listening played a stronger role in communication, which was largely face-to-to face; less than half the population had telephones. Reading and writing were essential to the other main form of communication; letters were highly prized. Families and lovers had to wait patiently for word from their members who moved away.

I am grateful to my character for his insistence. I reveled in the historical sociology of the decade in which he lived, but of course, that is not why I wrote it. I am fascinated by the human condition, how we are human, our need for connections and how varied they are despite our similarities.

Winchinchala

Boston Massachusetts
January 11, 2012
November 1, 2013

Illustrations[2]

---

[2] Photograph Source: United States National Archives and Records Administration, (NARA); the Library of Congress, (LOC); the United States presidential and military archives and German National Archives unless otherwise noted. Artwork or collages based on other images are sourced only if recognizable.

[3] PD-Public Domain images are those which fall under the definition in the U.S. copyright law title 17 of the United States Code.

The Life & Loves

of

Mariner

JACKIE VIK

1

Running Away
into the Arms of Destiny

ackie Vik knew the meaning of hard work. Work was life. His was on a Merchant ship at sea which he had come to consider his home. With a contented heart, he spent much of his time on deck with the salt air in his hair and the weather of the world on his face. Hard-earned experience as a seafarer and his good nature contributed to his success in overseeing the perpetual care of the vessel, the quality of the work and the morale of his crew who performed it. The rich length of his days and nights had carried him to distant shores with a crash of men and laid him merrily tipsy in a patchwork of promiscuous sheets with a delightfully unholy glory of women. Once in a while, the future came to him in flashes; he saw unusual phenomena and beings and carried on telepathic communication with animals. This, his mother claimed, was due to his sixth sense, klarsyn, in his family's native Norwegian. At times, all he had to do was see a person or handle one of their belongings; scenarios of buried pasts, mysterious futures or present thoughts played out in his mind. A little insight was fine. Déjà vu diminished shocks for him, but he didn't like the flashes from the future because determining the likelihood of their unfolding with any degree of certainty was impossible which made them more unnerving than helpful. When any premonitions did come true, they played out exactly as they had in his mind. Over time the psychic glimpses mingled with the vast swath of reality he had seen and provided him great insight into human behavior, which he thought largely the same everywhere.

Jackie divided that sea into two streams, one sparkling with bright hopes for success, happiness and love and the other running dark with fears of loneliness, failure, pain or incomprehensible mysteries such as klarsyn. On occasion an animal might tell him something or others' secrets, pasts or futures unfolded for him, but he kept what he heard or saw to himself as his mother had suggested when he first discovered his keen intuitive ability. He liked people and he didn't want his powers to make them leery of him. One of his duties was aboard a vessel whose captain believed, as mariners sometimes do, that cats are good luck.

The captain had a cat named Liberty, and it usually stayed in his quarters. He had raised him from a tiny kitty, and he had a picture of him asleep on his hat. Not all the men were fond of animals; some were superstitious, and a few expressed their displeasure about Liberty being in the galley, but the captain defended his pet.

"Liberty's a lot better lookin' than the rats running around, don't you think?"

No one said anything after that, at least not out loud. Jackie liked Liberty who came to visit him in his quarters and curled up right next to him. Jackie sensed when he was approaching and left the hatch to the foc'sle open. One afternoon Liberty hurried in, but rather than hopping up with Jackie as he usually did, he meowed ferociously and paced around.

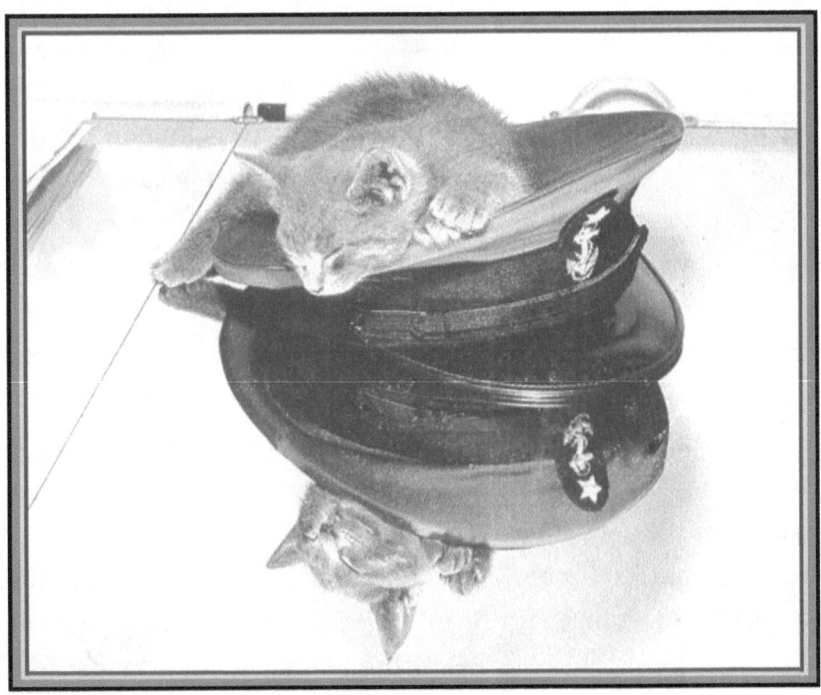

"Hold it. Everybody shut up a second," Jackie said. "What are you saying?" he asked Liberty softly.

The cat started toward the hatch and came back a few times.

"He wants us to follow him," Jackie said.

The men muttered their amusement but traipsed behind Jackie. The cat rushed ahead stopping to wait for them until he arrived at the hatch to the fiddly deck. There he screeched and yowled and then sat and stared at Jackie.

"What's he wanna dry his collar up there around the funnel or what?"

"No. Something's wrong. What is it!?" Jackie asked.

The powerful engine noise dominated the air, but Jackie thought he heard a loud, rhythmic banging which was out of place. Liberty continued to smooth himself against the hatch.

"You and you check down here," he said pointing, "and we'll go check up around the fiddly dee."

As soon as Jackie stepped through the hatch, the cat pattered up the narrow metal ladder and the banging grew louder. On the fiddly deck, Bart, one of the greenhorns, had taken a spill; he was on his back writhing in pain and pounding the railing with one of his clogs. Jackie took it and removed the other. Bart's foot and leg had blown up to twice their size. Unsure of exactly what injuries he had sustained, Jackie didn't want to risk moving him. He dispatched a couple of the crew for the medic and a stretcher, and the rest to their respective duties. He was alone with Bart.

"When they ask you where your shoes are, say 'somewhere.'"

"No they're .. ." Bart began.

"Just do what I tell you. The captain's liable for your ass, that's why he's big on 'your shoes fittin' right,' as he says. On duty, you have to wear gymnasium shoes or the black leather,'" he paused, "anything but clogs. Got it?"

"Yeah Boats, I got it."

The medic and one of the crew took Bart down the ladder to the infirmary. Jackie heard them ask.

"Where's your shoes Bart?"

"Somewhere around here," he answered.

Jackie gave him a thumbs up and lagged behind on the main deck. When they were out of sight, he flung the clogs overboard and went to Bart's quarters to get a different pair which he dropped off in the infirmary to make it appear that he had been wearing the correct shoes. Liberty followed along. A shot of morphine allowed Bart to temporarily dismiss the pain and welcome Jackie with a smile.

"Purser says he can't tell where the break is till the swelling goes down."

"Sorry kid. Whaddya wear those clogs for anyway?"

"I'm only five-six and a half without 'em," Bart whispered.

"So. How tall do you have to be to hang a pair of skivvies for crying out loud?"

"It's just habit," Bart said and hung his head in embarrassment.

"Habit knocked you on your ass. You're only seventeen. Men grow till they're in their twenties."

"Oh yeah? Is that when you got so tall?"

"Well no. I was always this tall."

Bart laughed and drifted off from the painkiller, so Jackie left with Liberty in his wake.

"Good job sailor. Maybe you'll get a promotion," he told Liberty who meowed in response.

Ever since that day, a couple of members of his crew were a little leery of him because he could "talk with animals." He worried that if the crew really thought he had mysterious powers, it might cost him their respect; an essential component of his repertoire as Bo' sun, a position he held dear and one he had paid his dues to get.

With mild embarrassment, he recalled his initial mariner's days several months after the end of the war. He marveled at the massive size of the ship, at least four hundred feet plus long by fifty odd wide with a mast so tall he was certain it tapped into the stars. The one in training had not reached anywhere near a hundred feet, and it had to be scraped and painted like every other inch of the vessel, a terrifying task. To alleviate the insecurity and dizziness and to bolster his courage, he indulged in a fantasy his mother had put in his head. In her playful way, she once announced she was the Goddess Frigg who could fly when dressed in a golden falcon's robe. As her son, he assumed the pantheon of gods had a watchful eye out for him, and in this way, he was always safe and never alone at sea. Gulls and albatross or a glean of fish flashing neon green were the spirits of mariners or those lost at sea. Veils of fog brought apparitions of angels. Mermaids and Nereid's could sing him safely to shore or one of the gods and goddesses of the winged theocracy were there for him, though he would never tell the seamen.

Most were good guys but as is the case with any group, there were exceptions. Jackie sensed this with the burly, profane mariners who burned with fires in their souls which needed to be stoked by confrontations and violence with the weak to prove themselves and to feel alive. They preyed on the greenhorns or those they thought they could beat. As a fair-haired teenager, he had received lecherous stares, been invited to the showers and threatened when he declined. His innate strength was evident in the ease with which he handled the fifteen-inch-around hawsers, but he knew that would not mean much against more than one man. Aboard ship he took to sleeping with his back to the bulkhead and a knife under his pillow, a habit which he always kept.

He lay awake in the hot, cramped, dank foc'sle battling claustrophobia in the lusty perspiration and foul gasses of eleven other seamen and questioned why he abandoned his footloose life on shore for the restricted one at sea. Every minute of his days was scheduled. Alone on deck, in the middle of the ocean, the infinity of clouds and water rolling toward the intangible horizon reduced the enormous ship to a dot. It was a belief that stayed with him and saw him though the routine of his chores as an able-bodied seaman and the years it took him to rise to the rank of Bo'sun. With the winds of time and place lapping across his cheeks, he stood as a seasoned mariner observing the ripples and laughing at his younger self who had placed him there more out of a desire not to work on a farm rather than expressly to work at sea. Rumors floated that he had joined up because he was running from the law. He never denied it. The truth paled in comparison and could be found in a phrase he often used.

"At least this ship isn't a farm."

✳ ✳ ✳

Each summer for as long as Jackie could remember, his parents packed up their curvy, black Chrysler and drove up to the leaning, green pines of the Adirondacks. They dropped him off at his Uncle Rolf's farm where the elements of good and bad balanced perfectly on the scale of experience until he approached his teens. Then the heavy hardship of separating from his friends in the city tipped the scales down on the negative side so did the shift in his chores. When he was younger, he and his cousins were unofficially charged with licking frosting beaters, tending to the vegetable garden with his aunt, collecting eggs, chasing chickens, cloud watching and crawling through the clover hunting for a four-leafed treasure. The beautiful dandelion-dappled field grew rapidly into hay which had to be cut, dried and baled and that became their jobs. This monumentally arduous task began with prayers for a stretch of dry weather because if the hay got wet, mold and rot set in, though a bit of dew brought out its sweet fragrance. The job he detested most was mucking. The barn animals used the hay underfoot as a toilet, so it became a soaking wet, foul-smelling mat of filth. Knots tied around his stomach and gagged him every single dawn which sometimes inspired bouts of insomnia. The animals knew they were the cause of his distress. It upset him to see the big bovines, Vipper and Minvenn, lower their eyelashes in shame and apology.

Vipper and Minvenn

"Aww come on. Don't take it to heart," he advised with an offering of leftover dried pears. "It's us humans' fault for cooping you up in here."

They mooed in reply.

"I don't suppose you know where India is, do you? I read that cows roam free there. You two could walk right down the middle of the street. Cars have to stop for you. Pretty girls make marigold necklaces," he paused and stroked Vipper's nose. "Maybe in the next life," he told her, and she mooed.

Minvenn nudged him for her fair share of attention which he provided after he finished mucking. He never got used to the stench. It clung to his clothes and loitered in Uncle Rolf's pickup truck, so whenever possible, he rode out back in the open air.

He was of a mind to confess to his mother that he didn't like to go to the farm, tell her he loved Uncle Rolf's clan, including the animals, but his chores didn't challenge his mind, and one made him ill; he could not bring himself to say anything. The fossilized cycle of their lives had already been cracked by the war; he didn't want to be responsible for further damage. He needed another way out of it. The armed forces had given presentations at his high school before graduation, and he lined up afterwards along with most of the males in the senior class. The army recruiter asked him a few questions, but upon learning his father was already serving and Jackie was an only child, he advised him to "give some real thought" before leaving his mother on her own. Thinking deterred his action for a while, but the sight of his buddies' older brothers in uniform, the olfactory memory of the muck stench and a seminal wanderlust fueled his desire to join if not the army, another organization. He had heard the Merchant Marine was under the auspices of the Coast Guard and run by private companies, so the commitment allowed greater flexibility than the military; he could ship out and return regularly. His mother wouldn't be alone for long, and it gave him a valid and noble reason for not going to the farm. A Merchant Marine poster lured him into the recruitment office. He listened to the spiel about doing his part and seeing the world, and then he filled out the application on the spot.

"Swell, but you're not eighteen," the recruiter pointed out, "so you do need to have your mother sign, and we can get the ball rolling."

That evening at dinner, his annual sojourn to the farm came up. Jackie smacked his forehead and attempted to feign having forgotten about going somewhere he had gone every summer of his life. This was the first time he had not been open with her, in part, because her klarsyn usually tipped her off to what he was doing. He hoped that was not the case on this day. The air he needed to project his voice was trapped in his throat, and though he pushed, it only came in a low, sheepish tone.

"Oh sorry Mor. This year, I can't..."

When the word, "can't" struggled out of his mouth, it instantly unlocked the knowledge she had long ago cached in the dark recesses of her mind. Almost from the moment of Jackie's conception, she felt he was Neptune's son and would inevitably be drawn to make life there. "The sea is his destiny," she told her brother Rolf when he visited summers and watched Jackie running into the foam at the shore. Her words were true. Now, he was sitting in front of her reporting he was going to sea. The sensation of her husband, Paul's hand on her belly swollen with their energetic baby came to her with the pangs of labor and her boisterous newborn's cry which was so loud, the midwife covered her ears in jest. Every single day for the years since she had delivered Jacob in the upstairs bedroom, she had seen him, fed him, hugged him and watched him grow into a handsome young man. She set her fork on her plate, lowered her eyes to her lap and with unexpected nonchalance spoke.

"So the sea has called...,"she said with a weak smile.

Her calm demeanor indicated to him that she had no objection, and he bounded out of his chair to embrace her and give her the document. Suddenly he stopped.

"If you want me to stay...need..." he was too excited to think.

"You have to live your own life Jackie, but do think about it. It's a big decision," she said, walked to her pen and ink, signed the application and tucked it between the salt and pepper shakers.

That night, he did reconsider his list of options on which, out of fairness, he included the farm, but he crossed it off immediately. College was next. An in-depth study of mythology and folklore appealed to him. His grades were excellent, but he hadn't applied anywhere because of the war. He had intended to continue in Vik's Woods, the family's shop for wooden arts and carpentry; he had always worked there part-time. After graduation he turned full time, and being inside all day was stifling. The workers complained no one could find him for twenty minutes or more when they needed him. That left going to sea, being with men and "doing men's work," as the recruiter claimed. One of the Navy recruiters at the high school had hushed his voice as if he was letting him in on a big secret.

"In the Navy, there are brothel boats that'll bring the girls right to the ships."

"I don't need any help with girls," Jackie blurted out reviewing the carousel of women with whom he had exchanged kisses in Times Square on V-J Day.

His naïve honesty flicked the grin off the Navy recruiter's face, but he thanked him, shook his hand and left.

Still he worried about his mother. From his bedroom window, he watched her hat bobbing with the motion of her hands tending to her garden, her precious garden where she was one with nature. Peacefully pruning, weeding or watering, she was the personification of contentment as was her way whatever she was doing. Cooking at the stove, shopping or working in the store she hummed. Painting the town with their family friends, Larry and Nancy, she chatted cheerfully. They had become regulars at many of the jazz spots. They saw Billie Holiday often enough for her to greet them as if they were old friends.

Jackie chuckled when he heard Billie speak because her language was rife with hot swears, "colorful language," as Nancy preferred to say. Larry said, "She could make a sailor blush, but she's a sweetheart." Jackie's favorite photo of her had been taken in her dressing room with her dog Buster. Two large gardenias, her personal signature, adorned her hair and Buster, who had the most human- looking eyes of any dog he had ever seen, wore a wide leather collar. He perked up when Frigg came into view; she invariably had a piece of lamb tucked in her purse for him. On the brink of changing his life, a little twinge of sadness crept over Jackie as he realized, his mother was fully occupied and probably did not need him. How like the yellow roses she grew delicate and soft to touch yet able to survive the winds and the first snows. She would most likely be fine without him. And so he picked, option four, the sea.

The next stop in life was the Sheepshead Bay Training Center. He wrote home on a weekly basis. Part of one letter read, "Just came back from the two-week training at sea. It's swell Mor. It's a little like Uncle Rolf's farm. There aren't any animals, but we have chores every day. I guess wherever I go, there will be chores."

Not being caged in the furniture store or standing up to his ankles in reeking animal muck saw him through his rise from Ordinary Seaman to Able Bodied Seaman. Every now and again when tedium or homesickness set in, the question of why he was there came up. In the beginning, his brain always replied, *It's not the farm*, but overtime it spotlighted sights whose magnificence had seared themselves into his memory in detail: a glorious melon dawn silhouetting the tropical trees of a faraway coast; the Great Barrier Reef awash in brilliant azures or snatches of the sultry brown beauty and a kittenish green-eyed blonde whose sumptuous curves he had recently explored with his face. Promises of more ravishing shores and their cache of comely girls eager to dance and laugh and be bedded rendered the hardships of life at sea into trifles. While he had joined to escape the farm, see the world and save money, he stayed because, after the subsequent handful of years, he had developed his intimate bond with Okeanos, the sea.

He had shipped out many times and met dozens of mariners. They all had different reasons for being there, traveling, catching or losing a woman, chasing adventure, maybe running from the law, but only a rare few were on board because of that bond. The greenhorns brought out all of his empathy. Being away from wherever they called home was stressful: jumping at commands from an intercom, the Bo'sun's pipe and clanging bells, working regularly at odd hours, living in crowded quarters, scraping rust, painting and scraping rust again easily wore away even the most impassioned of neophyte spirits, but not his. He enjoyed it all, and he tried to bring others to that frame of mind, keep the deck crew upbeat and out of the doldrums, though it was not part of his official duties. He sometimes brought his record player with him. They knew Jackie was aboard when they heard Georgie Auld's swinging, "Stompin' at the Savoy." Anyone who worked with him considered him a Bo'sun who was fair, well versed in the laws of the sea and an "all-around good guy," so crewmen never openly confronted him. His size was a deterrent though anyone who thought about it. At 6' 4" without his cap, he was more than a head above almost all men in any given room. He had long legs and a long torso squared off with broad, manly shoulders.

The pride that came with his official, silver Bo'sun's pipe and sleeve patch, after he earned them, lengthened his striding farmer's gait. One female admirer, of whom there were many, ran her eyes up to his head, down to his feet and back up to his razor sharp jaw.

"You ooze power. I wouldn't want to scrap with you if I was a guy," she said, pressed her warm body against his and cooed seductively, "Lucky for me, I'm a girl?"

"Lucky for me is more like it."

With playful passion, he dipped her on the dock. Part of an Irish saying from a menu ran through his head, '*A pretty girl and another one,*' and then he hoped, *maybe this trip to South- ampton, I will meet my love who is more than a love.*

II

Ashore

in

Plymouth, England

II

Ashore, in Plymouth, England

ackie's entertaining canon of tales was borne of his exten-
sive readings and trips to spots as faraway as a desert
fortress overlooking the Dead Sea to Pier 57 on 15th Street
close to his house in Chelsea, New York. No matter what
ship he was on, there always seemed to be one or two seamen
who knew his yarns, and they would attempt to ignite his mood
for sharing which was not easy to do. If the story was too well
known, it didn't give him room to embellish, or if it was too sad,
he couldn't be persuaded into telling it.

"Hey Jackie, tell us about that guy. What's his name?"

"Guy? I need more than that."

"The American Indian guy? He was holed up in the Philip-
pine jungle and…!"

"Oh Lieutenant Colonel, Edward McClish, U.S. army, a Choc-
taw. I don't know enough about it. There is a book about him."

"What's the one about the Jews burning themselves up?"

"You mean the one at King Herod's fortress? It's too hot to talk about mass suicide by fire. But what a damn shame. Guess it was better than being had by the Romans, what a gruesome bunch, considering what they did to Jesus."

Whether he gave the short or the long version of the horror of Herod's Palace, his audience always offered exclamations of disbelief and somber rumblings of sympathy for the hundreds who were driven to kill themselves. The listeners' reaction was the reward for him. No one knew it, but he practiced his stories and reaped satisfaction from his ability to hold the people in suspense or get them to react at a particular point. The legend of the young lovers of Guam was one of his personal favorites to tell. He had perfected his delivery so the audience was absolutely captivated, at least until he got to the epilogue. There, the spell inevitably broke which always bothered him. Over the years, to no avail, he tried to adjust his presentation, so he could suspend disbelief a little all the way through. One afternoon, a possible solution popped out of the big cigar box where he kept odds and ends, and he decided to try his story again the next time an opportunity came up.

It did one night when he and Smitty, the third mate and a life-long friend from home, went carousing. At a pub on Union Street in Plymouth, England, they floated into the river of murmured banter punctuated with loud greetings and good-time guffaws that ran beneath the jukebox music bouncing off the walls of the half-empty room. They cozied up to a comfortable table and observed the early birds unwittingly strike poses along the bar broadcasting their availability. Jackie listened to Smitty's usual monologue on his favorite and least favorite topics, his son Joey's intellectual and athletic accomplishments and his impossibly ill-tempered, Italian wife, Gina. She had the ability to drive him to the brink of violence with her shrill voice and slaphappy hands. Jackie paid attention for the first five years, and then he let it roll off his back. He knew he couldn't help and Smitty wasn't really expecting him to; he just needed to unload. When he was done, they dipped into a silence and sipped their pints. Surreptitiously they sized up girls in the place and those on the way in. They hoped for that millisecond of eye contact igniting a spark of mutual attraction. Two caught their attention at the same time. They traipsed in clinging tentatively to their coats and purses. One thrust her jaw up in greeting at the bartender.

"Colin," she said and wiggled her fingers, "Duncan around?"

He shook his head. The girls' eyes flitted around for a spot to sit. Behind their hands, they consulted and then occupied the table adjacent to Jackie and Smitty. To have a good view of the room and space for their legs, they moved the chairs away from the table. One was smoking and twirling her hair. The other one was swinging her bag and scanning the door every thirty seconds or so. Jackie admired the scanner's fingers as she fondled a charm sparkling like a star over the deep ravine of her cleavage. With a tiny jerk of his head, he indicated his preference for her. With Smitty as his companion, Jackie was confident their night was going to be a success because, though Smitty was shy at times, he was easy going and good-looking. Smitty cleared his throat and addressed the girls' backs.

"Hello there. Could I ask you something?"

"Oh brother," Jackie muttered. "Real smooth," he added when Smitty didn't get a reply.

Smitty presented his face to Smoker by leaning his chair back and into her space where he balanced unsteadily on its two hind legs. He tried again.

"Hello there."

The girl shot him a coquettish glance. Their eyes met, and the hoped-for spark of attraction ignited and held his body there longer than the chair legs were willing before dumping him on the floor.

"Oh!" the girls exclaimed and leaped up.

Jackie's chest and shoulders shook with stifled laughter, and he offered Smitty a hand.

"You're supposed to break the ice man, not your ass," he told him under his breath.

Undeterred, Smitty dusted himself off, tapped Smoker on the shoulder and beamed, "Sorry to bother you again."

"No bother. Are you quite all right?" she asked twirling the ends of her hair.

"Quite," he echoed. "Thanks. Could I ask you a question?"

"Depends. . . Is it, 'Can I buy you drink?'"

Smitty shook his head.

"Is it, 'Hey Angel, are you lookin' for your way back to Heaven?'"

He knit his brow in disapproval.

"Is it, 'What's a nice girl like you doin'. . .'"

"I am hopin' you're not that nice."

"Is that so?" she tittered.

"Guess what I do?"

Jackie laughed to himself and tried to think of a line that would get them back underway after Smitty ran them aground.

"All right then. A sailor,"

"Seaman," he corrected her.

"Seaman," she echoed.

"Yes. And a magician. Let me show you."

Smoker uncrossed her legs and rested her chin on her hands

with interest. When Scanner swiveled around, the glint of Jackie's Bo'sun's pipe caught her eye. She had never seen one quite like it, silver and so ornately decorated with Chinese dragons, even the lanyard was unique. She followed it to Jackie's powerful arms folded across the solid wall of his body and up the ribs of his turtleneck sweater to his waiting gaze.

"Nine two five. That's for silver, right?."

"That's right. Know what it is?"

"That's easy," she answered and tapped his Bo'sun's insignia with her red lacquered nail. Without taking his eyes from hers, he waved his hand at the barmaid for a round.

With exaggerated fanfare which included a small bow from his seat to each of the three, Smitty pulled a coin out of his pocket. Jackie softly blew his Bo'sun's pipe to mark the beginning of the trick. Smitty borrowed the cigarette Smoker was about to light.

"May I?"

Very carefully, he applied pressure to the filter end first, and pushed it straight through the coin. The girls gasped in amused surprise.

"How did you do that then?" Smoker asked.

Jackie gave a big laugh, "All the years I've known you and I never saw that one before."

"I can't tell you everything," he said with a wink and returned the cigarette to Smoker.

"Give it," she demanded and held out her hand.

"Can't. Trade secrets," he replied but pulled a coin from his pocket.

"What is this?"

"A coin, a magic coin from Guam. You been there Jackie, haven't you?"

"Sure. Couple times." The barmaid arrived with a pitcher and two extra glasses. "One of the most incredible stories I ever heard is from Guam."

"About the dragon that ate that boy?" Smitty asked seriously.

Smoker tutted. "Oh go on. Dragons?" she said in disbelief. "There's no dragons..."

"You say," Jackie cut in, "but there are," he flung his arms out, "and they're eight, nine, ten feet long, right Smitty?"

"That's right. And a few hundred pounds."

"And they eat people?"

Smitty lunged forward and planted a noisy, sucking kiss on her neck. She squealed and squirmed in her seat.

Jackie noticed Scanner's eyes still moving back and forth to the door. He didn't want to be a third wheel to Smitty and Smoker, so he returned the sultry gaze of a petite brunette on a stool at the bar. Feeling his gaze running down her shape, she arched her back. The glint from Scanner's charm recaptured him.

"Are you telling the story or not?" Smoker asked excitedly.

"I don't know. It takes a while, and there's just the two of you..."

"Two?" Scanner asked, took a breath almost heaving her breasts out of her blouse and counted, "Three. I'm here."

She and Smoker dragged their chairs closer.

Encouraged, Jackie began with his prologue.

"There's a sea captain in it. He could be from Spain or France or Japan. Whaddya want?"

He always invited his audience to choose, so when he imitated the accent poorly, they recognized it. Since Pearl Harbor, Spanish was usually the pick. He made voices for all his characters which helped him captured his listeners and set the scene.

"Let's do a little time travel and head for the 1890's out on an island in the middle of the Pacific; although, it doesn't really matter when we get there. A tropical paradise is always a tropical paradise. It's what you call lush with palms swaying in the air full of plumeria and jasmine; there are bright orange and white striped fish gliding through water, light blue here, turquoise there, dark in the middle. The beach is white sand, pure white, soft like confectionary sugar. Gorgeous and peaceful. Suddenly, a girl comes, running and giggling, all arms and limbs, no top on, so her island pleasures are bouncing on her chest. She's running from a young, island buck, right behind her, handsome son of a gun. Big. And all over, you know?"

He grabs the wooden pepper mill and holds it straight out from his crotch, and they all laugh.

"Oh grinding love. That's the best kind," Smitty interjects, and the laughs rolls on.

"Don't I know it? Anyways, so there they are, their teeth filling up their faces with happiness. A couple of clouds drift in front of the sun and dim the day. Together they say, 'Taya' mina'lak sin hinemhum.' I heard it means there is no brightness without the darkness. They go on with their flirting."

Smoker lights another cigarette, and Smitty drops his arm around her shoulder. Scanner has forgotten about the door and sits with her elbows on the table and her chin in her hand.

"The wind is streaming their long, black hair behind them. The skies and everything are grey, but not around them. They radiate that," he snaps his fingers to recall a word, "aura, that sunny glow you see around soulful people and star-crossed lovers."

A good-size group had gathered around the pub table, and Jackie got a little nervous. He knew well that there were countless stories of tragic love that had been told and retold. The only difference was the names of the location and the man and the woman. Undoubtedly everyone had heard one version or another, especially seamen, so he felt pressured to add small details and deliver it with more than usual theatrical flair.

"Inina, the girl, is from a local family, not too much dough and they have four daughters. This one is a real knock out. Inapo, the boy, really loves her, so he goes to his family and says he wants to marry her. She's the one. To his face, his mother argues, 'Inina? No Inapo. No dowry. And she's too pretty. The pretty ones never want to do their share of work.' His father agrees and asks him what is wrong with his cousin, Tadtasi. Inapo blows up. 'I don't love her, and one of her eyes doesn't open all the way. That's what's wrong with her. You don't understand,' and he storms off. Behind his back, his parents laugh at how upset he is cuz they're just teasing him. In the meantime, along comes the new Spanish Captain, takes one look at Inina, and he wants to marry her too. He's been to enough islands to be wise in the ways of their courtship. He puts on his dress uniform with the fluffy tassels and brass buttons to present himself to the father. 'That's kind of you Mr. Captain, but there is no dowry,' he tells him. The captain is shocked. 'You gonna pay me?! Your daughter is so beautiful, I will pay you.' He clapped his hands and his crew dragged in a trunk full of small mirrors, dishes, cooking pots large enough for an entire goat's head and bolts of fabric. It was a whole lot of nothing' that looks like something if you don't have much and you never saw it before and..."

Jackie reaches in his pocket and throws out a handful of coins that bang on the table with a jingling clatter.

"And of course there was silver and gold, not much to the captain but it was a lot to the father. It could be a dowry for his two younger daughters. Across the room his wife is waving off the deal. Little tears run down her face. The father goes to her. In his ear she tells him, 'I got enough pots. What about Inapo and Inina? They are in love.' Her voice tugs at his heart, but not his business sense. He shakes the captain's hand. Later on he explains the logic to the Missus. 'Inina has to suffer marrying the captain, not so old, not that bad looking. She can endure being rich, so her sisters might get good husbands too.' The wife is not pleased, but she accepts what he says because she is an island wife, but she does insist he tell Inina. When he does, he speaks very softly. Inina shakes her head back and forth, but he talks and talks and talks. He uses words that she has to listen to such as honor, obedience and respect. By the time he finishes, she is nodding. That night she tiptoes to Inapo."

Jackie taps on the pepper mill and winks.

"The next day when the captain shows up? Inina is gone."

A sailor, agitated with the music in the pub, hollers over to the bartender, "Colin. Col! We can't hear!"

Jackie's gestures, voices and facial expressions had the desired effect and the group before him sat spellbound. He waited for the volume to be lowered and repeated a couple of words.

"So Inina is gone. The captain shouts '¿Qué? You have my money. ¿Donde está mi novia. Bring her or, I gonna kill you!'"

Jackie demonstrates by grabbing Smitty by the throat and pretending to choke him until his tongue falls out the side of his mouth.

"To save their father, when the sisters spot Inina, they tattle, 'We saw them on the beach!'"

Jackie holds up his fingers to count off.

"The father, the captain, Inapo's parents, the soldiers; the whole village heads over. All morning they go in the caves, beat the bushes, even shake the cocoanut trees, but they don't see them. The captain smells a wild goose and draws his sword, but one of the sisters yells, 'Up there!' All eyes turn to the cliff. There they stood, Inina and Inapo sharing a kiss. That aura was shining like a huge diamond halo over their heads. They had woven their hair together in a fat braid that hung right in the middle of them. 'Inina!!' her father cries, but he was too late. She and Inapo jump. And right there in front of the whole village and their mothers and the midwives who brought 'em into the world, they left."

To create the sound of their bodies hitting the ground, Jackie dropped himself down hard on one knee.

"And then silence. For a whole minute," he whispered, "nothing moved. No birds. No wind. No waves. The ocean was perfectly still, just a mirror full of grey sky."

Slowly he rose to his feet with his Bo'sun's call in his mouth piping *The Still,* used to demand silence on the ship. He played it for a full seven seconds.

"And you know what? They never found those kids' bodies."

"The Komodo Dragon ate them!" Smoker guessed.

Scanner blotted away a tear. A few compliments ricocheted among the listeners. Smitty who now had Smoker nestled on his lap, gave Jackie a congratulatory punch in the arm.

After basking in his success, Jackie held up his hands.

"Wait. Wait."

Jackie pulled out his epilogue.

"The thing is, over the years, anybody who went to the spot heard voices, and not just the locals, visitors from faraway places who didn't know about Inapo and Inina. The reports were always

the same, 'Laughter. It sounded like two young people laughing.'
After a German woman and an American man said they heard,
'Taya' mina'lak sin hinemhum,' in addition to the laughing. The
story spread through the village that the two lovers were living
in the caves, so the mayor sent a crew to investigate. You know
what they found?"

"The Komodo Dragon," Smoker blurted out.

"Forget about the dragon. They found Inapo and Inini. They
were fossils, covered in limestone, lying right there next to one
another."

The disbelief began.

"Aw go on," came from several directions.

Jackie acknowledged the naysayers, "I know. I know. It's
incredible," I didn't believe it either, but..."

He reached inside his coat, snapped out a black and white
photograph and laid it on the table. The power of the image
morphed the remarks of ridicule into those of astonishment.
Eyes were widened with surprise or narrowed with suspicion in
examining the image of what appeared to be two humans
covered in a dusting of limestone in a cave. Jackie swaggered by.

"I took that myself last time I was there."

He followed the picture as it was passed from hand to hand
among the audience. A wave of perfume from a newly formed
constellation of girls chattering at the entrance distracted some
of the men. As they moseyed toward the bar, they pat him on the
shoulder.

Jackie, vindicated of his earlier failed endings, gave himself a
congratulatory pat on the back. On the chair where Scanner had
been sitting, he saw a scarf which he collected, and then he
joined Smitty. The girls were engaged in a conversation by the
wall that involved vigorous head shaking and arm waving.

"Did they get away?"

"Let's give 'em a minute. You've been working on that story Jackie."

"It's the picture."

Two small pins on Scanner's blouse sparkled with the jiggling of her breasts.

"Let's have a drink while they decide which one gets me," he declared slapping his chest and grinning.

"You already picked, besides Smoker gave me the signal."

A ruddy-faced Royal Navy sailor as tall as Jackie and a half breadth wider barged into the pub and jerked his head back and forth.

"Over there Duncan," the bartender called out loudly enough to warn Scanner.

He headed right for her, and at the sight of him, Scanner lowered her head and inched behind Smoker. Duncan grabbed at her and ended up with a handful of sweater which stretched as she pulled away. Duncan followed the trajectory of her gaze through the maze of drinkers to Jackie.

"What? Him?"

As soon as he released her, she hustled over to Smoker who had joined Smitty. Jackie and the sailor assumed a combat posture, eye to eye with their feet firmly under them and their arms folded high on their puffed up chests. The girls were too short to see what was going on. Smitty gestured for them to stop straining, and he craned his neck to see.

"They are just standing there," he reported.

Smoker inched in closer to him. The force of the men's steps thudded toward each other, a table crashed and banged onto the floor and the patrons cheers topped it off. The bartender hopped up like a Jack-in-the-box over the bar and pushed through.

"No punch-ups in here," he announced firmly and disbanded the crowd.

Smitty asked the girls to wait outside, and he tried to find Jackie who had disappeared. He found him in the head with Duncan whose face was contorted in pain. Jackie had shoved him against the wall and twisted his arm behind his back. When Jackie saw Smitty, he let the sailor go and leaped back. The sailor straightened himself out and knocked into Jackie as he left. Jackie threw some water on his face and calmed himself down.

"Let's get out of here," he told Smitty.

They bought a couple of bottles of booze and resumed their evening at the girls' flat. As singers and actresses at one of local theaters, they joined right in when Jackie shook a tune out on their tambourine and belted out a Norwegian shanty. A few of the words were Norwegian which Jackie sang and the rest of them muddled through.

"Kan du danse Polka?" until they got it. "My dear, Annie Oh, you New York girl Kan du danse Polka?!"

The lyrics ran around his head the next day as Scanner's fine silken hair spilled across his bare chest and tickled him. He stroked the soft strands and nestled into the warm spot his body had made in the bed. He felt at peace with the world. She yawned. The light streaming in the window glinted off that charm on her neck which Jackie saw clearly for the first time; it was an anchor with a diamond on it. He flicked it a few times and it illuminated a memory from his childhood. His mother was at the kitchen table writing a recipe. A bracelet dangled from her arm with a similar charm. He toyed with the anchor around Scanner's neck.

"Anna? Is that your name? Anna?"

"It's Asta. You have the most remarkable eyes," she said as

more of an observation than a compliment.

"I got 'em from my parents. Thank you."

"If you had a beard," she studied his face, "and you were a couple stones heavier, you could be that big statue in Florence. I think it is Perseus or Neptune."

"Oh. You mistook me for a god. Is that what got me in bed with the prettiest girl in the place?"

Asta giggled, searched the ceiling and said, "In part. My mind was not made up until the last moment. I do have a fella, you know?"

"Ha. That joker Duncan?" he interrupted. He whipped the sheet and it billowed like a great white cloud over them. He rose to his knees and admired her body. "Look at you—you're gorgeous. Duncan doesn't deserve you."

"Who said he had me all to himself?"

"Everyone you are with should deserve you," he told her as she toyed with the hair on his chest. "So what else about me?"

"The photographs were quite unexpected. A big burly seaman like you with little pussies in his pocket."

A couple of smart remarks came to him over her British use of the word "pussy" for kitty, but he didn't want to be vulgar even though he was leaving and unlikely to see her again. He wanted her to have a good impression of him because she was a genuinely sweet girl.

"Did I tell you? That hole in the gun where the cat is sitting is only six inches."

"Inches? How many centimeters is that?" she asked.

"This many," he replied and made a circle with his hand. "It's dangerous to have the animals aboard, but we seamen love 'em."

"Yes. Duncan said..." she stopped herself, "I wish you could stay."

"I can, but just for a little while."

In the pale grey shadows of the lace curtains, they basked in the quiet comfortable, closeness of long-time lovers.

"Say. What do you do, you Merchant Marine fellas? You're not soldiers, but there are plenty of you in the war."

"Nice pillow talk," he replied with a grin propping himself up on his elbow. "Too bad, we won't know us longer," he said and traced her lips with his finger and continued, "There's something about you... 'We deliver the goods,' that's our motto. It's like the theater, same word even, Pacific theater, European theater. The producers are the governments; the actors are officers and soldiers. And just like actors, military guys need... you know..." He knit his brow trying to recall a word.

"Props and sets you mean?"

"That is what I mean. Merchant Marines are the stagehands in the world. I been on ships full of rum or grain, sugar. In the war, those guys took tanks, boots, and medical supplies. I didn't start 'till after that, but a couple of years ago in 1954, we evacuated a few hundred thousand people…"

"From North to South Vietnam. I read about that" she interjected.

"You like to read?"

"Goes with acting," she said and bussed him on the mouth.

Wrapped together, they fell back asleep until her alarm clock rang. Asta went directly to the closet and he to the bathroom.

"Asta, I had a good time," he called out. "I mean it."

"So did I. It's an open rehearsal if you want to come."

From the doorway, he caught sight of her just as she was donning a colorful robe.

"Hold on a minute," he ordered sternly.

Curiosity widened her eyes and tilted her head and he grabbed his camera.

"Damn! No more shots left."

"Make believe," she suggested letting the robe fall around her shoulders.

He adjusted the settings, and she struck several seductive poses throughout the room.

"You are something."

For the last one, she hopped up on the velvet cushion by the vanity table. On his knees he approached her for a low angle. He slid his head between her feet on the cushion, and delighted in the view.

"Just one more, a close shot of the kitty"

"I'll give you a close shot," she said and meowed cutely.

Slowly, she lowered herself toward his face, but she lost her balance, and they collapsed onto the floor in paroxysms of unbridled laughter. Each confirmed that the other was not hurt, and he buried his face on her privates for a moment and then pulled away.

"I have to go."

With a hearty swipe, he cleaned his mouth on the back of his forearm and crawled up her torso to kiss her, but she recoiled.

"No!!! Not with that gob. Come on."

"I am sorry I can't make the rehearsal. Never forget you, er, ah…" he snapped his fingers. "What's your name again?"

"Asta!" she shouted playfully, and then mimicked him. "Yeah, what's your name again?"

"Me? Depends on where I am. Sometimes, Darling, and Sweetheart, sometimes aboard ship, the guys call me Boats, you know for Boatswain, but mostly I'm Jackie. Jackie Vik," he said and struck his bare chest with his palm.

Asta rolled her eyes and led him to the shower. A half an hour later, he emerged refreshed, shook off like a wet dog and pulled on his clothes. At the bedroom door he paused and considered asking where the theater was or exchanging addresses, so they could stay in touch.

"Bye Asta!" he boomed instead.

"Cheers then, Jackie. . . Jackie Vik!"

Her smiling voice inspired his desire to stay, but he ignored it and snatched open the door. Smitty was outside on the steps smoking a cigarette.

"Man is it cold," Jackie noted.

"You don't have to tell me," Smitty said, and rubbed his hands together.

"What a nice broad."

"Yeah mine too…" He offered him a cigarette, but Jackie declined.

"I have a good taste in my mouth."

Smitty shot him a curious glance and asked, "Jackie, before I forget, what did you do to that guy?"

"Guy?"

"In the pub last night, The Royal Navy guy? You turned his arm into a pretzel."

"Ah Duncan. As Roosevelt once said, 'When you see a rattlesnake poised to strike you, do not wait until he has struck before you crush him.'"

"What did you do to him? He just walked off."

"Look, this is exactly where we are standing," he said plucking a postcard from the spinner. He held it up and compared the view to the card. "The cars are a few years older, but...I'm getting this for my mother; show her where I've been."

"You always do Jackie. So what did you do?

"Nothing. We came to an understanding."

"An understanding?"

"Right. He understood he needed his arm," he said with a smirk.

Smitty kept looking over his shoulder. He stopped and waved.

"I knew she would come out to the street."

"What do you care? It's not like you're going to see her again. Say good-bye and shove off!" Jackie said and smacked him with his cap.

"Ow Whaddya do that for?"

"Knock some sense into you. Don't get stuck on one skirt. Go for *all* of them and your ding-a-ling will always have a triangle to beat. Go for just one and you'll end up making music all by yourself in your foc'sle or whatever you do."

"I have Gina, so..."

"A wife you can't stand? And not for nothing, but you're the only man I ever met who can't swing adultery in New York, so he can get the divorce he wants."

"I told you. I could beat her bloody, and she wouldn't give me a divorce. Gina's not just Catholic, she's Italian."

"What's that mean?"

"Divorce is a mortal sin."

Jackie shot his eyes back at Asta's apartment where they had spent the night and said with a grin, "I got pictures."

"Me with some chick in a pub…"

"Pub? No this is the little striptease on the kitchen table," he chuckled recalling the moment and grinned. "Yeah. That was a good time."

Smitty watched the ground and shoved his hands in his pockets. Jackie slapped him on the back.

"Just don't take any shit from Gina. She punches you or throws things, leave or you'll end up in the slammer. Remember, my house is your house Smitty."

"Thanks. I may take you up on that."

Jackie then heard the soft tintinnabulation of bells, and he was certain he was going to see a yellow rose. That's what happened before, the bells rang and the rose appeared. One shivered in the sea breeze, and he ran to it in a panic and snatched it up. His head oscillated like the needle of a compass first searching around and then he looked up and scanned the sky. All he saw were clouds and birds.

"Jackie you're nuts," Smitty told him with a laugh.

"You know Smitty, I think you're right."

Aboard ship he bellowed out a poem as the gulls screeched and glided overhead.

"'Goneys an' gullies an' all o' the birds o' the sea, they ain't no birds, not really, they're not mollies, or gullies, nor goneys at all, but simply the spirits of mariners living again,' or something like that."

The men had grown accustomed to Jackie's recitations. He swore to anyone who would listen that the screams, sighs, tears and laughs of those who wander alone and grieve by the sea, perish in it or love in its presence are memorialized by it.

"For all eternity Okeanos churns and tosses their sorrow and pain, their joy and passion for all to hear. You just have to listen."

When he wasn't on the sea, Jackie gravitated toward it. He read the messages written on the surface in ripples, wavelets, crests and whitecaps. They told of the depth, the location of rocks or objects jutting up to the surface and just what kind of relationship the water was having with the wind that day. Was it peaceful and reflecting the whole sky in a great glassy picture? Was it fanned by a soothing breeze and sighing out streaming ribbons of grey and silver? Was it frolicking in intermittent gusts and kicking up a mirth of white caps? Or was it pissed off from the pressure, foaming at the mouth and shooting spindrift in the air? For hours he observed the interactions of the wind, the sun and the moon with the sea, his home.

When will I find my love who is more than a love? he asked himself.

Fifteen years of dating had paraded a pageant of beauties in front of him, every size, shape and temperament: waitresses in aprons; ladies in furs; island girls in leis; Asian dolls in dresses slit up to their fortune cookies and on and on around the world. He separated them in two, day and night. Day-girls were sweet, possessed of an almost palpable vulnerability. Their soft hearts overflowed with nurturing kindness and their heads with pastel fairy tales of the pure loves they had but lost to the war or other unfortunate circumstance. They often became martyrs and enjoyed the attendant sympathy and respect, so it was in the guise of accepting his help in the house they sought his companionship. They seemed compelled to convince him they were "not that kind of girl," one who picks up or is picked up by men. Yet the sugar from which they were made melted on the hot iron skillet of his manliness. By morning, their pillows were invariably under his head and their bodies tucked by his torso. Night-girls were impertinent, racy, and callous. They were the scorned and the promiscuous, slumming debutantes; the career barmaids; the too-tipsy hussies or the outcasts. Being perceived as desirable and spinning their sugar into the fluffy fun of perishable cotton candy was the obvious name of their game. Tingling first night flirtations fast became last nights by dawn, so they could walk away physically satisfied and emotionally untouched. Girls, by day or by night, were available for a dash of flattery, a smattering of attention or a sturdy shoulder. Each was a land unto herself, and as with the ancient ruins, he exploring them wholeheartedly, all of them. In slaking his desires, he felt as if he was combating the tragic pandemic caused by loneliness in the world, but he had grown weary. He returned home once more with the delightful memory of Asta and the renewed hopes of finding a girl with whom to settle down and share true love, the kind his parents, Frigg and Paul had.

Neptune Fountain, Florence, Italy

III

Young Lovers &
A Son who
Sees Beyond

The Beach in Norway

III
Young Lovers &
A Son who
Sees Beyond

On her way up the stairs, Frigg Vik, Jackie's mother paused in front of the sketch of the Norwegian shore on the wall, a gift from Paul, her husband. Viewing it took her back to the summers of their teens when they frolicked on that exact spot where the sea meets the trees, and their friendship revealed itself as love. Magical clouds of morning fog floated on the forest floor and softened the path to the verdant clearing leading to the beach. Onto the mounds of rockweed and out to sea they streamed and then hung in the air until they were lifted to the sky by the slim, hot fingers of afternoon sun. The gritty sand would tickle Frigg's feet as she walked to the fringe of the water, an uninviting 60 degrees even in Midsummer. The only rule she made, which she insisted Paul follow, most adorably he thought, was that he not chase her into the icy sea. It was a promise made but broken at moments most unexpected by his mischievous, adolescent spirit excited by her squeal. Frigg's request and the tingling anticipation of Paul's pursuit were the prelude of their romping sand dance. She participated enthusiastically until one day at the end of the second summer when, as usual, Paul threw seaweed and chased her into the water. Instead of giggling and running away, her face reddened and she threw pebbles at him. The birds flapped out of the trees with a chorus of caws. Apologies bounced back and forth between Paul and Frigg, his for not keeping his word and hers for frightening the birds.

The image of that shore warmed her heart on the stairs of their home as much as it did in the long-ago reality; his careful pen had captured it so well. She could see herself with Paul pausing under the tree's canopy to admire the sun's brief departure. It was there she had fallen under the spell of his piercing, blue eyes; they twinkled in the match flame he put to the very first cigarette she ever smoked. He plucked it away and pressed his lips against hers in their first kiss. Many more followed, ebulliently sought and shared, propagating their feelings for one another throughout the Scandinavian summer nights full of bright daylight. When the season ended, they carried the memory of their giddy smooches across the Atlantic, held them in their souls and reminisced in letters about their days by the shore until June came again. This act of their lives ran for two more years. They always met at that same spot on the beach near their grandfathers' homes where they were separated by a field rather than the hundreds of miles between their homes in the United States, hers in Hudson, New York and his in Leesport Pennsylvania. By the time she was sweet sixteen and he almost eighteen, they realized they had an unbreakable connection which extended into the past and future beyond the beginning and end of the universe and time.

They basked the summer away in the light of each other's company. They bicycled, canoed and lolled in the hay every chance that presented itself. As the days inevitably grew darker so did their spirits because it meant their imminent separation was drawing near. One of their last nights, they put their heads together to come up with ways to meet in the States but ended empty handed. In the overnight hours, Paul found one. This trip, he was going to New York City, to live with his uncle who owned a furniture store, *Vik's Woods*; he signed on as a woodcarving apprentice. Frigg sat in silence, so he clarified. He had a naturally deep and commanding voice, but he tempered it to speak to Frigg.

"New York City is half the way to Hudson."

She understood. They would be much closer, and she emitted one of the squeals of which he was so fond. A burst of excited energy boosted her onto the big, smooth, rock they usually shared together. Anxiously, she inquired about the earliest date he could come to Hudson. Instead of answering or climbing up and joining her, he paced back and forth and dug in the sand with his heel. A smattering of fear mingled with her elation as she waited nervously for him to say something.

"Papa told me last night, I will be working long hours. New York City is nearer to Hudson, but…," he stuttered and stammered in English, but she wanted to hear it in Norwegian.

"Fortell me i norsk Paul," she urged impatiently.

"Jeg tenkte om oss, og jeg tror...

"Ja. Ja…" she said impatiently.

"Vil du gifte deg med meg?"

"Ja. Jeg vil gifte meg med deg min elskede," she answered his unexpected marriage proposal and leapt down to kiss him. "

"Men hvor?"

"What do you mean where? Here."

"We want our family in the United States too."

"Here and there. Both. Why not?"

"With the enthusiastic glee of the freshly engaged young girl she was. she agreed. In that blazing, white summer night, they enjoyed another first and conceived Jackie.

On the stairs of the home they made together in New York, her eyes traced the lines of the drawing framed on the wall, and she was there again. She felt again the sensation of the ground on her back and the, thick tendrils of fog which had arisen from the icy water on her face and breasts. She was sure it was Njord, the god of the sea because his apparition had lumbered onto the shore and ghosted into Paul's body before they gave themselves to one another. They had not made love before, but they had been intimate, and Paul's approach to her body was awkward, slightly clumsy and impatient. That night was different. There was a power in his hands, a tension in his muscles and deliberateness to his actions, and at the climax, he roared uncharacteristically. The fog lifted and then, as if struck by an arrow, Paul grabbed his chest and collapsed on her justifiably spent. A stork flew in front of the moon, and they joked about it being a sign that they had, "made a baby." As it turned out, their playful words were true and hastened their weddings and the beginning of their life in New York as Mr. and Mrs. Vik.

The pregnancy cast a euphoric spell over Frigg and painted apple son her cheeks. She felt a deep psychic connection to the new life she carried and was sure they were communicating telepathically. A calm came over him when she strolled by the sea, and he kicked in delight over their music. Paul played the fiddle and she sang. At her urging Paul would put his hand on the curve of her belly to feel his son kick. Despite relatives and friends' belief the baby was a girl, Frigg was positive he was a boy.

Young Lovers & a Son who Sees Beyond

"I am sure of it," she argued. "He will be a big, strong, manly Viking who will travel the world like his grandfather."

Frigg was eager to welcome her son who she decided to name Jacob in honor of her father's family name, Jacobson. All the usual questions gnawed at her. How would he look? Would he have Paul's handsome jaw and sparkling round eyes? And to herself, she hoped he would he have her klarsyn, though she knew those with a sixth sense faced challenges. It spooks people without it, but those who share it, have a special connection. She had that with her grandmother who, according to her grandfather, passed it on to Frigg. She would love her baby whether he had it or not. Her true desire was for him to have all ten fingers and toes, and twenty digits were present ad counted aloud when he entered the world weighing a whopping 10 lbs 6 oz.

As soon as Jacob could hold up his head, he tipped it to the side and focused his captivating blue eyes as if listening intently. Visitors often remarked that he was a "good baby," because he only cooed and never cried. Frigg attributed this to the connection she had with him which allowed her to tend to all his needs before he had a chance to fuss. If he awakened hungry during the night, she was sitting next to him. She carried Jacob along with her throughout the day in his white, wicker bassinet. If she was gone from view for too long and he wondered, as baby's do, if she was coming back, she sensed it and presented her proud face. After he outgrew the bassinet, she moved him to the walnut crib Paul made for him. It was a sturdy crib, not at all portable, so she had to leave him two flights up while she tended to the house. Being away from the baby heightened her hearing, but on one occasion, the sound of silence raced her up the stairs two at a time. She paused in the doorway. Eighteen-month-old Jacob was sitting in the corner of the crib quaking with sobs squishing a piece of banana she had given him, another was at his feet. It was whisked away by a small, dark hand with long thick claws. Frigg gasped and sneaked slowly closer. A raccoon, bigger than the baby, was sitting in the lower corner of the crib gobbling up the banana. With the speed of a spark, she had grabbed a nearby blanket, tossed it over Jackie and stood in the kitchen with him in her arms and the raccoon locked in the room. That evening, Paul trapped the animal and drove it to Central Park where he let it go.

By the time Jacob was eight, Frigg had let thoughts of his having psychic abilities fall behind all the other considerations in raising a boy. She saw what she needed to see, that he was healthy, intelligent and happy. To her delight, he was also very curious; she thought that was an important quality in a human being. He asked about everything. When reflections danced fairy-like on the ceiling, they searched for their sources. The most recent was traced to an anchor charm on her bracelet. He manipulated the light by tapping it as she sat reading a recipe in the kitchen. She rarely wore it for fear that she would lose her only memento of her younger sister Anna. When they were children, Anna had contracted consumption which was highly contagious, so she was sequestered in the guest room. Frigg was forbidden from seeing Anna from a distance closer than the door which upset both sisters because they had fallen asleep next to each other every night of their lives. To assuage her insomnia, Frigg visited with Anna after the house went to sleep. They chatted in whispers until they felt tired and said, "Goodnight." Anna was not improving. The next evening she didn't say "Goodnight," but "Good-bye." Frigg inched closer than she had ever been allowed or ever dared. Anna's plump cheeks had waned to hollows. She had grown so thin that her favorite bracelet slipped off, and she kept it under her pillow. She slipped it into Frigg's hand and asked her to keep it until she returned. Love trumped fear and warnings of illness, and the young Frigg leaned over and kissed Anna's face. In the morning, Anna was whisked away to a sanatorium; Frigg never saw her again. She didn't know why, but the family never spoke of her sister; there were no photographs. It was as if she had been an imaginary childhood friend. She felt guilty for having almost forgotten her. Young Jacob kissed her hand, and Frigg returned from the past to the kitchen.

"What happened to that little girl?"

Goose bumps ran down to the ends of her fingers and toes.

"What girl?" she asked nonchalantly.

"The one that coughs and coughs."

Frigg did not wish to excavate her little sister from the recesses of her brain, but it was obvious, Jackie had inherited a bit of the sixth sense. To avoid the topic of Anna, she completely distracted him with an offer of his favorite treat, Eplekake, apple cake.

Two years later Jacob had a clairaudient experience that brought his teacher, Miss Reed and the principal, Mr. Warren to their front door. They were in pursuit of an apology from him.

"He told other students Miss Reed is in a family way," Mr. Warren charged.

He pushed his glasses up on his nose. Frigg was aware of the law dictating female teachers be unmarried and the damage a rumor of being with child would do to a woman's reputation and career. She feigned shock and anger on behalf of her "wildly imaginative boy," and promised to speak with him; he did after Miss Reed and Mr. Warren had gone.

"Is it a boy or a girl?"

"A girl," he beamed. "So *you* believe me? Not them. Don't they want to know?"

"Gutten min, what people know, what they want to know, and what they want others to know is complicated."

When he scrunched his nose in puzzlement, she leapt up and playfully flung her shawl over her shoulders.

"Jacob, you are the son of Frigg, patron of marriage and motherhood, Norwegian goddess who was very clairvoyant. That means once in a while, you may hear things or see things in your mind that others cannot. It's klarsyn. It is best to keep it to yourself."

"So if something bad is going to happen, I am not to tell?"

"It is not a fact, only a sound or a vision; it is not fortune telling. You cannot change what will happen. It is a prologue to what might happen or has already. A fire for example. You sense a fire; see the orange color, maybe you hear a person scream. Stay away from that place or leave with your friend, maybe you will save yourself. If you yell fire and nothing happens, you will upset people, make them doubt you."

Experience proved his mother right. Plagued by the sound of fire truck sirens and firemen discussing Hansen's Market, the corner store owned by their family friends Fred and Nora Hansen; Jacob ached to warn them. Frigg's warning prevented him from saying anything, yet he didn't think he could live with himself if there was a fire and he hadn't at least mentioned it. He asked his mother.

"Should I keep *that* to myself?"

"Do you know a hundred percent there is going to be a fire? One hundred percent."

He shook his head. He said nothing. The big fire never came. A week later Nora was visiting with his mother in the kitchen, and she had a bandage on her hand.

"Oh, it's nothing," she told Frigg. "A candle fell over, and we had a small fire in the kitchen."

Jackie and his mother exchanged a knowing glance. Jackie was relieved, but he was not sure he wanted to have psychic flashes; they were very anxiety inducing. Eventually, he noticed they didn't come if he kept his mind occupied which was not difficult to do.

His parents encouraged his curiosity, intelligence and talent very chance they got. When his fascination with the artistry of his father's Hardanger Fiddle escalated to interminable questioning about how to make the sounds, his father bought him one and showed him how to play. He was determined to master the fiddle as he had so many other skills. He could do almost anything he set his mind to but learn the instrument. Discouraged and too embarrassed to ask for help, he put it away. Paul and Frigg told him about Fossgrimen, a supernatural spirit who lived in the waterfalls and whose violin talents were unsurpassable. He would give lessons to aspiring fiddlers who found him providing they brought him a good piece of meat, but he was far away in Norway.

"Some say your father plays as good as Fossgrimen," his mother said and whispered, "and he is very fond of cookies."

Jacob screwed up the courage to go to his father; he took a handful of freshly baked cookies. Paul laughed when he saw them and began the lessons right away. Hundreds of cookies later, Jacob was still struggling to produce a something other than a ghastly screeching on the strings, but the sound kept his psychic visions at bay, so he persevered.

A sense of pride filled him for a whole week after he and "Mor and Far," as he introduced his mother and father to the pupils at his school, performed for show and tell. He played a very short tune and concluded by deprecating himself.

"I'm just beginning. Okay, now this is how it really sounds."

Paul dazzled them with blazing fingering and bowing. The excited students stamped their feet and at the end whooped and applauded. Jacob wanted to be as good as his father and to spend time with him, so he practiced more and more.

Bryllupsdagen i Norge/Wedding Day in Norway © Winchinchala

IV
Big Changes &
Small Observations

Happy Birthday Jacob

IV
Big Changes &
Small Observations

nder Paul's tutelage, the sounds Jackie produced on his fiddle were eventually musical enough for the woodworking door to be left wide open. He closed his eyes and lost himself for hours and hours. Frigg and Paul were most supportive. The only time they asked him to stop was for the "Fireside Chats" broadcast from the Whitehouse to which they listened as a family since Hitler's invasion of Poland in September of 1939.

The Vik family tuned in and sat around the radio rapt with attention. Mr. and Mrs. Vik wanted the United States to follow the British and French example and declare war on Germany, and end the madness. The president admitted he had been awake until four thirty in the morning praying for a miracle to "prevent a devastating war in Europe and bring an end to the invasion of Poland by Germany," but to their utter disappointment, the remainder of the speech gave no hint of military assistance. On the contrary, he insisted on the United State's continuation of neutrality and referenced a book to which he thought all could relate.

"The New Testament -- a great teaching which opposes itself to the use of force, of armed force, of marching armies and falling bombs. The overwhelming masses of our people seek peace -- peace at home, and the kind of peace in other lands which will not jeopardize our peace at home." He closed with firm hope to keep "the United States out of this war."

Germany's occupation continued to the land of the Vik family grandfathers, Norway and to France which she and Paul had visited together as school children. Photographs of citizens' staring bewildered and frightened at the Nazi's barging into their cities touched the Vik family.

President Roosevelt's "chats" were heartfelt and compassionate. He did agree that the European countries needed help, so he urged citizens to offer it in the form of donations to the Red

Cross. He went on to assure listeners that the country's burgeoning arsenal of weapons and military personnel were ready and available to defend them and that he was appealing to God to end the conflict.

"Day and night I pray for the restoration of peace in this mad world of ours," was his conclusion.

"Ecclesiastes 3:8, 'a time to love, and a time to hate; a time of war,' is better my dear President," his mother said to the radio.

"Give him time Frigg. Believe in our old grandfathers. "

The knowledge that they were living under German Occupation gnawed at their souls, but they had to forge ahead, so they buried their heads in the sands of routine. Paul ran the store; Frigg ran the house and Jacob went to school and practiced music. To prevent themselves from obsessing about the war every day, Frigg and Paul limited discussions on the topic to once a week. Jacob was assigned the task of culling relevant articles from the magazines and papers and setting them aside. He also took the liberty of cutting out photographs which fascinated him, not the black and white depiction of events but the emotional reaction of those experiencing them. Why the cameramen was allowed to shoot them and how he could do so instead of sobbing or running away in terror was a mystery to him. The faces of mothers, children and grandfathers who could have been his own family were victims of war, not just soldiers.

A letter came from Grampa Vik postmarked London a week before Christmas. In addition to glad holiday tidings, he urged them not to worry because things were a little easier in the countryside where he and Grampa Jacobson lived than in Oslo, and assured them they were strong. "Vennligst ikke bekymre oss. Vi nordmenn er sterke. Det er ikke så vanskelig i landskapet som det er i Oslo."

President Roosevelt began his Fireside Chat, December 29th, 1940 with, "This is not a Fireside Chat," His mother sat in eager anticipation of an announcement declaring immediate action by the United States. The president delivered praise for the valiant fighting being done by the British and the "heroic Greek army" which was supporting them with "all forces of all the governments in exile." Frigg was very disappointed to hear him hold firm to his policy of non-involvement because, from what she understood, he didn't think the Axis powers were very strong. He remained unwilling to declare war.

Agreement and disagreement with his approach provided the foundation for many arguments among the Vik's friends who had immigrated to or been born in the United States. The last was a heated row that almost escalated to fisticuffs. It was the summer of 1941, and they had yet to hear from President Roosevelt which was fine by Frigg. She deemed politics and the war checked at the door of her house and expressly excluded the topics from Jacob's upcoming birthday party. She wanted his rite de passage from boy to adolescent to go smoothly. He was turning thirteen, though most people mistook him for sixteen because he was so tall. At times she felt silly introducing him as "my boy."

Just before the big day, Jacob strode in and announced to her and Paul that he was changing his name.

"Don't you like Jacob? We have called you that your whole life."

"He hugged his mother. "I do like it. I will always be Jacob, but it's a little formal. I want a friendly American sounding name... Jackie."

"You know Jacob is for my father and..."

"Okay Jackie," Paul exclaimed and cut Frigg off. "It might take us time to get used to, right?"

"Yes, Jackie," added his mother and mussed his hair, "Jackie, my handsome American son."

He shocked them a second time when he asked about the party guest list which Frigg wrote.

"Is Larry coming?"

"Of course," she answered baffled. "Why."

"Because...well he's Jewish, right? Should we have him here? What is wrong with them anyway?"

Paul and Frigg sat down with him to make certain he understood there was nothing wrong with the Jewish people.

"So how come Adolf Hitler has so many supporters?"

"He is their führer. He tells he doesn't like Jews; they are bad. They just believe him."

"That's stupid. Hitler should meet Larry. He would like him. Everyone likes Larry."

Paul and Frigg were disappointed Jackie's schooling had not taught him They took turns to sum up. "Nationalism is ingrained from a young age." "The German citizens were misled into believing the Polish army attacked them." "Germans are suffering from economic difficulties, and Hitler has "a special way to sound like he has solutions." An interesting discussion ensued and they were impressed with their son's thinking. He was, indeed, becoming a young man.

A "grown-up" gift was on Frigg's list for weeks, but she had failed to come up with one. She had clothes in mind, but he was already fitting into his father's hemmed hand-me-down trousers; they didn't have to spend the money. Paul thought a set of chisels would be good.

She agreed but dismissed the gift as too impersonal. Having watched him scrutinize the newspaper photographs so closely, she suggested a camera.

"Such an expensive gift Frigg. He's still a boy."

"No he is not. He is a teenager."

Frigg talked long and rationally and sweetly but was unable to persuade Paul until she told him she knew where they could get a "really good one, for free." That place was his workshop where he had three cameras which he hardly used because he was busy with his sculpting and the business. He thought it was a great solution. They put the original yellow box in a much larger one, so Jacob couldn't guess what was inside. On his birthday, the big gift challenged her to wrap it. She didn't have enough paper to go around it. Feedsack cloth fit, but left her unimpressed. Aluminum foil jazzed it up to her satisfaction. On top, she placed the tag, "To Jacob, Love Mor and Far," and set it on the table. All morning while she was cleaning house and preparing for the party, the shiny square called to her. She stopped and stared at it with her hands on her hips waiting to for her inner voice to give her a clue as to why, and then she saw it. She put an X through Jacob and wrote Jackie in large letters.

Grinning broadly, he lifted the lid. It was not any old camera; it was his father's best camera, the Kodak Regent. Paul noticed him hesitate.

"It's yours, son. Happy Birthday—Jackie," he said.

Jackie's mouth hung open in awe as his head moved back and forth between the camera and his parents. The expression on his face was thank you enough, but he said it at least two dozen times before he dashed out, with their blessings, to try it out.

"Don't stray. Guests will be here in a half an hour. You have to change," Frigg called after him.

The sun broke through the grey clouds and bathed the small, brick, front porch in diffused sunlight. He marveled at the clarity with which things appeared in the viewfinder. After he shot the leaves shimmering two feet away, he turned the camera toward the street. He wound the blurriness out and brought into view a lanky redhead and a plump little blonde about his age.

"Hello," chirped the red-haired with a tip of her head.

"Hello," added the blonde very shyly and averting her eyes from his face.

The pair played with their curls and dress hems. The little redhead struck a mature calendar-girl pose, but the other fiddled with her fingers.

"Come on! He doesn't have all day." her friend bossed.

They bat their eyes cutely and Jackie clicked the button on the camera. The redhead waved wildly across the street to a threesome of girls who rushed over.

"Take one of us girls all together, okay?"

They all mounted old Mr. Jamison's big, black Packard and perched on the fenders and hood; the red-haired girl sat in the middle. Bending her knees to push herself back placed her panties in clear view. Immediately a surge of blood throbbed in his groin and perspiration moistened his fingers; dainty white triangle in the shadow of her thighs had hypnotized him. Images of naked women's bodies he had seen at the peep show, oil paintings at the museum and French Risqué cards in the back of Mr. Mann's bookstore whirled in a Zoetrope strip in his head. None had hardened his body or awakened his desire as much as that dainty, white triangle. His involuntary physical response prevented him from moving in closer, as he wanted. He crossed one leg over the other. A prickly warmth came over him as he recalled the first time he had had that experience publically.

It was in the spring of the precious year. Larry and Nancy invited him and his parents to "the dinner hour at that clip joint on 52, Leon & Eddies." It was a music venue known for its burlesque acts usually late at night. That fine March evening Sherry Britton, a stripper unexpectedly performed during the dinner hour which meant children were present. The patrons assumed she would probably peel down to a set of flimsy undergarments, but she did not. To the strains of classical music with playfully dramatic eroticism, she removed every stitch of fabric except a tiny g-string, and then balanced two shot glasses of water on her firm bare-nipple breasts. From the corner of his eye, Jackie saw his mother shoot an inquiring look at his father who smiled and then to Jackie. He could not look away from the exciting figure of female perfection. His mouth froze open. He couldn't have moved a muscle if he wanted, though one had erected a tent in his lap until he pinched himself under the tablecloth. The porch provided no place to conceal himself, so he conjured up the image of the decaying cat carcass he and Bird had come across in the alley a week earlier.

"You are too far over," he told the red-haired girl on the fender and focused on the cat's raw guts oozing out of its stomach and nose and mouth when Bird dragged it across the dirt road with a piece of wood. It worked. Jackie stepped to the edge of the porch with his eye on the prize, spun his focus wheel and captured the sight with a click.

"Did you take it?" the red-haired girl whined impatiently.

He lied and said, "No," so he could get her to drop her legs and take one that was more presentable.

He kept his eye on the viewfinder.

"Say cheese, but..." he paused and gestured for the redhead to lower her legs.

"Sally!" The girls in front cried out in embarrassment pushed her legs onto the car and further screened her by leaning their shoulders together.

He clicked again. Old Mr. Jamison popped his head out of the window across the street. No one knew his exact age, but some say he was over eighty, and that he had fought in the Civil War. Jackie watched him push on his upper dentures in his mouth.

"Get off my car! And I mean now!" he boomed with a mighty gust of breath that blew the girls onto the ground and on their way, except the immodest redhead. She took ditzy little steps to the porch railing.

"So did you see? You saw, didn't you?"

Stathing the urge to grab her and hold her, he hung back, occupied him hands with the camera and made note of Mr. Jamison watching them. Undoubtedly, he would show up later to tell his mother that Jackie had girls sitting on the car, more because he wanted a reason to visit than tattle on him. Whatever behavior he was there to report, he usually forgot in about two minutes or as soon as Frigg served him coffee.

"You saw," insisted the girl saucily.

When he didn't say anything, her impetuous tone softened into insecurity.

"Didn't you?"

He leered at her, and almost under his breath answered, "I saw."

"I'm Sally," she beamed. "Who are you? Do you go to that high school on Bleeker Street? I live down there. Where do you live?" she fired at him rapidly, and then giggled at herself. "I suppose you live here."

"Yeah. I do. I'm Jackie, Jackie Vik, and I..."

He didn't want to lie and say he went to high school, but he didn't want to tell her the truth. She might run away if she learned he was only in the seventh grade.

With the graceless clomping of heavy, little girls' shoes, the round blonde dashed up and tugged at Sally.

"Come on," she whispered through her teeth.

The wind kicked up and he hustled down the stairs to see if their skirts flew up which they did.

"Good-bye Jackie," Sally called out.

"Good-bye."

When he waved, the camera swung on his neck, and he reached down to protect it.

I'll take one more picture, then I'll get ready, he thought.

Just then he heard the soft tintinnabulation of bells, not a lot, just one time through several notes. They sounded as though they were coming from the ground across the street, but all he saw was an enormous yellow rose. It tumbled softly in fragile, beauty on the rough, grey summer sidewalk. He centered it perfectly but sneezed. Lining it up again, he noticed a gentle nimbus with a pair of, pale slender hands in the middle. A visible aura shined, and he saw an apparition, a woman with long light brown hair. It hung to her shoulders in waves that rolled like the sea. He knew it was impossible, yet he could see the curves of the wrought iron fence behind her right through her blouse and skirt. The camera shook so much, he could hardly take the photograph, but he did. He wanted to snap another, but he heard a child squeal, and a man's voice yell out.

"Stop at the curb. Right there!"

Half way down the block, he saw the haphazard birthday-guest-parade approaching. The men wore hats and carried package-store paper bags and long-playing records. The women wore gloves and carried platters of food, and the children wore polished shoes and held hands except for his friends.

"Jacob!" Charlie yelled.

His father's hand delivered a swift whack to his head for shouting in the street. Jackie waved back, and turned quickly to catch a second photo of the woman, but she was gone. He looked around, but there was no trace of her or the rose. If the others were arriving, he should already be dressed, so the mystery of the woman and the rose would have to remain unsolved for the moment. He waved again and stole through the narrow passage between the buildings around to the back door, up the stairs and into the shower while the guests filed into the kitchen.

"Jacob can't be thirteen today. He's tall as tall as me," Larry declared.

"Who is Jacob?"

"I mean your son Jacob, Frigg."

"Oh. You mean Jackie?"

Larry laughed, "Oh brother. He really is thirteen," he said and turned to the others. "Did every one get that? Jacob is now Jackie."

"Thank you Larry," she said playfully and then made the introductions. "I think all have met before, but just in case, this is Larry Argent, our Mr. Art and Jazz."

"Right here. Right here," he said with a wave.

"He has a gallery in the village with three of Paul's sculptures."

Larry ran his palm over the wooden head of a doe and a fawn sculpture standing by the icebox.

"That one is mine Larry," she warned wagging her finger at him and pointed to Nancy. "This is…his…" her voice trailed of in hesitation because she knew they lived together but they were not married, "…our friend Nancy," she drew in a breath then blurted out excitedly. "She is studying for a doctorate in literature at Columbia University."

Eyes went from Larry's grey hair encircling a bald spot to his wrinkles to his paunch and then to Nancy's fresh face and youthful figure.

"You're wondering if she can cook," Frigg continued, "and yes, of course, she can; she brought the smoked salmon canapés and

Mousse de Sardines. This is Charlie and Ilta Muller and Bob Mann of Mann's Books," she pointed to the youngsters and prattled on, "the one who looks like Charlie is Charlie junior and the tallest is Bob's son Éan, it means Bird; Bill Edwards there is the pharmacist next to his wife, Phyllis. You have to try her vegetable turnovers," she said pointing them out, and "Fred and Nora Hansen, from Norway like us," she concluded, slipped her arm around Nora's waist and kissed her cheek, "my best friend who lives one block away."

Polite nods went around the circle as she finished.

"We made the scalloped potato and tuna casserole, and the rest. Help yourselves. And please, no politics today. Please!" Showered and composed in a crisp white shirt, and a double-breasted suit, Jackie strolled in to a cacophony of glad greetings and congratulations. Frigg brought out the cake to oohs and ahs and made sure everyone saw the name, "Jackie" written on top in blue icing, so when they sang Happy Birthday, they would get it right. He blew out the candles, cut the cake and directed the youngsters to the smaller table on the other side of the room.

Once the adults' jaws were sufficiently lubricated with light wine and heady gin, they buzzed on about the usual topics: their children's brilliance; the benefits of the new safety glass windshields; the last good movie they had all seen which they agreed was the comedy, *The Lady Eve* with Barbara Stanwyck and Henry Fonda. They all remembered "the honeymoon scene in the Pullman compartment," Phyllis and Nancy squealed in unison and laughed themselves to tears. Blotting hers away, Nancy lessened the levity by recommending a book, *For Whom the Bell Tolls* and giving her opinion of its author.

"Before I read Hemingway, I envisioned him to be a man who prefers the company of others like himself, gruff and rough with guns, drinking rum from bottles, on of those men who consider women accessories. The more I read him though… well… I still think he's rugged, but I suspect a sad loner, like his characters, vulnerable, susceptible to love. I haven't finished it yet, but… it is a case in point for war making strange bedfellows."

"It sure does!" Phyllis exclaimed, "Look at that Unity Mitford and Hitler. A high society British lady and … and… and… a crazy man who…"

She never had a chance to finish. The mention of the Nazi dictator's name veered the discussion headlong into the gravelly ditch of the politics and the war. A firestorm of emotionally charged opinions erupted into squabbles over the Nazi's advancements which Larry called "German events" in Antarctica, Greenland, Iceland, and the Cape Verde Islands.

"Look, Nazi's are closing in on the Western hemisphere. Is that close enough to merit action?" Fred asked.

"Did you guys read about the rumpus at La Guardia that Scottie dog…" Larry interjected attempting to change the subject.

"The Nazi's are close enough. We *should* help," Fred insisted.

"You want to help? Give to Red Cross, generously, like Roosevelt advised," Bill, suggested a hands length from Fred's face.

"Give to the Red Cross? Bill, if the Nazis win are ruling the world, there is not going to be any damn Red Cross."

"Hitler is not going to win. That's the point. He has to actually get a foothold in South America and…"

"South America? My elders are in Norway and…

"What I think Fred is that there are a hundred thousand of our boys' graves and a couple hundred thousand more missing a limb or part o' their mind from WW I and…"

"At least two graves have my uncle and my cousin. Don't…"

"Bill held up his left hand, "This is the United States," and extended his hand with the glass of gin as far away from his body as it would go, "and this is Europe where...."

"Where all people in United States come from, so..."

"Not American Indians Fred!" Jackie hollered from across the room.

"He means all civilized people Jackie," Bill said swirling his drink in his glass.

"You sound like Hitler," Jackie quipped, and everyone laughed at his cleverness.

"Sweden is right next door to Norway Fred. Maybe they will get over their chicken shit neutrality and help you. Why us?"

Fred was visibly upset and muttered to his drink, "Look Frigg, is right. No politics..."

Bill broke into a big smile and jabbed him in the arm. "Take it easy Fred. We're just talking."

"Ja well..." he pulled Nora close to him, and she patted his back, "This week, a couple of men came to our store from the War Department. U.S. is going to help."

"What's a couple of guys? That doesn't mean...."

Flustered, he lost his command of English and blurted out, "War Department informs us our telegram machine what we use for flower orders and money grams is now for receiving notifications. You know. Those Nora and me will be deliver when a boy or husband or father is wounded or missing. Happy now? You got your wish Bill. United States *is* going to war!"

"Mor. Mor! Mor!" Jackie repeated louder and louder deliberately interrupting.

Frigg's eyes crossed the room to the somber expressions of the youngsters who had stopped playing and sat listening. She clapped her hands with enthusiastic vigor and sang out.

"Partners please. Partners!"

Paul picked up his fiddle and played vigorously, so no one could hear anyone. They paired up, but Bob Mann was alone, and Larry took his hand and danced with him which helped recapture the festive birthday atmosphere. Frigg saw Jackie still sitting in his chair and took him a glass of ginger ale.

"Mor, Far is going to. . . it will be bad for him. I feel it," he hung his head.

"What an awful thought on your birthday."

"I saw him on a tropical island Mor. He was a mess in tattered clothes and the American Indians were ..."

"American Indians? Palm trees? Gutten min, listen to yourself. This is fear, your imagination. Come on dear. Enjoy your party. Who was that pretty girl I saw you with?"

'Don't you care about Far?"

"What? Jackie you know I do.

"Sorry. Jeg beklager Mor. I just worried," he said his voice resonating with regret and pulling her into his arms.

"Me too Jackie."

"So Mor, that pretty girl? I think I love her. I love her with all my heart."

Tingling with the thrill of hearing about her son's first love, Frigg moved her face close to his. "Love? You do? Tell me."

With a smile as wide as the street, he replied, "You! She is you, Mor!"

"Oh Jackie," she blushed and wagged a finger at him. "I see you are growing up to be a charmer like your grandfather Magnus."

Having broken the spell of discontent with his fiddling, Paul laid down his instrument. Larry put on a record, and Jackie danced with his mother until his father cut in. Paul enfolded

Frigg into his arms. His chin rested in her hair, and they danced elegantly as one. Their bodies and their psyches were in touch; this was their way.

She would sit on his lap with an arm slung around his neck and coquettishly offer him a tasty bit of this or that from the table, even if they had company. They finished one another's sentences, and on occasion, shared a simple glance that would send them into sputtering laughter over some secret they shared. Sunday's at the shore, one of their favorite places to go, Jackie's contemplations of the clouds and the behavior of sea were interrupted by the two of them running after one another or sauntering along holding hands like infatuated teenagers. If one of them went away, the one left behind changed. When Frigg would visit her brother on the farm, the scents of sawdust and linseed oil that rose from Paul's workshop were the same as any other day, but the sounds were not. The usual rhythmic chiseling of his wooden art by his careful craftsman's hands and the happy humming produced by his contented heart became a staccato of hits and misses and swears of frustration. Instead of being focused for hours at a time, he was discombobulated and the slightest noise on the porch hurried him up the stairs, outside, and back again.

When his father was on a hunt for the fallen trees he sculpted, Jackie saw him stride through the woods quite unfazed. He talked to Jackie about the trees in the low voice
one uses in a museum.

"Such mighty creatures, but a bolt of lightning can crack one right in half... Or a big gust of wind can blow it over. Only use the fallen, never a living tree."

Jackie liked that idea. On their last trip they came across trees felled by the wind, lighting and a beaver's busy gnawing; none was what his father wanted. That one they found early in the afternoon. Jackie followed him as he walked around it, rolled it over, and he contemplated its usefulness before selecting it. They sawed it into more manageable pieces which they dragged out to the car on a tarp. In a shady spot, they sat on a couple of weather-smoothed rocks and ate the lunch his mother had packed. Jackie wondered if she was flitting back and forth to the kitchen door as his father had when she was gone. He learned she was not when Paul went on another trip, and he stayed at home with her.

Well before daylight, she produced the dissonant clatter of several metal pots and glass mason jars in the kitchen. Jackie had to eat breakfast sitting on the couch because the table and counters were piled with crates of fruit. On the way home from school, the sweet aroma of preserves was noticeable a block away and became progressively stronger as he neared. Inside bushels of fruit covered the kitchen floor and chairs. Frigg had attached the apple corer and peeler to the counter and wound it with such vigor that wild strands of her hair hung onto her brow. Pots were steaming on the stove and so many pans of preserves sat cooling, one might have guessed a dozen women had been working, not his mother alone. She asked him to take the two cases of preserves to the cellar to shelve and to return with the box. She had been working hard. On the shelves, which were empty, last night was a double row of apple preserves.

Before another trip his father took, the manager of the Safeway and Fred Hansen at the corner store both asked Jackie jokingly if his mother was going to start selling bread. She had all but cleaned them out of butter and flour. He chucked and told them he doubted it, but their questions suggested she must be up to something. His return from school proved him right when pungent fishy vapors wafted over him on his corner. A wave of heat billowed through the front door which was propped open with one of the bowls lined along the porch and into the kitchen where there was a crowd of motley, crockery draped in feedbag cloths and dish towels. Frigg was bent in front of the open double oven with one of his neckerchiefs, which he thought he had lost, tied around her head American-Indian style; it was soaked through with perspiration. Five fish pies were visible on the racks in the oven, and by the time his father's trip was over, it had yielded at least three dozen more, mostly salmon, sardine and tuna. Larry Argent, Nancy and Mrs. Hansen bought at least a third of the pies and two cases of preserves and apple butter, but there was still plenty left. His mother offered them to his friends when they came home with him.

"Fish pie? No thank you," Charlie said.

"You don't know what you're missing," Bird told him with a full mouth.

They all tasted them and declared them favorites. The next time he accompanied his father, they came home to find his friends all sitting around the kitchen table with forks waiting for the pies to come from the oven.

When Jackie's parents saw each other after being apart, a powerful, magnetic force united them in tidings of kisses more worthy of a rising from the dead than their returns, hers from a visiting her brother or his from the woods. They embarrassed him because they didn't peck each other on the lips as parents usually did but cooed closely and kissed deeply right in front of his friends. He felt as if they were staring, but they were not. They were too busy with Frigg's cooking to pay much attention. Their mouths were chewing; their eyes were on the last few pieces on the platter.

"Jackie. You should try these fish balls," Charlie said spearing one and holding it up.

Wes noticed his parents kissing and leaned in to ask, "Gee Jackie, how long has your father been gone?"

"Couple days."

"Are you sure?"

"Sure I'm sure. You know Edgar Allen Poe?" the boys nodded. "He wrote that poem about 'love that was more than a love.' That's them."

"Not my parents," Charlie lamented.

Jackie already knew Mr. Muller and Aunt Ilta, as the kids called his mother, had problems. She often nagged her husband who hushed her with accusations of jealousy. And one time, at a party, he gave Jackie a hearty side hug. The heavy touch of his hand flashed a vision in Jackie's head. He saw a dimly lit hotel room. A healthy pin-up-type girl in high heels, a sailor cap and a bikini jiggled her head full of curls. She opened a cigarette case with the name Violet engraved on it, took one and then held it out to a person in the shadows. Charlie Muller senior emerged buck-naked. Jackie gasped and shook his head like a wild horse to evict the image. When Mr. Muller asked, "What's the matter boy?" Jackie didn't answer; he heeded his mother's advice and kept it to himself, but he liked woman's name and said it a loud quietly, "Violet."

"What?" Mr. Muller snapped suddenly serious. "What do you know about Violet?

"Violet," Jackie stammered, "I was thinking about a girl in my class. She ate a piece of bread and jam that had ants on it the other day. They walked all over her face." No sooner had the lie passed his lips and Mr. Muller boomed, "Violet! There you are," and grinned from ear to ear. He introduced her as his cousin.

Jackie compared Aunt Ilta to Violet. She was much younger

and prettier, but everyone loved Aunt Ilta. Her kindness was as legendary as her whiskey pie that she always allowed the boys to have when they visited Charlie Junior. Jackie decided that while Aunt Ilta and Charlie Muller senior were married, and were, perhaps once in love, they did not have "a love that was more than a love." None of his friends' parents had it as far as he could see.

Bird's mother Julia died and his father, John began dating a few short weeks later. His name ignited so much gossip in the community, Bird was ashamed, disgusted and anger. At least, that's what he told Jackie when their turn to buy candy came up.

"My father is such a jerk!" I he exclaimed slamming his foot into the snow. "I hate him Jackie."

"Since when? You always told me you loved your Dad." The truth silenced Bird. "And I think he's supposed to meet girls. 'Women mourn and men replace,' that's what my mother says."

"Is that right? What would your father do if your mother...you know...went to Heaven?"

"My mother?!" Jackie shuddered as the words came out of his mouth. He spun his tweed cap around and tightened his scarf around his neck. "My father and mother are like a walnut?"

Bird laughed.

"A walnut? Jackie you say the strangest things sometimes. How are your parents a walnut? "

"Like a walnut. Like. Like one. If you crack it in two, it's two halves. Can't put 'em back. They dry up and rot away. That's what would happen. He would dry up and rot away. Her too.

ALA CARTE MENU

SANDWICHES

Tuna Fish Salad	.35
Ham and Cheese	.40
Club Sandwich	1.00
Hamburger	.50
Bacon,lettuce,tomato	.70

DINNERS

They all come with: cole slaw,
roll and French fried potatoes.

Fishsticks	1.25
Scallops or Shrimps	1.59
Chicken	1.35

SIDE DISHES

Cole slaw	.35
French fried potatoes	.25
Soup	.35
Rolls(give you 3)	.25

THE DRINKS

CHAMPAGNE

Whole Bottle	5.95
Pint	3.00

COCKTAILS

Manhatten	.50
Old-Fashioned	.60
Martini	.50
Gin Fizz	.60
You Name It	.60

if have the ingredients, we wil
make it for you.

WHISKEY

WHISKEY	.60
WINE	.35
BEER	.40
COFFEE	.10

SALTY DOG TAVERN

TELEVISION
in the bar

"Here's to a long life, and
a merry one; a quick death,
and an easy one; a pretty
girl, and an honest one;
a cold beer -
and another one!"

Ocean Avenue... ...Telephone 72

V

A Pantheon of Friends & the Rocky Road of Love

T he friendship among Jackie Vik, Bird Mann, Smitty, Lucky Louis, Charlie Muller, Wes Arnold, and Seamus O'Reilly had been forged in grammar school. They cavorted away their childhood bellyaching about homework, playing games and teasing girls who they believed God had placed on Earth for that express purpose, that is until a surge of hormones altered their belief. In Junior High the mere sight of a pretty face or a soft sweater snugging the mounds of a well-developed classmate or shop girl veered their thoughts, whatever they were, off track, and from as far away as across the street, a shapely backside could stem a heated debate over whether Atom Man or Super Man would win in hand-to-hand combat. When they pilfered booze and tippled it in secret behind the O'Reilly family bar, they toasted a list of favorites. All but two of them concluded with a drink "to the prettiest one of all," the wholesome, young violet-eyed star of the films, *Courage of Lassie* and *Black Velvet*, Elizabeth Taylor.

"I wouldn't kick her out a bed, but I got my girl," Jackie told them after he first saw Sherry Britton. To his surprise, the only one of TOP thunderstruck by her was Charlie.

"Hubba hubba!" he exclaimed and laid his lusty, adolescent eyes on her luscious curves.

"So firm, she could hold a glass on 'em, full of water," Jackie told him.

"Yeah, we should see if we can get in that club where she works some night," Charlie told him, and nonchalantly slipped the photograph in his book.

"No. No, you don't!" Jackie said and snatched it back. "Get your own."

A Pantheon of Friends & the Rocky Road of Love

The boys' disparate tastes were not limited to girls, but they considered that part of the reason they were the best of friends. Collectively, they considered themselves as accomplished and powerful as the gods of Olympus. Thus, they called themselves, The Only Pantheon, TOP. The unwritten oath was that differences of opinion, money and girls would not come between them; they would be there for each other through thick and thin, and that is exactly what they did. Without forethought or even listening at times, they held conversations about health, the weather, families and news tidbits. They repeated them so often they knew them as well their grandfathers' stories. Jackie's lines were among their favorites and most often quoted in smiling unison in his absence. The perfunctory greeting, "How ya doin' today?" was met with Jackie's positive rising tone, "Better than yesterday, but not as good as I'm going to be tomorrow." If a new acquaintance asked why he went to sea, TOP cried, "It isn't a farm," and they laughed —every time. TOP's shared life experiences had simmered away differences in class, religion, occupation and intelligence, so staying together was not difficult.

On the rare occasion that they found themselves free at the same time, they roamed the streets of New York shoulder to shoulder like a pack of wolves trotting from party to party or bar to bar, not to flirt but to revel in the glory of each other's company. The last time was a winter's eve when the temps dipped down to record breaking cold. The night came to an expected and abrupt end when the new barkeep suggested it was time to go. Giddily they paid up and reeled and teetered unceremoniously into the street. There they tested each other's ability to stand on one foot in order to determine who was in the best shape to drive. A dusting of snow sparkled on their black automobile parked in the shadows on the side street. It was Charlie's car, but Seamus had the key. That meant they had had the conversation earlier and deemed him the driver. He questioned the wisdom of assigning an Irishman such a sober responsibility and asked again if he was supposed to get them home, but they were too drunk to recall and too cold to care. Seamus took the key. Tiny icicles hung from the door handle and covered the lock; inserting the key was impossible. TOP jumped up and down and rubbed their hands together up while Seamus and Wes blew on the frozen keyhole to no avail.

"I gotta take a leak," Jackie and Smitty said at the same time.

Exchanging a look confirming they were thinking alike, they strode over to the car and urinated on the lock. TOP broke into raucous laughter. No one wanted to touch the steaming chrome, so the boys used a few handfuls of fresh, clean snow to wipe it down. Impatiently, they huddled together near the car so they could jump in quickly. The key remained useless. Wes stepped up to contribute his defrosting solution to the cause. In the quiet of the wee hours, its purl over the chrome lock was all they heard.

"Hey!" a sharp anonymous man bellowed. "What the Hell do you think are you doing?"

A group of five young men, as inebriated as TOP, glared menacingly at them from the rear bumper.

"What's it look like? The lock froze," Jackie said.

Suddenly, the gang of five rushed TOP; a mêlée broke out.

"We don't have any money," Seamus yelled.

"So you break into my car?!"

"Your car?" Jackie asked from the hood where he had jumped to pounce on one of the men.

"Yeah *my* car."

All the young men stepped back. The owner slid his key into the lock with ease. His gang piled into the car and drove by; one of them flipped TOP the bird as they passed. TOP's tension gusted out in laughter amid a round of confirmations each had survived unscathed. They were. Memory dawned on Charlie. They had walked to the Eighth Avenue Subway after "Seamus mentioned something about an Irishman, and we decided one should drive." They all acknowledged with nods. "We spent all our dough. What now geniuses?" In any other season, they would have walked, but the subzero temperature incited a fleeting discussion of hopping the turnstile which went nowhere because the subway wasn't even running.

"Hold on," Jackie ordered.

He slipped along the icy sidewalk almost falling twice. Burying their faces in their collars and their hands in their pockets, they fended off the frigid air and waited and waited and waited. Bird was finishing his second cigarette when a heavy, black Chrysler Crown Imperial Sedan crunched through the street.

"Be nice to get a lift in that," Smitty said and excitedly added, "Look!"

The automatic window rolled down, and they saw Jackie in the back seat.

"Get in," he beamed.

There were jump seats, so they all fit comfortably. An older, clean-shaven, colored man in a stiff, blue-grey chauffeur's hat adjusted the rear view mirror.

"You didn't say anything about all these people," he commented. "Five bucks was for you and your friend to one address. That's all I got time for. If my boss doesn't find me waiting for him on a night like this...." He shook his head, and then assessed their inebriation and fatigue. "It's twenty dollars...for all, or you fellas are gonna have to find another car, FBI or not,"

Murmuring "FBI?" quizzically, TOP shifted uneasily.

Jackie took off his watch and hung it on his index finger over the driver's shoulder. He glanced at it, but he didn't take it.

"Twenty dollars," he repeated sternly.

"That's a Timex, same one 'the Rock couldn't stop,'" Jackie defended.

"Good for Rocky Marciano. Joe Louis had a Swiss watch."

"Oh. You were rooting for Joe Louis? What a beating he..."

"Joe Louis was ten years older and retired, so Marciano didn't *really* beat him, and that watch wasn't but eleven dollars and ninety-five cents when it was new... Still twenty dollars."

Except for Wes, each of the others put his watch forward but none was worth much more. They turned to Wes.

"No. No. No. No. This was a birthday present from my father."

Their concerted effort removed the Bulova timepiece. He

grabbed it back, and TOP issued several grunts of disappointment. Jackie asked them to understand that it was a gift, and reminded them of their godly status.

"Keep it Wes. We're The Only Pantheon. What's a freezing, cold night to us?"

With that, Wes reluctantly dropped his watch onto the front seat. As soon as the driver saw Bulova, he stepped on the gas.

"Ten dollars each," too pay for the watch was the promise TOP made, never kept and always remembered by Wes.

"My father will never stop asking me 'What time is it?' and you guys still owe me sixty dollars and fifty cents," he reminded them from time to time.

✳✳✳

Originally, they had all lived in Chelsea or nearby Greenwich Village, and eventually, life moved them around, but the friendship had a permanent home at Seamus' tavern, The Salty Dog. No "Ladies Invited" sign hung outside. Seamus firmly believed, "Chicks bellying up to the bar is bad business. Me and McSorley's are the last ones with any sense." He did allow women in who had business, a designer or accountant, and the waitresses hustled through the swinging doors from the bar to the dining room where women were welcome. If one of TOP had a particularly attractive girl, he might bring her in for a minute to show her off, as long as she didn't sit at the bar. Charlie brought his fiancée Patty. With a smug gleam, he swaggered in on the pretense of asking Seamus if any one had found his cufflink. He could have taken her to the back office, but he left her waiting obediently on display by the wall. Clutching her handbag tightly, she cast her large hazel eyes television light highlighted her cheekbones as Charlie returned patting his pocket and grinned before walking her out. From time to time rage or desperation or both shoved a wife, who they did not rank as a girl, through the swinging doors to collect her soused husband, and that was it.

At The Dog, their beer-soaked sanctuary overlooking the sea, they were free to cuss, belch, tell off-color jokes, smoke pipes and cigars, guzzle booze, roughhouse, make noise talk about broads or just sit quietly and read the paper or watch the action on the pier. They were men sharing their lives, celebrating and commiserating being men with other men.

Maddy, Grandfather O'Reilly's beagle, was nicknamed the Salty Dog; he was the bar's mascot. Long ago, he had died of natural causes but he lived on in a photograph taken while he was sitting cutely in a lifesaver. The story behind the snap told of the day he had saved Grandfather O'Reilly life. It was one TOP had heard many times since they were children. The very idea made them laugh because he was quite a portly man, and the beagle was so small. Weeks before the Salty Dog was complete, Grandfather O'Reilly and his cronies spent the day on the water and had a late-night feast aboard one of their fishing boats. Upon returning from the head, he slipped and fell overboard, "completely bollixed," Seamus always interjected. Maddy barked and barked for attention. Getting none, he grabbed the lifesaver by its rope, jumped into the water and swam out to the grandfather with the knotted end between his small teeth. Once the old man had the lifesaver, he caught his breath and hollered, "Help!" Fortunately, the motor wasn't running, and his friends heard him. Amid their good-natured ribbing, they pulled him aboard with Maddy cuddled in his arms.

"He's a right salty dog," he bellowed and held the dog on high.

When Seamus took over ownership of the pub, he questioned

his grandfather's best friend about the veracity of this story. He confirmed it and added to the little, departed Maddy's role in his grandfather's life.

"He tells me Grandad opened this place not long after he stepped off the boat from Ireland. When his friend was waiting for him to go to city hall to file the documents for the pub, he and Maddy sat watching him. He patted his palm on the newspaper, the counter, the cupboard, and his pockets. 'I can't find my glasses Maddy. Do you know where they are?' he asks her just joking. Maddy leaps off the chair, runs under the tablecloth and returns with the glasses. At City Hall, he scratches the name O'Reilly's Pub off the papers and writes the Salty Dog."

On the sign outside and on the menu underneath Maddy the beagle, an old Irish saying was written.

> "Here's to a long life, and a merry one;
> a quick death, and an easy one;
> a pretty girl, and an honest one;
> a cold beer - and another one!"

Inside The Dog, a picture window stretched from floor to ceiling and the length of the wall. It offered a view of the piers' activity and people, in particular girls by day and the lights of the harbor at night To TOP's dismay, Seamus was toying with a new interior design intended to replace the view with a wall and a mural of it, and that made absolutely no sense to anyone, but Seamus. He claimed he had to cover the picture window for one reason, to save money. Even with the fireplace lit and the furnace going, The Dog was frigid in the winter, covering the window would keep it warm. It was the talk of the bar for weeks. The

members of TOP each took a turn accusing one another of having instigated the change by bitching about the cold. The truth
was revealed; no one had complained, not even Seamus himself.
They went over the time line of the complaint and traced it back
to the appearance of the interior designer, Michaela. She had re-
fined features, a head of thick, permed curls and a long slim
waist beneath, "a couple of luscious honeydews indeed," Lucky-
Lou grunted.

"Her fruit," TOP declared was the culprit

Seamus' had a well-known fondness for fruit, especially mel-
ons, and though that, no doubt, played a major role in his
decision to consult with Michaela, they defended him.

"Yeah, Shannon's been putting on the pounds, right Smitty?"
Charlie pointed out.

"Every other year, he's got her in the family way."

"So a wife putting on weight is a reason to throw away money
on a reproduction of a view to replace an actual view?" Wes
asked.

It didn't make sense to them. Late one afternoon, TOP tallied
up how much they spent at The Dog in a year multiplied it by
their lifetimes and arrived at a figure that led them to believe
they were "pretty much co-owners of the place," and as such, they
were entitled to a say in what goes on. They had an impromptu
meeting with Michaela when she accepted TOP's invitation to a
friendly drink. Sipping hers, with an umbrella as she requested,
they offered her a big shot of their collective opinion. TOP was
all for change, but they did not want the view, their view,
blocked off. They urged him to have her "look again at her little
recipe. Come up with a design that includes the window."

"There's nothing out there," Michaela responded sweetly.

"Nothing out there?" Lou echoed.

They all leaned and stared out at the sea stretching to the horizon and then at each other.

"That's the ocean, all of life, and there's ships and yachts with broads," he struck a sexy pose," and grinned out of one side of his mouth, "And that's everything.

"I thought you were goin' to take a leak," Charlie said, and Lou left.

"TOP?" asked Michaela tipping her head to one side.

"Actually, it's T. – O. – P. for The Only Pantheon," Wes explained. "You know, the gods all together."

In a snap, she had run her eyes over the bunch and said, "Gods, I see. So keeping the window is to save the Gods' view of the ocean?"

No eyes were on the window or boats or the ocean; they were all on Michaela's top button which had come undone with the last deep breath she had taken. Bending toward the bar for her glass, she unintentionally gave them a peek of her shiny red satin bra with the lace trim.

"Don't you fellas want to save God Seamus' cash? If you want to see the boats, you can just step outside."

Their eyes were so fixed on her blouse that she lowered her head.

"Oh would you look at me, I'm naked for Heaven's sakes," she declared and buttoned up. "You're going to love it. You'll see."

From the back room, Seamus was lilting out her name.

"Michaela. Oh Michaela."

She excused herself and went to join him. Lucky Louis returned to hear TOP speaking among themselves in low tones.

"What'd I miss?"

"Vavavoom!" Wes said and elbowed Smitty.

Smitty recounted what they had seen, but in the retelling, one button became, "all her buttons had come undone, and we saw them—in a red brassiere... the ones with the lace!"

"Red!" Lucky grabbed his head and let out the anguished groan of a man who had lost two weeks pay in a poker game.

"Okay. Louis, take it easy. Now listen! Seamus and Shannon have seven children," Wes pointed out, "and Smitty and me have one each and. . . "

"We know how many kids we have," Charlie said.

"Yes, and our wives don't mind our being out working but if they thought we were consulting with Miss Red Brassiere all hours of the day and night..."

"What? Are you saying we should tell Shannon that Seamus is up to something with... " Smitty asked.

"No," Wes clarified. No one talks to Shannon. We tell Seamus to keep the window or we *will* tell her about his schedule with the red brassiere."

Smitty slid off his seat and ran his hands nervously through his hair.

"We can't do that. Seamus is one of TOP. Are we messing with that for a view of the harbor?"

They reviewed and revised their thinking. Indeed "pretty little Shannon," as they called her when she and Seamus were sweethearts, got married right after high school. And nine years later, she has pushed out a good portion of her charm in the delivery of their half a dozen children, but he loved her. He would never do anything untoward. Trying to muscle him over to their idea would be wrong, a violation of the rules that bound TOP. "What is he supposed to do?" Wes asked.

"I don't get it," Lucky Lou said rotating among them for a clue to what they were talking about.

"Seems like all Seamus has to do is wave his magic wand and

presto bango, Shannon's got another bun in the over," Smitty explained.

"Seamus has a magic wand?" Lucky Lou asked.

They didn't try to explain.

"That's why Seamus is here all hours. Well, I'm here all hours, and I only have one child. Imagine having seven," Smitty said.

They blamed her undone button for inciting their malicious, underhanded thoughts of betrayal, but their problem, saving the window, remained unsolved.

"Where's Jackie?" was their chorus.

On his fingers, Smitty counted off the possibilities, "Home, with a chick, the Five Spot, the bookstore, the Union Hall, Bremerhaven, one of those places."

Jackie arrived two days later. They briefed him on the window situation and warned him of Michaela's wiles.

"Big knockers don't scare me."

He insisted TOP go to the bar across the way and leave him alone with her. He borrowed Smitty's lighter to break the ice by lighting her cigarette.

Without any warning, Smitty lunged forward and held Jackie in his arms, and then he kissed his cheek. Jackie pulled back.

"I almost forgot. That's from Asta."

"Good thing, I thought I was gonna have to deck ya," he replied turning his eyes up to revisit her in his mind. And then he gave Smitty a noisy wet kiss.

"That's for Asta."

"None of that in here lads," Seamus teased from across the bar.

They waved him off. Smitty suggested that Jackie "might wanna get a ship over to Plymouth and visit the poor girl. She's still very beautiful."

He confided that he had actually thought about it, but South-ampton was on the American Merchant Line and he was going in the opposite direction, "South on the Pacific Argentine Brazil Line.

"What's all the suspense?"

"She wants to tell you."

His curiosity was peeked.

"That was some night, wasn't it?" Jackie asked, smacked his chest and lamented not having returned, "She had something that Asta…."

Smitty kissed him again.

"Get out of here!" he ordered shoving him away.

Jackie turned the lighter over and over in his hand. It brought a vision of a woman and two blurry figures in a mirror. The woman washed her hands and threw her shiny black hair back revealing eyes as blue and vibrant as a tropical ocean. One of the other figures came into focus. He put his arm around her; it was Smitty.

So that's what's going on.

He sat his Manhattan down, and let time tick him into the dead zone, an indeterminate length of time when sound and mo-tion ceased to exist. In a bar, it usually came after lunch and before Happy Hour. Without customers, there was no music coming from the jukebox, no clunking glasses or matches being lit, no banter, no chairs and feet thumping on the floor, and no smoke, so the fan was off and so were the waitresses. The zone made him very uneasy and filled him with a sense of fear that a spell had been cast on him because he was frozen as well in the unpeopled place, and if no noise came, he would be trapped for-ever. Relief always washed over him when a floorboard awakened with a creak or a playful ray of sun danced on a bottle.

Such an infinitesimal noise or movement was all it took to re-animate the world and let him breathe. Today it was the outer door; it squeaked and banged. Slowly, the waitresses' yakking in the next room became audible and animated him.

The scent of perfume caught him and he saw a woman enter who he was sure was Michaela. Even though there was no one else at the bar, she chose the seat next to him. When she scooched by, the stiff fabric of her bra rubbed his arm, and his body hair stood up. Seamus appeared yawning deeply and threw a hand towel over his shoulder.

"Two of my favorite people. Another Manhattan for you Jackie and...wait...don't tell me," he snapped his fingers, "Reverse Manhattan," he hit the bar with his palm.

"Reverse?" Jackie shot a glance of curiosity at Michaela.

"Easy. Two vermouth and a half of whiskey. How do you think she stays so sweet Jackie?" Seamus asked as Michaela took out a cigarette.

"Jackie of The Only Pantheon?" she asked.

"That's me, Jackie, Jackie Vik," he replied, and as planned, used Smitty's lighter.

"I'm Michaela," she said and shook his hand.

She watched as Jackie, like most men she encountered, dropped his eyes to her bosom. Out of habit, she ran her fingers along the divide in her sweater. A boisterous post-work conversation blasted into the room followed by two men swaggering with self-importance, so he took her by the hand and led her to the privacy of a booth. Under different circumstances, he might have sat a little closer, but she was with Smitty, and he knew he had to focus on his mission.

"I imagine an uptown girl like you redoing a fancy living room or a hotel or something. What made you want to take on…"

"Anyone can do those. This is a challenge, and I want to…"

He slid the lighter across the table toward her.

"Be near our friend Smitty?"

Michaela gasped. "What? Smitty? Did my husband's family put you up to…"

"Your husband was wounded in the war, right?" he asked following his intuition.

"Smitty told you?!" she declared completely stunned.

Unsettled by Jackie's knowledge of her situation rendered her malleable. He explained to her that people have trouble with change and how TOP felt the DOG was their home.

"We spend more time here than in our houses sometimes, so we know a thing or two about it. You can make a change that will save one person a few bucks but cause the rest to grouse, or you can make a change that will make everyone happy. Isn't that the challenge?"

Michaela agreed, and offered to think about it. He assured her Smitty had not betrayed her confidence; he had guessed her circumstances. Jackie reported to TOP that he had a plan to save their ocean view, and he kept the details to himself. No one knew exactly what was going on. Michaela no longer spread her plans out on the table but kept them secret. Seamus avoided any direct questions about the solution

One night Seamus had TOP come specifically to make a big deal about presenting Michaela's new design for the Dog. Everyone waited, as they were told, on the restaurant side while they set up the bar. To add to the suspense, Seamus had turned off all the lights, including the jukebox. When they were finally invited in, they stumbled blindly and bumped into the chairs and walls and one another. They were prepared to be disappointed because they were certain Seamus had kept them in the dark metaphorically and literally and gone with the mural option.

"Hit it!" Seamus called and one of his helpers turned on the lights but there was no mural.

They all nodded in approval.

"What is that, a curtain or a sail?"

"Both," Seamus told them.

The curtains were in two layers, one for the summer through which the ocean was visible and the other for the winter. It was more of a heavy canvas painting to block out the money-devouring draft. Seamus worked the ropes raising it to reveal Michaela, in a glamorous cocktail dress on the pier. Her modest wave elicited a round of wolf whistles, whoops and hollers. They jumped and hugged each other with all the enthusiasm of fans who had witnessed their team making the winning touch down. Michaela entered to another round of appreciative applause.

"No No. Please. I can't take all the credit. Jackie was talking about hoisting sails, and I thought that would be the perfect solution."

With both arms, she gestured toward Jackie for a round of applause. Jackie hoisted the sail-curtains.

"I'm drinking to TOP because your belly-aching finally amounted to an idea."

"Jackie, the savior of the ocean. Hooray!" TOP responded.

And from that day forward, when Jackie walked through the door of The Dog, he was greeted with a loud cheer. It has waned in volume over time, but it is still given.

"There he is. The savior of the ocean. Hooray."

* * *

etween chomps on her gum, the new waitress at the Dog asked Jackie why he read so much, and TOP perked up and listened because in all the years they had known him, no one had ever asked.

"Those swell little postcards got me started."

"What?" she asked confused.

From his wallet, he snapped one out. It was a woman in a library on a velvet sofa in front of a wall of books. Other than an ethnic necklace with jumbo beads which he thought to be "ivory or wood," she was nude. Light flowed in from the window toward which she extended her arm. The waitress bopped by.

"She must be far-sighted; she is holding the book in Brooklyn."

"I'd hold it for her," he explained with a wink.

The waitress walked away with a flick of her ponytail. Jackie lowered his voice.

"When we were kids, me and Bird found a whole box of these in the bookstore. I guess they belonged to his old man. Thank God he was heavy on his feet. If we heard him coming, we'd grab the decoy book we had on the shelf. He was suspicious though. He quizzed me on mine, *Legends from around the World.* Turns out I was actually reading it. I must have impressed him because every birthday after that, he invited me to the store to pick out a book."

Passing by again, the waitress said, "You mean you stole the pic…"

"Seamus where'd you get this smarty pants broad?" Jackie yelled with a little smile, but received no reply.

The waitress read the card.

"Nineteen hundred eight?! She's probably in her grave by now. Why don't you join the 20th century and buy that *Playboy* like other men?"

"I ain't like other men. Besides, these broads are classier and they fit in my pocket."

He tugged on the edge of a bookmark jutting between the pages, and pulled out another card. Everyone gathered around. A wave of nostalgia rolled over Jackie recalling the particulars of acquiring the photographs.

"These were in one of those birthday books. I always wanted to find a girl who was, you know, smart and sexy not in a trampy way, but fun, and… this one with the camera…Be fun to take turns taking pictures. Or the one with the book…get me to read more. 'A good book on your shelf is a friend that turns its back on you and remains a friend,' that's what Nancy says, you know Nancy, the literature pro-fes-sor…," he emphasized her position every time he said her name.

"Who is Nancy?" Lucky Lou asked quietly.

"You saw her at Bird's when we were playing cards. Remember? Tall. Blonde. Bazookas out to here," Smitty cupped hands in front of his chest, "She's doing something up there at Columbia."

A mischievous grin slunk through Charlie's liquor numbed lips. "Pro-fes-sor Nancy reads naked, does she?…"

"What do you know about Nancy?" Jackie flared and grabbed him by the front of the shirt. "Just shut up about her."

"Just talking. Jackie. Just talking," Charlie responded coolly stepping backwards with his hands up to avoid a fight.

Every now and again, TOP saw Jackie with a girl, but none of them initiated or responded to any flirting with her because they acknowledge the basic hands-off-a-buddy's-girl man code. Like him, Smitty, Wes and Charlie were all attractive men of above average height, broad shoulders and classic head-turning, V-shaped physiques, though Wes was considerably slimmer. Their appearance was not the issue for Jackie; he knew he was handsome, but his ego suffered when he compared other aspects of himself to them. Though everyone acknowledged Jackie was the smartest among the group, people tended to believe their answers over his. Smitty didn't go to college, but otherwise, they had served in the military, earned degrees, had business cards, married beautiful women and started their families. At the Dog one afternoon when no one else was around, to Seamus' surprise, Jackie listed these facts and hung his head.

"So what's wrong with me?"

"Nothing. You're a special guy, so you're going to need a special girl. Least you found out before you got hitched."

Jackie had been engaged twice and, purely by chance, both fiancées were of Norwegian decent; Hilde was from Minnesota and Margrete from Wisconsin. Hilde said she didn't mind that Jackie was a Merchant Marine, but she devoted a considerable amount of conversation to when he was going to quit as he said he would, take over the store and stick around. When every date she picked for the wedding conflicted with his sea schedule, she suspected it was not a coincidence. After the usual two-year waiting period and trying to set a date for six months, she gave up.

"You shouldn't get engaged Jackie, not to me, not to anyone. It's bigamy. Okeanos, the sea is your wife," Hilde announced quite politely and tossed the engagement ring in the candy dish.

The painful ending to their relationship haunted him, so he limited himself to a few local girls and those on distant shores who liked to "have fun," which gnawed at him. He thought by now he would have found a "love that was more than a love," like his parents had. Smitty, and Seamus, who already had seven children, had gotten married the year they graduated high school because the girls had gotten pregnant. Wes and Charlie waited until they finished college. They chose their brides from their social circle because they were virgins, from good families. Wes' wife had the perfect all-American prettiness while Charlie's wife, Patty was flat out gorgeous. All were stay-at-home wives and, true to their marriage vows, were obedient, except Seamus' wife, Shannon who was more of a feisty loud mouth due to raising so many kids. No one had the rare love his parents had, but they were all content. In his heart, he longed for that "love that was more than a love," but saw clearly such a connection was not necessary for a happy union. A full year after Hilde left, he got deliberately pursued Margrete who while not "the one" had an alluring something he thought he could live with. She didn't speak much, but when she did, it was in a soft Norwegian accent that changed her "w's" to "v's" and lyrically inflected her sentences upward at the end. Bird and Smitty insisted, "She reminds me of your mother, the way she talks." To their faces, he took offense and disagreed vehemently but to himself, he confessed Magrete's voice and Frigg's were slightly similar. Not only was she a "total knockout," she could cook, garden, mend and accepted his love for Okeanos, but then Hilde did too, at first. To test Margrete, he deliberately made plans when he knew he had to ship out. Invariably, her reaction was a shrug of her shoulders.

"Okay, another time," she said cheerfully.

He didn't think he would do better. Friday night, he donned his best suit, put on some jazz, downed a shot of whiskey and presented her the ring on bended knee. She dappled him with a kisses which were a prelude to a carnal fugue performed on the floor. Nuzzling against his chest, she blathered gleefully about how happy he made her and that she couldn't wait until they "moved to the farm, and I..."

"Farm!? What are you talking about?" he asked gruffly.

From the lofty heights of the newly engaged cloud on which she floated, she explained again how she and her brother were expected to one day return and take over the family farm.

"You mean after I am dead."

"No, I mean so we can make our lives together."

"Am I supposed to give up, Vik's Woods and my friends?"

"You mean the girls like that Negro and your Columbia professor?" she quipped.

"Fana is a diplomat's daughter, speaks French, and Nancy ..."

"Oh you and your fancy city friends. You can make friends on a farm too."

"If I get a farm itch I need to scratch, I visit my uncle."

Jackie leapt to his feet, slid his legs into his pants, lit a cigarette and paced. They retreated into themselves at other ends of the room in silence. Eventually, the occasion of the engagement and the hours passing dissipated the tension. Margrete returned to preparing dinner and unintentionally whipped up delights libidinous by leaving her dress on the back of the couch so it wouldn't get stained and cooking in her flimsy, low cut silk slip. It rustled over her shapely rump as she beat potatoes in a pot at the stove. Jackie's hands explored her contour from behind and rested his chin in the nook between her ear and her clavicle. She applied a dollop of the mash on her sternum and presented it to Jackie. He lapped it up and slid his tongue down her breasts. He was about to place his mouth on her soft, white flesh, when the olfactory memory of farm wafted over him. It caused him to feel a flabby, cow udder in place of Margrete's firm breast which collapsed his desire.

"The goddess of winter ends up with the god of the sea. He loved the sea, and she loved the woods, but…"

"Njord and Skadi? Oh Jackie. We are people not mythological beings. You are asking me to completely abandon my family."

"Margrete, I am asking you to make one with me. You never complained about me going off to…"

"I thought you loved me…"

"I do love you," should have shot out of his mouth. Instead, her gentle remark silenced him. He realized he did not love her, not really. He was settling for her so he could get married like his friends.

Hoping for the "love you" to come, she searched his face and waited and waited. When it was more than evident, that he was not going to speak, she collected her clothes and dressed in the bedroom. When she emerged, she was in her hat telling him, they were over. The door was no more than twenty steps away, but hope that he might spring after her slowed her gait. Jackie knew it, but the only reason he would catch her would be to spin her around so quickly they would go back to the moment before they met and prevent this heartache. Unable to do that, he poured himself a drink, put the needle back on the record and straightened out his albums.

The engagement ring was in the candy dish again. Jackie sold it and used the cash for a Flashmatic remote for his mother and a new camera for himself. He showed it off to TOP, casually mentioned that the wedding was off and dismissed their condolences.

"Awww. Forget about it. Who wants a seaman?" he asked and dropped his head in despair.

"Smitty found himself a wife," Lucky Louis pointed out.

"He had to marry Gina...you know?" Wes sniggered with Smitty standing right there.

"You might not have if her father hadn't showed up. Remember. Mum was still alive then God keep her soul," Seamus said and they revisited that night.

Closing time at the Dog was Seamus' job on the weekend. His father was at war; his mother was in charge, but she preferred to work in the office late at night while TOP mopped and cleaned. Their adolescent energy shot them into the task, but to maintain their speed, they hit B3 on the Wurlitzer, "Stomping at the Savoy," their work song. They shook and wiggled and did the dosey doe. Jackie liked arms with someone and then let him go to wave his arms wildly The music stopped abruptly, and Mrs. O'Reilly, who had the electric plug in her hand, was the reason. Jackie's partner was on the floor. He was a small, round man with wavy black hair and a mustache brandishing a beat up Italian Beretta he pulled from his coat.

In a thick southern Italian accent he said, "Io sono Senore Gurgiolo, the father of Gina. Who is to be her husband? Or who do I shoot?"

Involuntarily, heads turned toward Smitty.

"Are you going to marry Gina?"

"Yes," Jackie whispered to him, "Say yes."

Smitty was completely tongue-tied.

"Yes, he is. We're celebrating," Jackie said.

Mr. Gurgiola squinted at Smitty, and then flashed a toothy grin. "Of course you are. I know my Gina found a nice boy."

He provided instructions as to how he expected Smitty to propose down to the last detail.

"Capisce?"

Mrs. O'Reilly shook her head as she watched him walk out, When he was gone, they all laughed, except Smitty.

After the marriage, he confessed, "It's all right."

TOP didn't see how living in a house with "your wife, her in-laws, two aunts, an uncle, two grandparents and five siblings," as Smitty reported could be all right for anyone. They figured he was trying to make the best of a situation. He hung out at the Dog all day on the pretense of looking for work, but in the end, he signed up for the Merchant Marine and left.

"The way things are going, that is the only way I will end up hitched."

"Jackie, the only reason we're still married is because you aren't. We love hearing about all those broads," He rubbed his hands together. The red head was my favorite."

"What red-head."

Seamus sighed with envy, "Look at that. You can't even remember. And you travel. You're a magician with wood," he pointed to a small carved deer between the liquor bottles, "and all the photos you take, the musicians you know. Jesus man. The last time I went uptown with you, it was like you was a visiting dignitary. Anyone of us would trade you places."

"I guess, as they say, the grass is always greener Seamus."

President Roosevelt signing the "Declaration of War"

VI

The War &

Casualties at Home

ecember 9th, 1941, at 10:00 President Roosevelt's voice came across the radio loud and clear.

"We are now in the midst of a war, not for conquest, not for vengeance, but for a world in which this nation, and all that this nation represents, will be safe for our children. We expect to eliminate the danger from Japan, but it would serve us ill if we accomplished that and found that the rest of the world was dominated by Hitler and Mussolini. So we are going to win the war and we are going to win the peace that follows."

The full impact of the statement announcing the country was "in the midst of a war," momentarily stifled their conversation. Paul reached out for Frigg's hand and she for Jackie's hand. Tears rolled down her cheeks. They held one another, and then Paul broke the spell.

"What happened to, 'Ecclesiastes 3:8, 'a time to love, and a time to hate; a time of war?' You always quote it Frigg. Here is the war. The military will fight and save our Oupas, and our beach."

"Our grandfathers...our beach Paul... and...and...our past," Frigg sighed fully embracing Paul.

Jackie wanted to give them their privacy and to process the news on his own. He bundled up and sat outside in the hollow of the porch. The winter weather was very calming, and it was colder than it had ever been. The weatherman had said, "It's a cold, cold, cold day." Moments he had had on the front porch dropped in and out of his mind. There was the big black and white Border Collie that walked up the stairs as if he lived there and stayed all day. TOP playing marbles right in the middle until sunset. The snowball fight they had last year when Charlie slipped and broke his thumb. Summertime reading on the stoop while his parents sat in the shade, Frigg embroidering and Paul carving. Viewing the mysteriously diaphanous lady with the yellow rose. Photographing the girls on the hood of Mr. Jamison car and Sally flaunting her dainty, white triangle. Lost in that thought he breathed heavily. The cold air turned his exhalations into a mini cloud of crystals.

Another freezing winter, and Far is going to war, he thought and shoved his hands into his pockets.

Paul and Frigg fantasized about the army stationing him in Norway where, of course, he would check in on their grandparents, though they knew it was unlikely. When the Burke-Wadsworth act passed through congress the previous year, men between twenty-one and thirty-five had to register with the local draft board, and that included Paul who was thirty-one. He asked how much time he would have to prepare but was told not to worry because married men with children were low on the list. Paul waxed patriotic at the board.

"It's only a year," he said.

Then, the Draft Bill passed. All men 18 - 35 were going, not for a year but the duration of the war. When he received his induction letter, it was not to Norway but to the processing station, Tuesday, December 23 at 7:30 am.

Prepare in Duplicate

December 23 1941
Whitehall Examining and
Processing Center
Manhattan, New York

(LOCAL BOARD DATE STAMP WITH CODE)

December 8 1941

(Date of mailing)

ORDER TO REPORT FOR INDUCTION

The President of the United States,

To _____ Paul _____ Lange _____ Vik _____
(First name)   (Middle name)   (Last name)

Order No. ___03775_____

GREETING:

Having submitted yourself to a local board composed of your neighbors for the purpose of determining your availability for training and service in the land or naval forces of the United States, you are hereby notified that you have now been selected for training and service therein.

39 Whitehall in Manhattan, New York

You will, therefore, report to the local board named above at _____
(Place of reporting)

at __7:30__ a.m., on the _____23_____ day of ___December___, 19__41__
(Hour of reporting)

Thi local board will furnish transportation to an induction station. You will there be examined, and, if accepted for training and service, you will then be inducted into the land or naval forces.

Persons reporting to the induction station in some instances may be rejected for physical or other reasons. It is well to keep this in mind in arranging your affairs, to prevent any undue hardship if you are rejected at the induction station. If you are employed, you should advise your employer of this notice and of the possibility that you may not be accepted at the induction station. Your employer can then be prepared to replace you if you are accepted, or to continue your employment if you are rejected.

Willful failure to report promptly to this local board at the hour and on the day named in this notice is a violation of the Selective Training and Service Act of 1940, as amended, and subjects the violator to fine and imprisonment.

If you are so far removed from your own local board that reporting in compliance with this order will be a serious hardship and you desire to report to a local board in the area of which you are now located, go immediately to that local board and make written request for transfer of your delivery for induction, taking this order with you.

B.D Woodward

_____
U. S. GOVERNMENT PRINTING OFFICE   16-18971-4   *Member or clerk of the local board.*

D. S. S. 1 (1/0) Left
(Revise 11-1' 18)

Mr. and Mrs. Vik changed Christ's birthday from the 25th to Sunday the 21st, so they could host their long-ago-planned Christmas party. The twenty-second, they decided, would be for their family traditions of church, opening gifts and eating Christmas dinner.

The Vik's base guest list consisted of those who attended Jackie's birthday plus their guests if they chose to bring them. Bob Mann was bringing a date, a woman named Shirley who no one knew but many envisioned as tawdry for going out with him, a new widower. To their disappointment, she was a shy, plump woman in glasses. Larry and Nancy brought their neighbors and a friend's teenage daughter. She was tall and strikingly beautiful girl coated in rich, dark chocolate skin and sheathed in a red satin dress. Her unusual and sensual appearance completely entranced Jackie, and he stood slack-jawed and wide-eyed in front of her. The thick cigarette smoke in the room swirled into a fog and the volume of people talking faded to quiet. Jackie heard birds chirping and music playing. He saw the young woman lying nude in his parents' big, brass bed. The crisp, linen sheets outlined her extraordinarily long limbs guiding his eyes to her lean, taut torso beneath her ample breasts. While he was lingering on her dark nipples, a sharp clap returned him to the Christmas party.

"Anybody home?" the dark girl joked flashing a beaming smile.

"Huh? What? Be right back," he said excusing himself with images of the dead cat again.

Outside he puffed on a cigarette and peeked into the room through the window. It looked like a wonderful movie. His parents' friends, dressed more glamorously than usual for what might be the last Christmas they would spend together. The men were graceful in their rigidly constructed suits, and the women rustled and scrooped in silk and taffeta cocktail dresses. Thinking of the dead cat had not succeeded in diminishing his arousal, so he stepped off the porch to let Jack Frost try. It worked. He took one last drag on his cigarette and rejoined them.

In the soft glow of holiday candles and tree lights, the guests sang harmoniously for the first time. Jackie considered the sound a reward for having written the lyrics to five hymns ten times in his best penmanship. He made a mental note to collect the pages later, so he didn't have to rewrite the lyrics again next year. Larry beckoned the others near and formally introduced the chocolate girl.

"This is Fana, a wonderfully spoiled Parisian who is visiting with her parents, my dear friends. They wanted a night out alone. Who could resist an offer to squire a goddess around New York?"

With a lascivious grin, he bopped her on her nose with his index finger. Nancy rolled her eyes and pushed her glass forward for a refill from Bill Edwards who happened, as always, to have the punch ladle in his hand. She took a healthy sip and separated Fana from Larry by inching into the small space between them. She removed his hand from Fana, put it at her own waist and held it there.

"Fana is in the last years of lycée. That's high school, but she is a gifted singer. Why don't you entertain us with a song?" she suggested in a voice bristling with envy and condescension.

"Entertain?" Larry asked disapprovingly, You mean treat us. And that would be lovely Fana. Would you treat us with a song?

"My pleasure. Lawrence," she told him sweetly with a peck on the cheek. "Perhaps *Sainte Nuit.*"

"Silent Night," Larry translated returning the peck, "Parfait."
"They know what it is Larry," Nancy snapped.

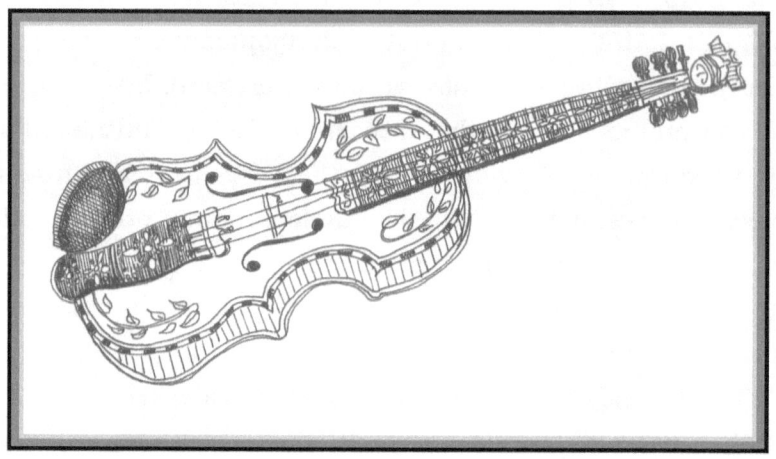

Paul knew his fine-tuning the fiddle would interfere, so he took it downstairs. Jackie caught himself again staring at Fana as she spoke; he had never heard anyone pronounce words so beautifully. To prevent himself from staring, he set his light meter, but walking around, he stumbled into an ottoman not only because he wasn't watching where he was going but also because he had drunk quite a bit of eggnog which had been spiked three times this year. Frigg had drizzled in an artsy flourish of brandy before she set the brimful, crystal vessel on the table. Larry came next, sampled the beverage, smacked his lips several times and deemed it, "too weak" which Nancy verified. He further fortified it with a healthy splashy and she mirthfully added another, "for good measure." By the time Bill came for his third serving, the bowl was half-empty, so he refilled the bowl with a bottle of rum before filling an eight-ounce tumbler full for himself and a saucer for Jackie. Bill insisted they toast Christmas downed his glass in a couple of gulps and said, "Oh no our glasses are full of air," and filled them up again before stumbling away. After the second drink, the camera instructions for shooting at night were all blurry. He called on God to help by reciting a little prayer. His father returned with the fiddle. In the viewfinder, Jackie found Fana posing demurely yet regally with her hands in front of her. Taking in a deep breath expanded her breasts in her dress like dark, rye bread dough rising in a bowl and he caught her with a click.

His intention was to photograph her singing, but her bright, emotional notes held him and everyone captive until her last note had completely evaporated into the smoky air. The intimate audience clapped. A man said, "Bravo," and she bowed her head. Jackie was going to tell her she was very good but tears were pooling in the corner of his eyes, and he had to use the bathroom, so did several women who had rushed to the door at the top of the stairs. Unable to wait, he slipped out front to a spot under the tree by the porch. The invigorating snow-sprinkled air smarted on his skin reminding him of the previous year's mercilessly frigid winter. In the shadow of the evergreen, he relieved himself carefully to protect his good shoes. The stars and snowflakes were a hazy jumble thanks to the alcohol vapors wafting in his head, and he rather liked that. To himself, he declared this Christmas party his parents' best because he felt fantastic, and then he declared it the worst because his father was leaving home, leaving him and Mor. A vision of jars of preserves and stacks of pies crowded over the stars and snowflakes, and he shook his head to get rid of it. The thud of a heavy car door and voices called his curiosity and caused him to linger at the tree. Shaking his leg, he zipped up and peeked out. A man and a woman passed within inches but didn't notice him. The man stopped.

"Put your gloves on Sally."

The little white triangle popped in his head, and his heart sped up. With tipsy stealth and cunning, he checked to see if it was the same Sally; it was. Stellar sparkles alighting on her hat and hair hanging over her shoulders added a princess-like shimmer to her cuteness as she lolled along catching flurries on her tongue. When she was near enough, he grabbed her by the hand, and she squealed.

"Shhhhh," he bubbled holding her between the wrought iron porch lattice and his body.

"Jackie," she whispered with genuine surprise. "What are you doing here?"

"Waiting for you," he fibbed with a sly one-sided grin. To his delight, the huntress as hunted was dumbfounded, and he gave her a kiss. Moaning softly, she received it. Her warmth seeped right through her heavy winter coat while he tried clumsily to lift it from the hem. Abruptly he stopped and he pulled away. In his mind, he saw Sally lying in large dark-green, metal tube in a hospital. There was a nurse standing nearby. Sally looked terribly ill.

"What's wrong?" she asked bringing him back to the cold, Christmas reality beneath the tree.

"Nothing. Snow fell down my back is all."

"Come on," she urged inviting him to another kiss.

It was broken by a voice that boomed so loudly it knocked the snow from the branches overhead, "Sally!"

"My Dad," she whispered in Jackie's ear.

Strangely, she tossed one of her gloves on the ground and ducked down to pass back to the street. He pulled her back and kissed her again before setting her free. Footsteps approached the tree. She righted her hat. With mischief and holiday cheer twinkling in their faces, she and Jackie mouthed, "Merry Christmas," to each other.

"Sally are you in there?" her father asked at the dark entrance of their cache.

GIVE A
WAR BOND
FOR
CHRISTMAS!

UNITED STATES WAR BOND

"THE BEST PRESENT FOR THE BEST FUTURE!!!"

Jackie flattened himself against the tree. His heart pounded in his chest. Sally put her index finger up to her lips and burst out to greet her father.

"Daddy? Daddy. The wind blew my glove away. Oh! Here it is," she said in a voice more childish than the one she used to speak with Jackie showed him the glove in her hand.

"I see. Come along. Your mother is waiting."

Jackie spotted the small navy glove on the ground on his way in. He thought she might have dropped it deliberately, so she could come back. He wasn't sure; he didn't want her small hands to be cold.

"Excuse me," he called running after them.

"Yes? What is it?"

"Excuse me sir, I noticed this on the sidewalk.

"Sally? I thought you found your glove.."

"I guess… Um… I dropped it…."

He handed her the glove and turned to Jackie.

"Thank you young man." They stood in awkward silence. "Is there something else?"

"Just Merry Christmas, sir, miss."

"Yes. Yes. Merry Christmas," Sally and her father replied.

✳✳✳

Fierce winter winds blasted through the frigid block of winter months and blew Sally, the singer, the Christmas party of 1941 and his father's departure into memories. Jackie kept waiting for signs of his mother's anxiety to arrive and produce preserves or pies; twelve weeks passed. They did not which he credited to his father being relative nearby on Long Island at Camp Upton, writing and calling. When he went further south to the Fort Belvoir, the training camp in Virginia, she sent more food than she had previously, and she sent several pairs of pajamas. He returned them and wrote, "The army doesn't allow pajamas." She was completely annoyed with the army and didn't think her husband was going to sleep well in the raw or in his uniform.

In the last letter he sent from training, he included several changes he had to make. The letters would not be as frequent as long or as detailed. He had to send them through Victory mail which meant several strangers would read them before she did.

"Letters are all censored," he wrote.

To get around that, he had written to her in Norwegian which was easier for him and more intimate, but that letter was returned. The rules demanded that letters be written in English, which frustrated her, especially since he was about to go the front and he couldn't tell her where.

"Troops don't know themselves," he wrote.

Over the following year, Paul did not seem to know where he was, or if he did, he didn't tell. As far as Jackie could tell, his mother was still fine. In one letter, his father bragged modestly he achieved the rank of corporal in an engineer company for no reason other than his superior skills in math and art. Eventually, he replaced the letters with parcels that arrived every now and then but spoke to his understanding of her and what she liked and needed. The last one came at Christmas. It was full of tiny glass birds and bells which rang. Frigg took great pleasure in hanging them in the tree. After the last one was in place, she surveyed her arrangement and made a couple of adjustments. When the guests arrived, she positioned herself by the ornaments prominently dangling on the ends of the branches where they were certain to incite inquiry.

"Aren't they lovely? It's Paul's idea."

The manner in which she said his name summoned his presence to the room and gave the impression that he could charge up from the basement with his fiddle in hand at any moment. Jackie was comforted by the feeling. He was also impressed by the women's creation of a proper feast in the face of food shortages and rationing. There were pots of vegetables and two roasted turkeys and a large ham pie. The Christmas dinner committee, led by his mother, had met on a frigid December morning at the kitchen table on Ocean Avenue. The women raised their right hands and recited the pledge plastered throughout supermarkets and grocery stores.

"I accept no rationed goods without giving up ration stamps."

Then they settled down to plan the meal with great seriousness, several packs of cigarettes and an urn of coffee. In front of them, they piled the government regulation coupons for coffee and sugar and the blue and red stamps for meat and butter for collective use. Each woman announced the dish she planned to make and read off the ingredients and amounts she needed. Phyllis acted as the secretary and took notes. Nora calculated the total quantities. After consulting, each saw individually and they all saw collectively, they didn't have enough sugar for what they considered a holiday staple, the desserts. "It just isn't Christmas without rum cake and pie," one of them muttered. The light coffee klatch atmosphere dimmed with frustration and cigarette smoke. Nancy got up and put her hands on her slim hips.

"Come on. We're a bunch of smart girls. We can solve this problem. We just need a little help."

From one of her book totes, she pulled a bottle of whiskey and plunked it on the table. Within an hour, they had reshuffled and reassigned; they were almost satisfied. Fana was truly upset she wanted to contribute but as a foreigner had no points or coupons to offer. She couldn't even bring the dish she wanted because she didn't have the right ingredients, the one most treasured, sugar.

I mean, I have sugar but the wrong one. My father brought it from France."

"What kind of sugar is 'wrong?' Nancy asked.

"Sucre granule, three kilos. I need powdered," she lamented.

When they heard, "sucre," the women's faces lit up, and then turned to Nancy for confirmation.

"Yes. Sugar… Apparently Fana has six pounds of it!"

"Six pounds," they echoed.

They thanked Fana, promised to show her how to powder the granulated sugar and toasted her father for buying granulated sugar, making Christmas desserts possible.

THIS STORE IS PLEDGED TO CONFORM TO THE
SUGAR REGULATIONS OF THE U.S. FOOD ADMINISTRATION

Your Sugar Ration
is 2 lbs. per month

SUGAR
2 lbs.

SUGAR
1 lb. 1 oz.

SUGAR
11 oz.

AMERICA'S VOLUNTARY RATION
ENGLAND'S COMPULSORY RATION

FRANCE'S COMPULSORY RATION

ITALY'S COMPULSORY RATION

**We must confine our consumption of Sugar
to not more than 2 lbs. per person per month
in order to provide a restricted ration
to England, France and Italy.**

UNITED STATES OF AMERICA
OFFICE OF PRICE ADMINISTRATION

WAR RATION BOOK TV

IDENTIFICATION

Mrs Paul Vik
(Name of person to whom book is issued)

361 Ocean Avenue
(Street number or rural route)

New York   New York   30
(City or post office)   (State)   (Age)   (Sex)

ISSUED BY LOCAL BOARD NO. New York   New York
(County)   (State)

(Street address of local board)   (City)

By
(Signature of issuing officer)

SIGNATURE
(To be signed by the person to whom this book is issued. If such person is unable to sign because of age or incapacity, another may sign in his behalf)

NOT
VALID
WITHOUT
STAMP

WARNING

1 This book is the property of the United States Government. It is unlawful to sell or give it to any other person or to use it or permit anyone else to use it, except to obtain rationed goods for the person to whom it was issued.

2 This book must be returned to the War Price and Rationing Board which issued it, if the person to whom it was issued is inducted into the armed services of the United States, or leaves the country for more than 30 days, or dies. The address of the Board appears above.

3 A person who finds a lost War Ration Book must return it to the War Price and Rationing Board which issued it.

4 PERSONS WHO VIOLATE RATIONING REGULATIONS ARE SUBJECT TO $10,000 FINE OR IMPRISONMENT, OR BOTH.

OPA FORM NO. R-121

✳✳✳

The wooden leaves expanded the kitchen table to accommodate the adults. The younger children sat at the two card tables across the room which looked very small to Jackie who now took his place with the grown-ups including Charlie, Wes and Bird. Frigg's stipulation that politics and war be left at the door kept the levels of harmony and levity high except for a brief dip into the horrors of the Cocoanut Grove fire in Boston.

"I heard it began over a kiss," Phyllis reported.

"You don't know what you're talking about," Edwards barked at his wife.

Jackie and his friends were worried that he might single-handedly threaten the longevity of the party by unleashing his imbecilic alter ego with drink, as was his habit. Attempting to keep him sober, they surreptitiously whisked his drinks away as soon as he put them down. They stifled their laughs as they watched him look at the back of his jacket and turn around and around like a dog chasing his tail.

"What happened to my drink? I could have sworn I put it right there," he asked no one in particular.

He preferred straight gin to the punch, but they had taken it off the table, so he had to ask for a refill. The boys politely offered to retrieve a bottle from downstairs, ducked out the back door and came through the front a few minutes later. The hope was he would forget about having asked. They didn't realize Bill didn't just want another drink, he had an uncontrollable craving that suspended all life around him until he got one. If it didn't arrive, he sucked the contents of every unattended glass, and when those ran out, he had a full flask in his jacket.

"How was the Cocoanut Grove fire about a kiss?" Nancy asked Phyllis with genuine interest.

"The way I heard it was there was a couple in a booth, and the fella kept trying to kiss the girl, but she was shy. Poor dear. So he dimmed the light by unscrewing the bulb. The manager didn't want that and sent the bus boy to get it going again. It was too dark to see, so he lit a match and whoosh,"

"What in the God damn Hell do you know?" he asked and slapped his wife across the face. The sound of his palm on her cheek elicited a collective gasp from those who saw it and her whelp brought the room to a standstill. With a booze-blotched red and white face and no remorse or even awareness that he was making a scene, he blasted his wife.

"You're always running your mouth," and he moved toward her, but Frigg stepped in and smiled.

"Phyllis I have to show you a dress I am working on," she said and ushered her upstairs.

Confused and swaying on his feet, Bill turned and saw all eyes on him.

"What are you looking at?" he asked.

In Paul's absence, Jackie had become the head of the house.. He rushed over to Bill and urged him toward the door. Bill was ready for a fight and confronted him, but Jackie opened his jacket and showed him a bottle of gin, and he became cooperative. With the sign language of close friends, Jackie was able to communicate to Smitty, Bird and Charlie that they were in charge and should keep the party going. Immediately Bird put on a record. Charlie grabbed a girl to dance and Smitty raised a fan of playing cards in the air.

"Pick a card, any card."

VII

Consequences
Sad & Glad

VII
Consequences Sad & Glad

enuine concern for Phyllis and Bill stoked the blaze of gossip about the abusive, alcohol fueled drama at the holiday party well into the following year. By summer's end, the women of Ocean Avenue still found amusement in slipping their names into conversations. Jackie was pissed that Bill, who was over the thirty-five year old age limit and had no children was not eligible for the draft.

"If they recruited him, he might straighten out."

"The military doesn't want alkoholiker Jackie. Would you give a drunk man a gun? They want good, healthy men..."

"Like Far."

"Ja Jackie, liker din Far."

Except for Phyllis, who was in denial, the Vik's friends all knew she and Bill had a problem. No one knew of a solution. To support Phyllis and provide excuses to be away from Bill, the women invited her to each and every dinner or event no matter how small, though she was disinclined to attend. Her last reason was veiled beneath an abundance of make-up over her blackened eye the last time she showed up. No one mentioned it. Little by little, Phyllis dropped by their house more often. If Bill was there, she was somber and withdrawn. On her own, she was convivial and talkative with Frigg. They exchanged never-ending tips on cutting corners, gardening and recipes while they listened to the radio. They readied themselves with beverages and cookies when it was time for one of their favorite programs *The Whistler.* Jackie was proud of his mother and the women of the coffee klatch for caring about their friend, Phyllis.

That's what TOP would do, he told himself.

Knowledge of his wife's visits brought Bill around at all hours, supposedly in search of her, but Jackie saw the way he looked at Frigg. He told her he had a bad feeling about Bill Edward's unpredictable and unwelcome appearances, but she pooh-poohed him and insisted he had "just lost track of time." Her farm-girl naïveté and hospitable nature let him in for "some strong coffee" before she sent him home; although, if he was too far in the bag, she served the coffee and called a taxi. Jackie repeatedly asked her to turn him away, but she insisted, "It's all right." As a newly honed woman in charge, she let him know she was pleased about him, her young son challenging her. He didn't say anything else to her or Edwards, but he annoyingly shadowed his every move and rushed him through his coffee into his coat and out.

Walnut carving

The latest delivery from his father contained two wooden crates, which Frigg unpacked with the business face she usually wore at the store. Larry and Nancy, who had become Frigg's constant companions, were on hand and advised her as to what she might sell or set aside for further research. The contents yielded a menagerie of carvings from "persimmon and box-wood," according to Larry. One was a walnut, each small enough to fit in a palm.

"Clearly Paul is in the Pacific Theatre," Larry noted.

He lifted an enormous lamp base resembling a bird and a lion at the same time, and curiosity rippled through all their faces. Jackie had gone into the kitchen to peel his apple.

"What a swell griffin," he said walking back in. They're as old as forever, from India and Greece. Aeschylus wrote about them in *Prometheus Bound.* The Griffin pulled Okeanos' chariot." Jackie ran his hand over the creature and he continued. "The head is an eagle and the body is a lion, so they're courageous. Perseus rode one to save Andromeda." He took a big bite of his apple. "The sea goddesses were mad the queen of Joppa said her daughter, Andromeda was prettier than them. So they complained to Poseidon who flooded the land, and sent a big seamonster. The Nereids chained Andromeda to a rock in the ocean. But when Perseus was flying by on the Griffin, he saw her and fell in love." He chuckled. "I guess her mother was right. She was prettier. He had to kill the seamonster to get Andromeda."

"I see," Frigg said to Jackie, though she didn't really, and she added with pride, "He's at the top of his class."

Larry removed smaller objects from the crates including several swords to which Frigg expressed her opposition. They were beautifully crafted works of art, the likes of which Jackie had never seen, and he begged her to let him keep at least one. Larry spoke up on his behalf and noted Jackie's good judgment in handling saws and wood-cutting tools, and she consented.

"You have no idea of where Paul is?"

Frigg was silent. Jackie shot Larry a look discouraging further discussion of his father. He was sure it would cause his mother to fall apart. Larry took the hint and discussed how he would display the extraordinary objects she consigned in his gallery.

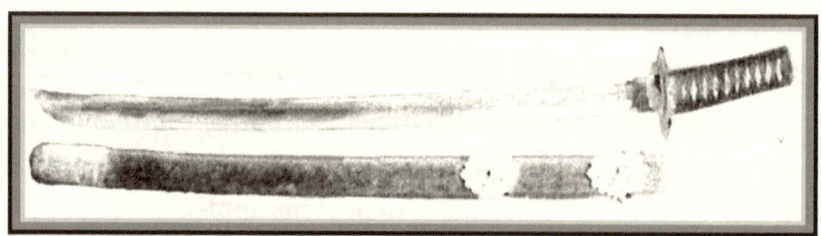

The Samurai Sword

Larry unsheathed the blade and claimed its twenty-four inch length made it a Katana and demonstrated how to use it. He held it over his head and sliced into the air with ease. With a mock ceremonial bow, he presented it to Jackie on his upward turned palms. Jackie placed his hands around the handle and discovered it was much heavier than he anticipated. He closed his eyes, took a deep breath to raise it, and he swung it downward just as Larry was bending to retrieve an object from the floor. The blade struck and he heard the grotesque sound of a butcher's cleaver hacking into an animal. The alien words, "Ketteitekina surasshu de aite o seifuku suru[4]," chopped out of his mouth, and then he saw Larry's head lying on the ground next to his body spurting blood.

"Argh!" Jackie cried out and dropped the Katana.

The women ran in and saw Jackie, eyes wide as saucers, staring at the rug. Larry was next to him, his head intact. Unaware of why Jackie screamed, he shrugged. Jackie was relieved to see him and realized the vision must have come from the sword. He feigned amusement and claimed he was "playing."

Frigg saw through him and that night suggested he cleanse

---

[4] Japanese: Conquer the opponent with one decisive slash.

the negative forces from the weapon by dipping it in a bath laced with sea salt. All the way to the tub, the hack that decapitated Larry haunted him. Once over the tub, the sword trembled in fear and resisted the plunge. Jackie had to dig deep to find enough strength to force it in and hold it under. It wriggled desperately in his hands and at one point reached the surface where it let out a blood-curdling scream. Resubmerged it heated up and within a minute it was so hot, he had to release it. He leaped back and stood in astonishment as the water boiled and the sword emitted a pulsing, blinding orange glow. Hideous wraiths ascended in swaths of steam frightening Jackie and urging a soundless cry for "Mor!" In the blink of his eyes, the light vanished and the sword rested peacefully under the water. When he took it out, it was much lighter.

The next day, he practiced in the mirror before he tucked it under the couch where he and he alone could find it and his mother would probably forget about it if she hadn't already. She was seldom home having busied herself with the store as zealously as she had the preserves and fish pies, yet her husband's absence had not turned her into a disheveled whirlwind as in the past. In its place was a composed woman. Prior to shipping out, Paul advised his employees at Vik's Woods a new manager was arriving, Henry Johns. Along with many of the men in the community, the military inducted him and unable to show up which the staff understood, so they expected a different man, not a woman. The idea didn't even cross their minds and certainly not his wife. They had a high opinion of Mrs. Vik because she knew her place and was adept at bringing their boss his lunch or lightening his mood, not replacing him. To ease the men's strong objections, which she feared would undermine the store stability, she assured them she was taking the reigns temporarily.

The truth was she was no longer interviewing applicants. Within a couple of days, it was clear to her that the position involved making schedules, buying supplies and keeping track of money, all of which she had done for years in caring for the household. Because she and Paul were so close, she knew as much about the quality of carvings and their woods as anyone, so she felt secure in the idea that she could run the business. The only challenge she saw was the male staff's resistance. They questioned her about every decision she made, but despite her nerves, she stayed.

"Once they get to know me, they will be different," she explained to Jackie after Joe argued with her in front of a customer.

He was so loud and disrespectful Jackie had stepped out from behind the counter to intervene, but his mother raised her hand and smiled.

"It's all right. I'm sure Joe is just tired, aren't you? You know how difficult it is for salesmen," she said to the customer who nodded.

Frigg led the woman toward a hand-crafted bowl which she purchased. It was obvious that Frigg not only liked being in charge but was good at running the store. Being there provided her a sense of worth and closeness to his father. At times her fingers dawdled on the wood, smoothed it as she had Paul's arm. Unfortunately Jackie observed the change in attitude Joe had displayed in all the employees. They were more supercilious with her than they had ever been with his father and came and went as they pleased rather than asking as they had before. At times, they were flat out dismissive and confrontational in dealing with her. Though her demeanor was publically unflappable, Jackie knew the men's' disrespect bothered her..

"Working is making her nutty," he confided in Bird.

In the middle of the night sometimes, he heard her in the kitchen rattling the cookware. The preserve shelf was full and the kitchen overflowed with so many pies she had to take them to Fred and Nora's to sell. One Saturday night insomnia thrashed him around in bed. The uneasiness of walking alone outside late at night followed him as he paced him back and forth from his room to the hallway. Upon his seventh trip, a blood-curdling scream made him jump. The only weapon he had nearby was the flashlight, so he grabbed it and bolted into the hall. He flicked on the light. No one. He charged into his mother's room. The light switch didn't work; he shined the flashlight on her bed where he saw her sitting bolt upright, her large, round, blue eyes staring blankly. Her breathing was shallow and rapid; her brow wept perspiration.

"Mor?" he whispered.

Approaching cautiously, he searched the rest of the room with the beam of light until he found the lamp. He turned it on; still she he didn't move. While he stood assessing the scene, she tore out of bed and down the stairs; he followed.

"Mor? Mor? What are you doing here?"

He picked up the phone and asked the operator to connect him to Fred Hansen.

"It's min Mor," came out automatically, and nothing followed.

The pitch and tone of his voice communicated such urgency that within a matter of minutes Fred and Nora were there with coats thrown over their robes. In low voices, they consoled Jackie.

"It's probably a bad dream. Don't worry. Everything is okay," Nora assured him.

Frigg's eyes were bulging out of her head. She was clawing at the sofa in exactly the same way a dog digs at the earth trying to retrieve a bone he was certain he had buried in that exact spot. Almost a half an hour had passed. His heart thumped more slowly. Then she screamed again and Jackie involuntarily jumped. Fred placed a comforting arm on his shoulder.

"Everything's okay boy."

Nora told them to "be still now. I shall try to get her back to bed." She spoke to his mother in Norwegian, "Frigg. Det er meg, Nora. Vi må gå i dvale nå. Kan du komme med meg?"

Fred told Jackie, "Nora said they had to go to sleep and asked if she would come with her."

After a long handful of seconds had ticked by, the sleeping Frigg reached out for Nora who led her upstairs. To Jackie's relief, Fred and Nora spent the night in the guest room. Sunday morning, Frigg was the first one in the kitchen, and she put the coffee on. She was completely astonished to see Nora.

"God morgen. Is Fred all right?"

"Ja. We are here for you."

The account of the previous evening perplexed her, and she was both embarrassed and sorry the Hansens had been inconvenienced over her. She had no doubts that it was true; the vision was quite vivid. She and Paul sauntered in a summer night's daylight on their beach. He lifted her to their rock, and then he Paul was swallowed up by the ground. Only his hand and face were visible. She jumped down to him and dug so frantically to unearth him that her fingers and arms ached.

"Oh! Are you hurt?" Nora asked.

"No. Why?"

"Your hands..."

Dirt rimmed Frigg's fingernails and fresh lacerations crisscrossed her knuckles.

"I was working in the garden," she said, but she recalled having been in the yard during the night for reasons unknown. To avoid further inquiry about the dirt, she changed the subject.

"Nora did you receive a new Point Ration Chart yet?"

"Ja. I bring it later,"

They prepared a heavy breakfast which Fred and Jackie devoured with gusto. Nora offered to stay with Frigg because they only opened the store a few hours Sundays. Frigg refused politely saying it would not be necessary because her brother Rolf was coming.

Nora had no bold or busy bones in her, so after church when Frigg and Jackie saw her on the porch with Fred, they knew there had to be bad news. In silence, all shuffled around the table.

"Fortell meg," Frigg demanded.

Fred laid a telegram on the table. Her eyes fixed on his eyes,. She raised the pale yellow telegram very, very slowly and read each and every single solitary word aloud.

CLASS OF SERVICE		SYMBOLS
This is a full-rate Telegram or Cablegram unless its deferred character is indicated by a suitable symbol above or preceding the address.	WESTERN UNION 1204	DL=Day Letter
		NT=Overnight Telegram
		LC=Deferred Cable
		NLT=Cable Night Letter
	A. N. WILLIAMS PRESIDENT NEWCOMB CARLTON CHAIRMAN OF THE BOARD J. C. WILLEVER FIRST VICE-PRESIDENT	Ship Radiogram

The filing time shown in the date line on telegrams and day letters is STANDARD TIME at point of origin. Time of receipt is STANDARD TIME at point of destination

WMUA7 44 GOVT=WASHINGTON DC

MRS PAUL L VIK
OCEAN AVENUE
MANHATTAN NEW YORK

THE SECRETARY OF WAR DESIRES ME TO EXPRESS HIS DEEP REGRET THAT YOUR

HUSBAND SERGEANT PAUL VIK HAS BEEN MISSING AND IS PRESUMED LOST

FOLLOWING ACTION IN THE PERFORMANCE OF HIS DUTY AND IN THE SEVICE OF HIS

COUNTRY. THE ARMY APPRECIATES YOUR GREAT ANXIETY AND WILL FURNISH

INFORMATION PROMPTLY WHEN RECEIVED.

ULIO THE ADJUTANT GENERAL

THE COMPANY WILL APPRECIATE SUGGESTIONS FROM ITS PATRONS CONCERNING ITS SERVICE

"What?! Far is lost?!" Jackie cried out.

"No. Manglet. Missing is what's there," Fred chimed in. "They can not keep track of those thousands of men all over the world. These telegrams come into the store almost every day."

Nora, knowing full well, he had just fibbed for Jackie's benefit, flicked her eyes at him to suggest he not go too far trying to prove his point.

Frigg's calm demeanor belied the tremendous internal turmoil the telegram unleashed in her. The Hansens lingered long enough to be comfortable that she and Jackie were okay and then return to the store.

"If you need to talk, just call," Nora whispered in Frigg's ear tenderly.

She lowered her head in acknowledgement. After the Hansen's ambled out, Jackie hung up his coat in the hall closet. When he returned to the kitchen, he watched his mother go completely to pieces. Tension had pulled his lips in around his teeth and clamped his mouth shut. He was stiff all over when his mother wrapped her arms around him. He didn't kiss her cheek as he usually did; he couldn't. Sobs wracked her entire body. Fearful of her falling, he accompanied her upstairs where she remained for days. In an effort to care for her, he ignored his own anxiety and brought her coffee and meals on a tray, but she didn't respond to his knocks, so he left them by the door where they stayed until he replaced them.

I thought she said Uncle Rolf is coming. Where is he?

The alternating silence and grieving wails doused the fires of hope he had kept burning for his father's return. Unwittingly seeking solace from her abandonment and his father's status as missing, he descended into the workshop. Stretching out on the cot in the dark, he inhaled the wood fragrances that transported him back to the days he and his father had spent in the woods hunting them.

What should I do Far? What should I do?

For three mornings, he ate breakfast alone in the cold kitchen, pretended everything was normal and went to school. A woman was in the kitchen on the fourth day who must have been his mother, but she looked more like one of the Valkyries, the beautiful women in the service of the God Odin who were responsible for collecting dead soldiers' souls. Those who had fought in battle were considered good and sent to Valhalla where they feasted. Those who were bad were sent to Niflhel where they froze. Had she been a Valkyrie, her tragic expression said she suffered the double blow of coming across a dead soldier who was her husband and then discovering his soul was bad. He greeted her, but his mother was not in the body in front of him.

By the end of the week, his posture slumped whether he was walking or sitting. After school, he was reluctant to go home. Destitute of the inclination to read or even talk, he lingered at the bookstore with Bird and his father, Mr. Mann mentioned he didn't seem to be himself and offered to help. The heartbreaking answer he gave that his father was missing and his mother was "behaving strangely" inspired Mr. Mann to invite him to stay with them for a few days. Jackie accepted, but he had to let his mother know. He heard her in the workshop, so he brought her a cup of piping hot coffee and a cookie. The small lamp was shining behind her and illuminated the ends of her hair as she sat fondling a window screen his father had been carving. Jackie turned on all the lights.

"Have you been sleeping here?" she asked faintly.

He nodded and pushed the cup toward her. "I made this for you. I ..."

"Is everything all right?"

For an instant he questioned his own sanity. *What does she mean asking me that? Doesn't she realize she has locked herself up for days and not made me breakfast or ... "*

Anger borne of confusion forced his words out very loudly.

"The men at the store think they scared you away. Everyone is asking about you, Mor. I don't know what to tell them. I understand why Far is not here. But... Why aren't you here? Where is my mother?"

"Oh guten min, I..." she said and held him in her arms, "I am sorry. I..."

Jackie pulled away, mustered his stoicism and announced, "Mr. Mann invited me to their house for a few days," and he walked out.

Softly, she called after him and stayed his steps but only for a moment. He couldn't bear looking at her, so he slept at Bird Mann's for a couple of days, and then, somewhat reluctantly, returned. He arrived at the exact moment as his big bear of an Uncle Rolf.

"Where have you been?" Jackie demanded nervously.

"Taking care of business nevø" he answered with a hearty hug. "A farm is a baby; you can't just walk away and leave it. You know that."

Jackie offered to get his mother, though he saw neither light nor movement in her room at the top of the stairs. Rolf held out his strong arm and blocked his path.

"She should bring herself down here. I would be at my door waiting for her if I knew she was coming," he stated, and then rubbed his stomach. "Must be some pies around, right?"

The familiarity of his request lifted Jackie's mood. Uncle Rolf had a reputation for being an enthusiastic eater. Anyone who worked from twilight to long after dark seven days a week would have be, but his ample girth divulged his epicurean leanings. He and Jackie laid a mini smorgasbord of deviled eggs, cheese, sardines, ham, and rye crisp crackers. Jackie had never seen so much food on the table for two people or four people. Uncle Rolf grabbed a handful of crackers like a deck of cards and death three to Jackie and a dozen to himself. Rolf scrutinized the table.

"What's missing? Something's missing."

He clapped his hands, leaped up and found two mason jars, pickled green beans and strawberry preserves, and they feasted. Rolf pointed out all the changes his parents had made to the house over the years.

"That's a great love story your parents have."

"All she knew was the farm, the animals, the smell of growing things, the sky at night, all of that. Gave it all up for your father. That's why he made the garden...for her. And then at night he would take her to Times Square to look at the craters on the moon."

Jackie laughed and echoed, "The craters on the moon," with a puff of incredulity.

"Ja Jackie. Sure. I saw them. There was a telescope there, twelve feet long I guess. You could put a dime in it and see the moon. On a clear night anyway."

The more Rolf spoke, the more Jackie understood the incredible depth of his parent's bond that began when his mother as an infant was put to bed beside his twenty-month-old father.

"So Jackie, if she is upstairs and you are here, what is the big emergency?"

Jackie retrieved the telegram from the drawer and handed it him, but he merely glanced at it.

"Oh the MIA telegram," he said matter-of-factly with a flurry of crackers falling from his mouth.

When Jackie snatched it back, Rolf realized he may have misinterpreted his nonchalance, and he laid his arm across Jackie's shoulders.

"I'm sorry Jackie. I really am. Be sad, but don't fall apart. Be a man my boy. Your Far is counting on us to keep things together," he waited a moment for Jackie to process his words, and so he could eat a pickle. "We got the same telegram and my mother, your grandmother, crumble like crackers. Your grandfather was off in the Great War, you know? So a couple weeks ago, we got one about my brother, Lars, your uncle."

"Uncle Lars? Really?"

"Yes, Uncle Lars. Mama thought about the whole thing all over again. You have his name, Jacob. Be a man boy," he said and delivered another dose of his healing bear warmth.

Jackie swallowed his feelings and invited Rolf to the work-shop. He put another deviled egg in his mouth, laid a pickle on top of the sardines on the cracker and accepted. Jackie played his fiddle, and after devouring every morsel of food he had brought, Rolf played along by slapping out a tune on his thighs and stamping his feet. Thumping upstairs interrupted them. It was the iceman. When he slid the block of ice in, he commented, as he always did, on the uniqueness of the icebox.

"My husband made it," Frigg announced beaming with pride.

Her face was pale and somber beneath her fat braid wrapped in a crown over her head.

"Sister," Rolf bellowed and threw his arms up in the air.

Usually Frigg did the same, but this time her enervated form was still. Her eyes ran over Jackie as if he wasn't there, so he donned his camera and left.

The Ice Box

Two hours later, he walked in and saw Uncle Rolf's visit had had the desired magical effect of resurrecting his mother's pleasant demeanor. She was smiling and cooking more food for Uncle Rolf. They were discussing the days of their youth, and he told Jackie what a strong, bossy sister and worker his mother had been.

"Remember when Papa gave you permission to run the tractor and Pete climbed up there first?" A mischievous smirk dawned on her face. "You had him out of that tractor, on the ground on his backside in two seconds."

Jackie couldn't imagine his mother challenging anyone, but Uncle Rolf said it was a matter of survival for a girl on a farm with no sisters and three brothers. He and Frigg had a couple of beers and chatted away the time and her gloom. A few days later Uncle Rolf was gone, and Jackie thought he had taken his mother's new stability with him. When he didn't see her in the morning, he feared a relapse. It weighed on his mind throughout the day. On his way to the furniture store, he opened himself up to the energy of the universe to receive her image. She was fine, but when he sauntered into an electrically charged atmosphere, he thought he might have gotten it wrong. Three of the employees were frozen in postures leaning slightly toward the direction of the office wall vibrating with a heated but muffled argument between his mother and Joe.

"Yes, you do have to do what I say," she said firmly.

Joe whooshed through the showroom grabbing his hat on the way out. A moment later, the area in front of the office lit up with a visible energy as Frigg entered. She was wearing a suit, and her hair was neatly arranged in a bun.

"In case anyone else is confused, the bar is down the street, not in here," she stated sharply and gave a quick tug to the bottom of her jacket. She winked at Jackie, but who was she?

He didn't know if it was his stay at Bird's, her brother's appearance, time passing, a combination of all or none of these that hauled her up from despair. Before him was the body of the woman who playfully called herself "goddess, Frigg," Mrs. Vik, his mother, but he did not recognize her without his father, their closeness and laughter and love. Just as she had morphed when she thought her darling lost, she morphed again. In her smart suit and bun, she was a slightly callous, assertive woman. Nothing bothered her. There was a small fire in the store. She put it out. Joe came in stinking of booze again, and she fired him, at least temporarily. One of the store's delivery trucks was stuck in the snow, and she put on her woolen trousers and galoshes and helped shovel it out. Under that strong veneer, which impressed him, beat the heart of his beloved mother. He hoped she was safe within for while his tough business mother was less feminine and abrupt, the ghostly Valkyrie mother was impossible for him to bear. He kept an eye out for her when parcels from his father, shipped long ago, arrived.

The most recent held drawings, one was of their beach in Norway hanging on the stairs and one was American Indians dancing in the sand under a palm tree. There was no note. Frigg got lost in the drawing of the beach. No tears were shed. As far as he could see, she was fine. She did develop the habit of setting a place for his father at the table, even when they had company, and she cleared the dishes and washed them as if he had used them. Jackie didn't complain if it kept her on an even keel. Normalcy returned in the house. He continued clipping articles for their weekly discussions. A headline about a soldier who escaped from a Japanese prison camp in the Philippines completely grabbed his attention *Seventy-five thousand. How is that possible?*

Envisioning his father or uncle or anyone being subjected to such cruel and inhumane treatment as having their heads chopped off stopped him cold. He took a breath and looked at the accompanying photographs. The cameraman had to have shot it from a great distance to get the hundreds of captured soldiers sitting on the ground. In another, the men's faces were tragically gaunt, streaked with deep lines of despair and wet with the mud of perspiration and dry dust. Their uniforms were caked with such thick dirt it concealed their nationalities, but from their faces, he assumed they were American.

Their emaciated bodies bulged through the inside of their clothes and the Japanese bayonets threatened to poke the outside. A chill ran through his limbs. Frigg wiped her hands and read over his shoulder. Every muscle used to express worry tensed, and she put her fingertips to her lips. He covered the picture and article with his hand to prevent it from yanking her back into the dark abyss of longing and worry.

"Thank you gutten min, but I heard about that. Obviously, the writer made a mistake. April 1942? Umulig Jackie. 75,000 prisoners for almost two years and no one knew anything about it. Not one newspaper wrote anything? That is umulig."

The New Yorker Newspaper

THE NEWS FOR TODAY   TUESDAY APRIL 3, 1944   ONLY THREE CENTS

ESCAPED U.S. PRISONER GIVES HORRIFIC ACCOUNT OF TORTURE AND STARVATION ON A DEATH MARCH AT THE HANDS OF JAPS!!!

By Godfrey Arnold

Two Years Ago- More Than 75,000 U.S. and Filipino troops taken prisoner. Bataan, The Philippines

"We walked day and night—night and day in unbelievable heat, many of us had no helmets to protect from the blazing sun. We had no food or water. We were not given any. Our fellow soldiers were brutalized in front of our eyes, beaten mercilessly just for asking permission to get a drop of water. I don't mean from a faucet or a well. I mean stagnant, putrid water with animal waste and oil in it. Any animal had the good sense not to think about it but that's how thirsty we were. We learned to stop asking after a couple of men got permission, wet their mouths and then had their heads chopped off. Men got bayoneted or shot if they fell down, so we tried to stay on our feet. If you didn't that's when the buzzard squad would get you. They're the Japs that bring up the rear and clear the bodies off the road. We tried to help the guys sicker and more exhausted than us, but after walking through days and nights for days, knowing if you tripped...They aimed the guns at us and forced us to stop for a man who had fallen. He could not take one more step. They forced us to bury him. It was the hardest think I ever had to do it my life. It was not the work. It was because he was not dead."

"Umulig? Impossible? I don't know mor. Seems anything *is* possible in war. What I don't understand is, we read an article about Bataan, a while ago. Remember? The Japanese were supposed to help stabilize it and. . ."

"The rules Jackie. Let's talk on the weekend."

He folded the page over and continued clipping, but the article did not make it into the discussion pile. He would spare his mother the horrific account. When he cleaned up, an angry power welled up in him and crushed the paper into a small ball.

Later that night, while reading in bed, he heard a sound that sent a shiver up his spine, the vigorous rustle of the trash. He had only heard one creature do that.

Another rat.

The last time he heard it along with the family while making breakfast one winter's morning, but as they moved around to find the source, it stopped. When Frigg opened the cupboard, she and the beast were mutually startled. She screamed and opened the front door, so she could run away if it came after her. The portly rodent clambered in dizzying circles of destruction unable to remember the location of the small entrance through which he had come. The squeaky-clean plates offered him no traction and he tumbled him onto the shelf below with the thud of a big man's boot; he was at least a foot long, not including its tail.

"I need a weapon," Paul declared and charged down to his shop.

In the moment he was gone, the creature dove to the floor and raced for the porch. Frigg slammed the door shut so quickly, she accidentally caught it. Suddenly a long narrow awl skewered it to the doorjamb. Paul had thrown it from across the room. Frigg covered her ears to block the rat's squeals of agony and went outside. The family left it and had breakfast in the coffee shop on 10th avenue. Paul headed home first to clear away the carnage. His mother's fear of disease and her desire to scour the memory from her mind, instigated a massive cleaning project. Every pot, dish and utensil as well as the cupboards, counters and walls were disinfected and painted after Paul had hunted through the cupboards, found the rat's secret entryways and stuffed them full of steel wool.

That's when they painted those roses on the walls in the kitchen, Jackie recalled.

Deciding he had procrastinated long enough, he grabbed a chair leg he was repairing and his flashlight. To prevent casting a shadow and tipping the rat off to his presence, he dropped to the carpet and slid on his stomach to the railing overlooking the living room/kitchen area. Rubbish and newspapers were strewn about, but there was no rat. Frigg sat at the table. She had painstakingly flattened the newspaper pages he had earlier crushed so thoroughly. She poured over the photograph in the Bataan article scrutinizing each of the soldiers' faces for a glimpse of her love, his father. It was impossible to identify an individual, yet unyielding love and desperation pressed her eye against the magnifying glass. He didn't want to intrude upon her private moment. Stealthfully, he repositioned himself to snake back to his room.

"Jackie?" his mother said as softly as if he were next to her.

He joined her and amid the wreckage of the paper, she held their son who, intuition told her, was all that remained of Paul. Her sorrow was palpable during their long, warm embrace, but they uttered not one word. He couldn't remember the last time she spoke about his father.

The Vik's community, carried on with their lives as if the war had not reached into their kitchens and their beds and snatched away their men. They never knew who would be next and prayed for peace and emotional survival demanded they believe it was soon. By the end of 1944, Seamus, Lucky Lou and Smitty's mothers had received the dreaded telegrams which a Major General began by writing it was his "sad duty to inform you of the death of your" son or husband, words which forever altered the families' lives.

TOP's steps were not as spritely and their demeanors not as mischievous as they might have been had they grown up without the anxiety of war. Regularly they met to read letters they received from any of their family's soldiers. Those from fathers were particularly poignant. They listened closely, their worried souls burning as hot as July's black-tar streets. "I'm all right," or "I should be home soon," sprinkled a refreshing shower on them. "Take care of your mother," puffed them up with a sense of manliness and purpose. Sometimes news of a soldiers' death arrived before the last letter he had written. With trembling hands and the odd escaped tear running down their cheeks TOP read them too.

Paul had stopped writing long ago, so Jackie had no letters. In order to participate, he brought his clippings. Over the months, casualties, invasion, and destruction appeared less frequently and small victories replaced them. TOP interpreted the early spring as a sign of the war ending. Instead, it raged on and right into their perfunctory norm. At times, they met and didn't mention the war at all which aroused a sense of guilt in Jackie until one day in Times Square. He had ditched school and planned to take a photograph of the smoking camel. No one was obsessing about the war; it seemed to be the farthest thing from anyone's mind. Hawkers, buskers and streetwalkers were peddling their various wares, and the crowds hustled about as usual. He turned his face up and basked in the beautiful spring sun. On 44th Street, he stopped to get a papaya drink. Rum and Coca Cola was blaring over the radio but it suddenly stopped.

An authoritative male voice said, "We interrupt this broadcast with breaking news. Flash: President Roosevelt is dead. The White House announced just a few moments ago that President Roosevelt died of a cerebral hemorrhage at Warm Spring's Georgia. We have no further details at this time. Stay tuned."

President Roosevelt is dead? I must be hearing things.

Slack jawed he spun around. At first, everyone was immobile but then the gravity of grief for the president's passing yanked them to benches and leaned them against the walls. Questions and comments rippled through the crowd. "What was that?" "Did you hear that?" "Oh my Lord, the president died?" Women buried their faces in their hands and sobbed audibly. *How are we going to get through this war now?.*

TOP thought the worst and questioned the existence of God and justice for allowing Roosevelt, the leader who defended freedom to die and Hitler, the one who challenged it to live. But they had faith in the United States. When they worked in the gardens in the afternoon, Jackie fanned the embers of optimism, patriotism and hope and quoted Roosevelt.

"Like he said, 'We have nothing to fear, but fear itself.' We're going to win this God damn war."

Sorrow for Roosevelt diminished as the scent and light of spring crescendoed into the luminous calm before a sudden storm of joy. It began when news of the dictator's death was struck in the biggest, boldest letters anyone had ever seen a newspaper use for two words, "Hitler Dead." No sooner had the nation's pulse returned to normal when President Truman announced Germany's surrender.

"This is a solemn but a glorious hour. I only wish that Franklin D. Roosevelt had lived to witness this day. General Eisenhower informs me that the forces of Germany have surrendered to the United Nations. The flags of freedom fly over all Europe." In his next breath, President Truman reminded the country not too get too excited because, "Our victory is but half-won. The West is free, but the East is still in bondage to the treacherous tyranny of the Japanese. When the last Japanese division has surrendered unconditionally, then only will our fighting job be done."

The Victory-over-Europe celebration, dreamed about and sandbagged within the nation's hearts so long, exploded. Nothing could have stopped it. War's weighty shadow was peeled to pieces by a cacophony of Church bells. New Yorkers clustered in streets and bolstered the tolling with emotional thanks and raucous gladding that day and in June when General Dwight

Eisenhower, the Supreme Commander of the Allied Forces in Europe, waved from a convertible to the masses. They were at least a million deep on Broadway. The roar of their welcome was so loud, Jackie thought it must have rocketed to all the Gods in the universe. At times, the throng of revelers lifted him and his mother completely off the ground; one was when Eisenhower passed right in front of them.

"If this is half-winning, imagine what the real end is gonna be like," he told Frigg.

Jackie was sure the spell of the VE Day festivities were intoxicating enough to last weeks, but he hadn't taken into account the sobering effect of the war raging on in the Pacific. It soon subdued New York to its tumultuous pre VE Day. Then the United States decided to take drastic measures and drop an atom bomb on Japan.

This political move threatened to disband TOP. They split into opposing camps on whether or not the country should blow anyone up. There was no tiebreaker because Lucky Lou preferred to remain neutral and not to have any opinion. Charlie, speaking for his half of TOP, presented the pro-argument that, "The Japs don't want to surrender. They're gonna fight to the death, so if we shoot or bomb, what the Hell's the difference?"

"Cold-blooded murder of civilians is the difference. Children are the difference, thousands and thousands of them. That shit is going to fry them alive. For what? Peace?" Jackie countered.

Tensions ran high and repelled the two halves of TOP, especially after not one but two Atom bombs decimated Hiroshima and Nagasaki. Charlie's pro-bomb contingent stood by their opinion. Social obligation eventually brought TOP and all the Vik's friends together at a gathering. Recent news pointed to the Japanese waving a white flag, and they wanted to be together to hear President Truman on the radio. He was aware that the nation was on tenterhooks, and didn't waste any time getting to the words, "unconditional surrender." He didn't really have to say them in

their entirety. When he voiced the syllable "con" of "unconditional," it triggered a frenzied exaltation among the United
State's entire population of humans and animals alike. Every
single ship's horn blew and automobiles honked and honked and
honked amid the startled pandemonium of ten billion birds taking flight and citizens ejaculating an ecstasy of relief. TOP
blasted into the streets where they gave and received hugs with
neighbors and strangers. Old Mr. Jamison was so overjoyed he
arrived on the scene without his teeth and waved his cane in the
air. Tears streamed down his face, and Jackie gave him a big Uncle Rolf hug and kissed him on both his cheeks. The boys
skipped along to the deafening of Times Square. The ground
shook mightily and the buildings swayed in the jubilation. By the
time an ounce of Jackie's wits had settled back into him, he had
run back to get his camera to "document history." The expand-
ing galaxy of revelers made it almost impossible.

"Only a few came out," he told TOP when he tossed the photographs down. I don't care. I kissed so many girls," he bragged
breathlessly, "God Bless America."

Kiss the War Goodbye

Consequences Sad & Glad

The New Yorker Newspaper

THE NEWS FOR TODAY   TUESDAY AUGUST 14, 1945   ONLY THREE CENTS

VICTORY!
JAPAN
DEFEATED

PEACE!

VIII
Difficult Departures

othing TOP did in the years since VJ-Day ever elevated any of them to an emotional summit quite as stimulating. Their weddings and the arrival of their children were thrilling but in different ways. After hours at the Dog one night, the seven of them sat together drinking and they decided to compare feelings, a word Charlie objected to.

"What are we a bunch of whiny broads?"

With further discussion "feelings" changed to "reactions." They came up with the questions to which they had to write a word or two about them: losing their virginity; standing at the altar getting married; holding their newborn child for the first time; learning a parent had passed; being away from home and stabbing or shooting a man in the army whether they killed him or not. Their outer differences had caused them to consider their camaraderie a mystery when all along their inner similarities had made it logical. An even greater sense of brotherhood grew among them. They expressed a true love among them.

"Brotherly love," Charlie clarified, and they drank a toast to TOP.

"The Only Pantheon. All for one and one for all."

"Be great if our children ended up friends, wouldn't it?" Jackie asked.

They agreed with another toast.

"And that goes for you and you too," he said pointing to Bird and Lucky Lou. You're next."

"Us? No. You'll be next Jackie," Bird said, "You always are, at least meeting girls."

The new one, he met in the most unlikely place, the Dog. Seamus hired Helen, a new waitress in the dining room, part-time for Fridays and Saturdays. She was a dancer the rest of the time. Her profession enhanced her shapely legs and her youth gave her a bubbly presence. When her eyes met Jackie's, the spark of attraction could have ignited a bonfire. She dropped the entire one hundred and three pound package of her enticements in his lap about a half an hour after he sat in her section. That same night, he was in her tiny apartment where she showed him how she could do full splits on the wall.

"So what can you do?" she asked brightly with her hands on her hips.

He strode over to her and scooped her up in his arms by her rump, and let her rest her legs on his shoulders with her back against the wall. She confessed she'd wanted to be with a man of his tremendous size to try out standing positions. Within a few weeks, the deep mauve wallpaper faded and peeled from the rubbing and perspiration of their bodies.

The dancing life had done for Helen what the mariner's life had done for Jackie, introduced her to foreign ports and made her a citizen of the world, so Jackie overlooked her disinterest in reading. They spent their months meeting in her place and comparing notes about cultures and exotic cities. She was an energetic and agile lover. At times they were blinded by the throes of their passion and neglected to take into consideration the pitfalls of her small room. Jackie collapsed on her one night, and he couldn't roll off. They had managed to lodge themselves under the bed, and he had to buck it off as a wild, untamed stallion would a heavy saddle. Another night, Helen found a good position for herself on the bed and grabbed a wall sconce, but it was not strong enough, and she fell over bending Jackie's "Ding-a-Ling," as he called it, all the way backwards. He let out several mighty yowls until it came loose and slapped his stomach with a loud thwack. The lingering ache terminated their horizontal dancing for a few days.

The brief break developed into a long break because Helen for an audition. All her sexual energy was transferred to practicing. Jackie complained that he never saw her. To satisfy his need to see her, and her need to dance, she invited him to join her. At first, he took it as an affront to his image as a man, a rugged, seaman who adored women.

"Dance with you? What in those fruity clothes?"

"Fruity clothes? What are you talkin' Jackie?"

"Right. No man is gonna put his dick in a pair of tights, pink tights unless there's a broad in them."

Laughing to herself, Helen shook her head in disbelief and assured him he could wear his own clothes.

"Haven't you ever been to a musical?"

"Sure I have," he barked defensively. "Larry took me and my mother to Oklahoma." He leaped and landed clumsily. "Farm hands don't spring around like that."

His move gave rise to Helen's doubts about the idea of his practicing with her, but she liked him.

"I'm not asking you to leave the Merchant Marines and become a dancer, I am asking you to help me, your lover," she cooed gazing up at him.

He acquiesced, but as soon as he stepped into the mirrored studio, he got cold feet.

What am I doing here?

A couple engaged in the Tango was finishing their session.. The male was dressed in a black shirt and trousers and moved with undeniable power and deliberation. The arrogant jut of his chin and the way his partner slithered over him and bowed to him fascinated Jackie. On the way out, the man slapped Jackie on the back, and they exchanged a hearty handshake. Helen didn't have any particular moves to rehearse; she wanted to keep limber, be prepared for whatever the audition might require. Thinking a familiar song more comfortable, might relax Jackie, she had him bring in a record he liked. Expecting Rock 'n Roll or swing, she laughed at the folk music that squeaked out. Jackie shushed her, tapped his foot and began to dance. Never having seen the moves, she observed with interest.

"That's a Valdres Springar from the south of Norway, usually done with a partner," he said and carried on alone.

"So you can dance."

Copying what he did, she was able to join him as he passed her for a second turn around the room. Helen changed the record and showed him another step.

"Slow-Slow-Quick-Quick; Slow-Slow-Quick-Quick," she said, and he repeated to himself.

Jackie had rhythm, and he was not only strong but he was limber enough to execute a few tricky moves. To trumpets blaring with the tempo racing at 150 beats per minute, he could lift her up in his arms and place her on one hip from where she slithered, snake-like, around his waist. She ordered, "Now let's go around the world," which busted him up laughing.

"Stop! You're going to drop me Jackie," she complained.

"All right. All right. It's just that means something else to me," he said squeezing her ass.

"Behave Jackie."

He did and after a while, he began to look forward to their sessions which he was sure were responsible for the tighter definition in his muscles. One night when he saw himself reflected next to Helen, the image of his parents dancing together floated by. Their fingers were interlaced, and they were lost in each other's eyes oblivious to their steps. In front of him, they stopped. His father moved his mother's hair from her shoulders and touched his vest buttons with a tenderness Jackie felt could only lead to soulful lovemaking. Dancing with Helen, who only looked at herself in the mirror, was not dancing with a partner. It was performing. This observation combined with the tension and the closeness of practicing eventually diminished the initial fiery magnetism between them. The only heat he noticed was in the studio. All the fan did was blow it around. Helen stripped down to her underwear; he wasn't aroused. Counting off steps obsessively, she ignored him while he sat on the sidelines until she was ready to work with a partner. They were there for hours and hours; she became a tired and passive lover, unable or unwilling to respond with a pleasurable clench of desire in response to his thrusts. He had to dig deep into his reserves to deliver himself to the finish. During their last sexual encounter, Helen lapsed into total non-participation; he stopped and received an unexpected blow to his ego. Because he was considerably taller, his chest formed a canopy over her and he bent his head to see the impact of his motions on her face. She had a blasé expression and exhaled a puff of smoke from a cigarette.

"Don't mind me," she suggested. "Go ahead."

The sight of her smoking beneath him affected him just like the image of the dead cat, so he closed his eyes, and thought of Asta. She never would have treated him that way. He pushed himself to climax and threw himself on his back in an uncharacteristically grumpy post coital mood. He contemplated going home; he hadn't been there in quite a while, but he was too tired. In the morning, he awakened to a make-up streaked pillow and the blur of Helen going from the closet to the suitcase, packing for her trip to Philadelphia. He showered and put on "Stompin' at the Savoy" which she asked him to turn off. In silence, he sat on the edge of the bed putting on his shoes, and she dropped on his lap and ran her fingers up his inner thigh to his crotch. She wanted to have dinner that night since she would be gone for a week. Her blasé expression from the previous night sent his blood straight down to his feet. Forehead to forehead, she looked into his eyes, and dawdled on his thighs but he refused to allow her to peak his interest.

"I'm not sure," was his disinterested reply. He removed her hand with an insincere smile. "I have to see what's going on at the store. I'll let you know later.

Jackie did not want to be alone. He reviewed the marriages

among TOP. Seamus and Shannon were an instant couple, two of a kind, breeding like Catholic rabbits. Wes married Susan after securing his parents approval. Jackie thought that was strange since they themselves were divorced. Charlie's father lived in a townhouse on East 67th but his mother lived in Chelsea, which is how he got involved with TOP. Jackie recalled the day Charlie returned from a church social and announced, "Patty is the one." He seemed to be right.

Even Smitty confessed to his marriage being "good at times." No one had held out for "love that was more than a love." Jackie realized such a holy grail was bestowed not sought and found.

What a dreamer I am, a dreamer on a fool's errand. Helen is all right. She is feisty, funny and flexible, and more attractive than Margrete or Hilde. Our children will be beautiful.

He dismissed her tendency to be contemptuous, standoffish and self-centered.

That's cuz she's doing that dance thing, dealing with those theatre people, bunch of gypsies. This is just a phase. She can't be a dancer forever. What kind of a life is that for a girl?

At lunch, he sat at the typewriter and clacked out questions to ask her at dinner. He already knew she was sensual, liked to travel and liked to read, so the list included questions about favorite foods, movies, colors, flowers; family; religion; number of kids she wanted and where she would live if she could live anywhere in the world. He called and told her to dress for dinner after all, and she was excited.

Rather than going up to the apartment, he heightened the tingling in anticipation of his little beauty's arrival by waiting in her lobby. Involuntarily, his eyes widened in delight as she twirled out in a soft black, chiffon dress. It was perfect for a white-table-cloth restaurant such as Lüchow's. Because he had taken many women there, the maître d' recognized him and greeted him with a warm smile.

"Mr. Vik, how nice to see you again."

"Yes, nice to see you again Mr. Vik," Helen mocked when they were seated. "I didn't know you went to places like this," she noted.

"There's a lot you don't know about me."

Over champagne, Helen gushed about her plans and where she was going to stay in Philadelphia. When she arrived at a natural lull in her monologue, he brought up the list which she thought was a great idea but suggested they both answer. They did; however, it didn't incite the getting-to-know-you-better discussion for which he had hoped. On a piece of paper borrowed from the waiter, she made a list and wrote down their answers. With a giggle, she balled up the paper and put it on the table.

"I guess we are an example of opposites attracting," and then she went on talking about the audition.

On the way out, he slipped the paper with her answers into his pocket because he didn't want the waiter to find it. He took her to one of his favorite places, The Five Spot Café on St. Marks. The entire establishment was about the size of his living room. Several times, he heard his name and waved without really knowing to whom. There was no privacy and strangers had to sit shoulder to shoulder, but everyone had a front row seat to the music. Helen immediately stated the obvious, that it was crowded and mentioned that jazz would not have been her first choice. Unwilling to watch her sulk, he apologized and led her out. She didn't say another word until they got to their next stop.

"The Pier? Jackie, we're at the pier," she stated as if he did not know that.

It was late and there were almost no people, just a group of colored men dressed in white shirts and dark jackets. Three sat quite close together on a bench with musical instrument cases were nearby, and one leaned on the railing looking out at the big, round, golden moon. Jackie felt a surge of fear ripple through Helen's body. She rubbed her arms, and he placed his jacket around her shoulders.

"We got here earlier than I thought."

"For what Jackie? You getting' on a ship in the middle of the night?"

"You'll see." An uncomfortable silence filled the space between them. "You know Athens?"

"Athens, Greece?"

"Yea. The water there is incredible, blue. I mean, truly blue. If you hold it in your hands, the color is still there. The buildings are gleaming white; it smells so good..."

"I think it's those meat sandwiches they got," interjected one of the colored men who moved closer to them.

"That's right. The souvlaki."

They exchanged introductions and shook hands, but when Theo extended his hand to Helen, but she kept her arm limp at her side and only nodded. Jackie cut his eyes at her disapprovingly.

"Such a beautiful place and I was just thinking about the power of music, you know?"

Theo nodded, "Yeah man."

There was a rich man there who loved music. He wanted to

hear the best musician, so he had a contest, offered a cash prize for the best. A guy named Arion won, a harp player."

"They had harmonicas back then?" Theo asked.

"I don't know. I mean an angel's harp. Arion got a bundle of money, new clothes and women while he toured Greece, but…" he pointed to Theo.

"Time to branch out, right."

"He goes to Italy. More women. More money, but he gets homesick. On the way…"

"Let me guess. Somebody wants that money."

"Right. The sailors on the return trip. So Theo, I ask you. What's the only way to steal from a guy and not have him turn you in?"

"Kill him," Theo said pointing at him.

"Yeah, but they took the money first and they didn't want any witnesses, so they told him he had to kill himself or they would kill him."

"Oh. Wow. No. Did they or did he…"

"Which would you do, kill yourself or be killed?"

"That's rough. If I was outnumbered and there was no other way…" Theo paused and then shook his head and said "Myself, long as I could jump over and take my sax. Then I might have a chance."

"Arion too. He put on his fancy suit and played for them."

"Thinking if he played good, they might change their minds."

"Are you sure you haven't heard it before? Jackie hit his hands together, "Bam. Arion jumped overboard."

Theo shook his head in sympathy.

"The ship sails out of sight, and the sailors are laughing and waiving good-bye. Arion figures he's a goner, so in the middle of the ocean he plays his harp. A giant dolphin hears it; they love music. This dolphin is mammoth," Jackie stretches his arms out as far as he can. "Arion climbs aboard the dolphin and plays his harp while the dolphin takes him home."

"Oh Wow. Wow.."

"Jackie it's cold," Helen complained.

He pulled her close and laid his jacket across her shoulders. "Just another second."

"For what?" she asked annoyed.

Jackie waved his hand toward the moonlight pouring into the water, and two big dolphins leaped into silhouettes right in front of the moon.

"Come here. Dig it!" Theo said to his buddies who joined them at the railing.

The dolphins leaped up twice more then swam in circles. A car cruised up and honked. The musicians put a few things in the trunk before squeezing in with their instruments.

"Hey Jackie, Jackie man," Theo called out of the window, "Come by the Five Spot…"

"We just came from there."

"Next time. We're there Thursdays."

Jackie gave them a thumbs up. One of Helen's brown curls had fallen on her spellbound face. She stared until the last ripple was gone. Disbelief chopped up her words before she spit them out.

"How did you…This is weird Jackie … The story. The timing. The dolphins. I mean…" she stepped away and eyed him with distrust.

Jackie had heard the dolphins clicking in the distance, and he shot a photograph of them. He was not positive they would show up again, so he asked. They said, "Yes." He had hoped the sight of them would toss Helen into his arms for a romantic moment but that did not happen. Instead, it rattled her..

What is with this girl?

He caught his jacket as it slipped from her shoulders, and she walked ahead of him to the street. She hailed a cab herself. They exchanged a swift, cool kiss.

"Good luck on the audition," he called after the cab, but he changed it to "break a leg," which she had once insisted was the way to bring an actor luck.

* * *

Straight, drunk, giddy and despondent, Jackie had walked home through the grey streets of New York at all hours of the day and night in every kind of weather. He couldn't recall his footsteps having echoed so loudly or echoing at all, not even in 1942 when the blackout orders forced the lights off and the city was cloaked in the still of a million black shadows. Clomp - Clomp. Clomp - Clomp sounded all around, and he couldn't stand it. He took off his shoes and walked the rest of the way in his socks. The front of his building brought him a sense of relief similar to the one he had when he saw the "Welcome Home" banner in the port those many years ago.

Evidence of his absence from his own life was visible in the withering ends of the plant leaves, delivered newspapers stuck in the various postures in which they had they landed, mail lifting the lid on the box and a thin layer of city dust from the yard sprinkled on the porch. He heaped the papers and mail on the kitchen table, and sat down. A letter from Uncle Rolf caught his eye. "Update," was written on the outside, which made him chuckle. All of the letters Uncle Rolf had sent over the last twenty-five years were the same. He could just as easily have sent a postcard and written, "Everything remains the same, and everyone is still alive," but he didn't. Jackie recalled having seen Uncle Rolf sit down to write when he was on the farm. Late at night in the cool, quiet of his room after he was ready for bed, he turned the desk lamp on. He would think, and then he would dip the pen in ink. He wrote a line. He thought some more and wrote some more always with the same calm movement of his arm. He enjoyed the act of sitting, reviewing his life and sharing it with someone.

Good old Uncle Rolf.

Fana had sent a card from Paris advising him she was sailing for New York the following day. Her family had been visiting when Jackie first met her at the Christmas party so long ago, but after she was accepted to Barnard College, Larry and Nancy's house which became her home away from home. Though she was four years his senior, they were very close. Her second note was on Argent Gallery stationary with no stamp or address meaning she was in New York. Nancy's messages were written on her personal stationary which were lavender in color and fragrance. One invited him to meet her for coffee and talk about "the book," but he had forgotten which one they were reading. The second, dated ten days later, expressed concern because she had not heard from him. He pushed the mail away and the edge of one stuck out. The stamps from the United Kingdom brought a smile to his lips because he knew it had to be from Asta. The stationary was pink and stained with a spray of jasmine perfume; he breathed it in before reading. She lamented not having "got in touch sooner," but she couldn't didn't have the address. She was "happy to Smitty came by with it and let me know you are shipping out on a different line. I am not involved in the theater anymore, and I should love to see you again Jackie." Her expressed desire quickened his heartbeat, and he was ready to charge to the Union Hall to sign aboard a ship bound for Plymouth until he read, "I should also tell you, I was married and we have a son." He didn't run anywhere that night but delighted in knowing thoughts of him had endured and were strong enough for her to write to him. Enclosed was a photograph of her on a chilly British beach in which she appeared to be the same knockout he remembered. He kicked himself for not having recognized her qualities and letting her slip away, possibly to the undeserving and disrespectful British sailor with whom he had fought.

"Either the connection is there or it isn't, right cutie?" he asked and kissed the photo. The Theater. Pfft. What kind of life is that, right? You got out, but this other dancer I met, this Helen..." over everything else and agitated him anew. He sorted through his records unable to pick one,

Her name brought the evening's failed date to mind, and he preferred to think about something else, so he sorted through his hundreds of albums. He couldn't make up his mind, so he dropped the needle on the record already on the turntable and hung up his jacket. Helen's question and answer page from the restaurant fell out. For some reason, she had abbreviated versus as vs. which, to Jackie, made it look like they were playing a competitive game. The first column was hers, the next his and then she had her remarks in parenthesis. "Food: Marshmallows vs. fish, (so stinky); Flowers: roses vs. jasmine or violets, (those are sort of small); Favorite Color: red vs. blue, (so romantic vs. so sad; Religion: Catholic vs. Lutheran; (He can convert.) Children: one day, one vs. five, (Never); Where: any big city vs. near the sea; (Finally, N.Y. is a big city and near the sea; Movie: *The King and I*, Yul Brynner vs. *Giant*, Elizabeth Taylor." (*Giant?* So long. Should'a been a play.)

"Ha. We got nothing in common," he said a loud and thought, *Break a leg, she tells me to say. Pfft. Like I don't know what to say— I'm Jackie Vik. I know what to say.*

Swigging a succession of rum shots, he boarded one of the ships, running day and night, crowded with lost souls bound for the unilluminated port of Oblivion. He sailed so far down the murky waters of aloneness, he was oblivious to the light over the kitchen table blowing out and sat in the dark.

Goddamn it! I should go over there. What'd she think: I am a God who can boss dolphins around? Just a practice partner. Slow-Slow-Quick-Quick; Slow-Slow-Quick-Quick Ha. If she doesn't get the part, she'll be back. Crummy way to say good-bye. ... I will go over there. God she was something.

He stumbled to the bathroom and on the way back slipped on one of the slick records on the floor. On his hands and knees, he crawled to the record player, and after three drunken attempts, he managed to set the needle down again. He upped the sound, closed his eyes and danced alone in the dark. Pleased with the way he moved, he complimented himself.

I got good. Forget you Helen. I'm Jackie, Jackie Vik. I'm movin' on! Going to England, see lovely Asta.

Intoxication and nothing else tickled him and he laughed so hard tears streamed down his cheeks.

Here's to a long life and a merry one; A quick death and an easy one; 'A pretty girl and an honest one; A cold beer and another one!' Yeah, a pretty girl and another one and another one and another one. God? What are you keepin' me for? You got someone special in mind? I sure would like to meet her.

He emptied the bottle and tumbled into the deep grooves of music and an alcohol-induced madness of mirth and melancholy. Around and around in a vertiginous whirl he twirled with his invisible partner until the phonograph needle hit the label, and his body hit the floor. The music stopped and sad, black quiet blanketed. A firm persistent rapping lifted it, and he blinked into the faint fragments of moonlight reflecting on metal knobs and handles in the room. Pain hammered in his head obviously because the room had flipped upside down, and he had to hold on tightly or fall to the ceiling.

"Jackie? Jackie? Je suis ici. Peux-tu ouvrir la porte? Jackie? Is it you?" asked a dark, svelte apparition in the door pane.

Fana? Ah Fana I would know her voice anywhere.

The simple thought of her lifted his spirits and guided him into the past and the first night they spent together. It began at a gallery opening when they both showed up to help Larry, their mutual surrogate uncle set up. Spending time with her, he found she was highly relatable and very quick to laugh despite what he called her "ritzy, educated style." When the opening bloomed into a party and exhausted the booze, Larry invited them to "come on over," to his house. Carefully holding onto their drinks and conversations, the ostentation of bejeweled revelers strutted down one set of stairs and up a second down two doors. Music was already blaring when they arrived. Larry declared a small bedroom the coatroom, and a mountain of cashmere, wool and fur piled up. Jackie took several photographs, and walked into the tower of Babel in the living room. Nattering, schmoozing and palaver on music, fashion, Paris, and painters in a variety of languages streamed in the air thick with the scent of liquor and perfume, cigarette smoke, and artificial levity. The pretentious uptown atmosphere contrasted sharply to his uninhibited good-times with TOP or his shipmates. He stayed for Larry's sake because he "I felt better when you and Fana are here," he sighed with an arm around each. Fana made it easy, surreptitiously reminding him how he was familiar with Mark Tobey, Jasper Johns, and Ginsberg and promoting him as a photographer. After at a jazz fête, she sent them to a friend at a French newspaper, and they published them. He was excited to thank her and finally, he spotted her in an aqua blue dress with the French-speaking clique. Cheek kisses were exchanged.

"God, are you a sight for sore eyes," he whispered into her ear.

Smiling brightly, she slipped her hand into his.

«Monsieur et Madame Dubonne et leur fille Isabelle, Monsieur Vik, Jackie Vik, Il est un photographe et un musicien. Jackie, Monsieur et Madame Dubonne. »

They leaned in to kiss him. Isabelle, a delicate teen with long hair, pulled him toward her by his belt, and rather than delivering a feathery European kiss; she pressed her lips on his cheeks and fluttered her eyelashes flirtatiously. Complimented and interested, he nodded.

« Il est très beau, » she gushed under her breath to Fana.

She ran her eyes over Jackie and saw that time had replaced the gangling, teen with a ruggedly, elegant man.

« Oui il est très beau, » she confirmed, and glanced around. Adding, «Oh. J'ai perdu mon verre de champagne. » before she led him into the coatroom.

He felt more comfortable in the diminished din, breathed and reclined on the mound of coats. Fana sat on the windowsill silhouetted by sunset, and he traced the lines of her long, dark legs and gracefully curving torso. The door opened and they dove out of sight on the floor beside the bed. A woman's high heels tacktacked on the wooden floor. "Larry! This is a grand total mess," complained their owner mirthfully as she tossed her wrap. Once she was gone, Fana tugged on the edge of a full-length fur.

"Talk about moola."

"Yes, my father's. He bought it for my belle-mère, my step mother, but I like it," she grinned running her hands over it. "Come."

She reached out to Jackie. He slipped his hand into her long fingers and followed her into the bathroom. The party vibrated vigorously through the door next to one he assumed was a towel closet. Fana opened it and revealed a narrow, dark passageway. She stepped in, and without any hesitation, he followed, but coughing in the bathroom, stayed them in their steps. Mischief danced in their eyes while they listened to the seat slamming up, a urine stream, the toilet flushing, and the faucet squeaking on and off. They burst out laughing and continued to a small set of wooden stairs that wound up to the third floor. With a key from her dress pocket, Fana let them into her spacious room.

The mahogany scent drew his attention to the floor protected with rich silk carpets, then to the bookcases beneath the vaulted celestial mural. When he looked down, she was gone. A twinkling chandelier hung from the middle of the ceiling illuminating every nub on the velvet tapestry curtains boasting a softness that invited his touch. The tasseled canopy hung low over the puffy bed where Fana had thrown the fur coat. Jackie caught his reflection in the mirror and admired how he looked surrounded by the luxurious room. Fana's reflection appeared and from her discrete gesturing he understood he had to take the coat and hide. He stuffed the fur under the pillows and slid behind the curtain. Their rose perfume tickled his nose, and he stifled a sneeze. He heard Fana talking with someone about a fruit platter, where to put ice, the glasses clinking and a match. Incalculable seconds ticked into minutes, and his heart beat in his ears. He had to know what was going on. Through the blade-like opening between the curtains, he peeked into the room.. Splashes of golden candle light caressed Fana's dark brown skin. She disappeared from view and reappeared, her nakedness partially covered by the fur coat. She admired herself in the mirror. He was not sure if he was supposed to continue to wait, but he did. As soon as he moved his head away from the curtain, she pulled it aside. All he could see were the beauty's huge black eyes and her full mouth upturned in a smile. Unbridled enthusiasm took charge of his desire, and he pulled her into his cache, slid his hands into her fur and kissed her hungrily, passionately and comfortably. He didn't have to bend to reach her because she was quite tall, almost eye-to-eye with him which he liked. His senses were further awakend on the soft coat and silken sheets which she threw off. They. Running his hand up her thighs to her own fur, she stayed his hand, and laughed nervously.

"Off limits?"

"Oui, mon chat is off limits."

"Chat?"

"Oui, kitty cat. I am always in my birthday suit at home. You not?"

Shaking his head, his ardor cooled. From the distant land of her side of the bed, she admitted she had never had "le sex," and he sighed and confessed to his purity as well. The tension between them vanished and, they relaxed in a sweet tête-à-tête over champagne and savories. In the morning, they were in one another's arms, and nature took its course. Penetrating her, he saw stars; they were a perfect fit. Her clench of desire in response to his thrusts was thrilling. The way she sighed and moaned and moved with him in the same rhythm, not just that time, every time over the past ten years made her his favorite lover.

Fana. Fana. Fana.

He heard breaking glass, but his head was too heavy to lift, so he ignored it and recalled it as a dream when he awakened in his bed. The wind was tossing balls of lilacs against his bedroom window and brought Frigg to mind, her careful landscaping of the small area of ground around their home. It provided natural vistas more commonly seen in the suburbs than the brownstone's urban location. His suit was not on the floor where he expected it to be but hung up and he was clad only in his underwear and a tie. Showered and dressed he left his room and surveyed the house for clues as to what he might have done the previous night. Strangely, his parents' bed was a mess. He walked in and out and in again to jog his memory.

Did I sleep here or…? I must have been out of it.

A hand touched his shoulder while he pulled up the covers. Fana's scent and her long, slender fingers gave her away, and he flung her gently onto the bed and straddled her.

"You took my clothes off and left me all alone?""

"You're welcome. I did not leave you on the kitchen floor."

"Touché. Why did you sleep in here? You did..."

"You were too drunk to...to...be good company Jackie"

"Fana! Fana! Fana!" He kissed her. "I missed you. Divorce Philippe and marry me Fana."

"Alors. Are you ready to come to Paris?"

"Paris, Paris Paris. Why? Why can't I love you here?"

fantastic spell, but of two who arrived at a mutual trust and caring for each other. She relisted her reasons for refusing to settle in the United States, including monolingualism, racism and bad food and wine. She once claimed to be "grateful for the stupid policy of segregation in the United States" because it sent talented Negroes to Paris like James Baldwin who she called "Jimmy" and Josephine Baker, the remarkable colored expat dancer with the Folies Bergère. Long ago, Fana presented him with a photograph of her in her famous faux banana skirt.

"Yes, she is the toast of Paris, but in the U. S.?" Her voice rose angrily. "She can not be served dinner at the Stork Club. A disgrace Jackie!

To soften her tone, Fana smiled. She loved Jackie, not in the romantic, heady manner of two people under its spell but as a fellow traveler in life with similar sensibilities. She paused in front of a framed newspaper photograph. Though widely seen in the States, it was new to her. She gazed at the man, a Chief Petty Officer playing an accordion for the devastating occasion of the train carrying President Roosevelt's body from Georgia to Washington D.C. The officer's face was awash with tears.

Graham Jackson playing "Goin' Home" April 13, 1945

"Sad. Sad and strange. "

"Not so strange. He stepped up, made changes so…"

À Paris, the news was that Negroes paying respects, but Jackie he got them lowly defense jobs? Is that so wonderful?"

Married to and the daughter of diplomats Fana was well versed on politics, and Jackie didn't want to sound bad. He ran his hands through his hair.

"Yeah it is. If the president gives the go-ahead for coloreds to work in the government for the same dough, regular companies are going to have to hire them too. Ha Ha. Otherwise they look anti-American. So it's a chip in the wall."

"Alors. Is it really possible to chip an invisible wall built of bricks, bricks fired in imperialism, oppression and hate?"

Desire for her and to change the subject, he kissed her.

"What would I do in Paris?"

"What do you do anywhere? I will make breakfast, but I can not stay. I will come back later."

"Why are women always leaving me?"

"I am leaving the house, not you."

When she returned, she explained her three-day limit was due to her husband's imminent arrival, but that in those few days she should be able to "fatten" him. Staying with Helen and dancing he was very thin. Fana cooked and cooked and cooked. Jackie didn't know the names of the dishes, only knew they tasted better than any food he had ever had anywhere. He ate and ate and ate, basked in the pleasure of her bright company and the familiarity of her body. The second night, they talked themselves into the inlet of insomnia between midnight and three a.m., and when other topics ran out, he told her about the exciting temptress Helen who was "confused, thinks she wants to be alone and not with me."

"I am surprised Jackie. You have so many women, but you understand none. Not all women want to be a wife."

The flat of his hand thumped when he hit his chest and she giggled girlishly.

"Mon Dieu. How does your head fit through the door?"

"What are you talking about? Helen had a…."

"A rival. You rival was her passion."

"If she married me, she wouldn't need one."

Jackie's inability to let himself understand combined with his stubborn side could have ended in an argument. To prevent one Fana brought up destiny and the eeriness of his having kept the house exactly the same as it was the day that his mother died.

"When will you make this the house of Jackie, Jackie Vik?"

From behind his position as Bo'sun he felt safe from her criticism, but he was not. She reminded him how she sailed back and forth among many ports, New York to Paris to Senegal and Brazil, and how regularly she redecorated her apartments.

Monday evening after work, he sat alone again at the kitchen table fortifying the right side of a shirt his grandmother had made for Paul; it was his favorite. Satisfied with his work, he slipped in his arm and took a few steps, but a thread had caught on a splinter and the side seam unraveled up to the armpit. The edges of the ancient garment were too tattered to restore unless he added a long patch.

"Damn it!" he roared a loud. "That's going to look ridiculous. Best to leave well enough alone. Imagine if I tried to fix everything in this joint."

He tossed the needle and thread in the drawer and several items leaped into sight. The telegram informing them his father was missing in action; his mother's anchor charm bracelet. He slammed it shut and rattled the treasured Staffordshire coffee pot on the top and his father's sculptures which had stood there in their places since his thirteenth birthday. Gently, as if touching his mother's cheek, he slid his hand over her loose-leaf recipe collection and lifted it up. Loose pages dropped to the floor, one was the article about Bill Edwards. The scar on his neck throbbed and that cold, September Saturday almost fourteen years ago came into view.

Central park had taken on the appearance of a Western movie set. Dozens of American Indians resplendent in their regalia were there for an unofficial, "American Indian Day." They paraded under the gentle shadows of the elms' autumn color lining the mall. Years before Governor Hanley acknowledged their contribution to "our society," meaning the war. He emphasized the disproportionately high number of men serving. He had also encouraged his constituents to support an official American Indian day to honor them. The politicians' absence at the gathering in 1946, the year after the war, suggested time had vanquished the sentiments, but supporters of the idea and the American Indians continued to meet annually on the meadow. Frigg approached a woman at a small table who was discussing the proposed legislation.

"Hello. My name is Frigg Hansen, from Norway," she said as she always did; even though, she was born in the United States, "and this is my son Jackie."

"I'm Robin, a Passamaquoddy from the north. This is my daughter, Tally. She just graduated from high school," she boasted, "and only seventeen, quite a good guitar player too," she concluded.

"Oh the same like Jackie, but he plays the fiddle."

He greeted Tally with a shy "Hello," and the women wandered away into their conversation leaving the two teens alone.

The incredible length of the girl's shiny, black hair fascinated Jackie. Even braided, the thick paintbrush-ends slid back and forth across her hips and mingled with her shawl's fringe. They drew him behind her when she strode to the semi-secluded stand of trees on the edge of the green. Excitedly, she gave him the happy details of the pow-wow she and her mother had attended earlier in the day in Brooklyn. Being among the American Indians brought back the vision he had had of his father with them on an unidentified, shore. With some guilt, he realized he had not thought about him for a long time.

"My father is in the army, not sure where," he told Tally when they spoke about their parents.

"I know the feeling."

Thunder rumbled in the distance, and a dark cloud rolled across the sky. Jackie lost his breath, astonished by what he saw, a colossal, shimmering grey-white wing hundreds of feet across dipping gracefully through the clouds. Conversations and laughter continued among the throng on Sheep's Meadow, apparently oblivious to it. Thunder rolled again and exploded so loudly he jumped.

"Ha Ha Ha," she laughed and shook her head. "Typical ikolisoman, scared of thunder."

"I don't what you just called me" but..

"White man," she smirked.

"Okay, but I am not typical, and I was not scared. I was surprised. I didn't expect to see…" He paused uncertain whether she had seen the wing, and he didn't' want to scare her. Within seconds, her spirit sparkled wholesomely in a golden glow, and he finished his thought, "I didn't expect to see a giant wing."

"Probably one of the Thunder Tribe," she remarked matter-of-factly. "Once they put on their wings and fly off to play ball...they make a lot of noises. I saw them flying over a lake like this," she demonstrated spreading her arms beneath her shawl and flapping it like wings.

"I think it belonged to Freya..."

"To what?" Tally asked crinkling her nose in displeasure because her explanation had not intrigued him as it had others.

"Not what, who? She is a goddess, and when she puts on her feathered cape, she can fly like a falcon."

His voice trailed off, and together they turned their stupefied faces skyward. An enormous, powdery, down-feather was floating earthward. They zigzagged a wide swath in the grass, as it wended through the air and right onto Tally's outstretched arms.

"Wow!" wafted out of them in unison.

Jackie scanned the clouds in vain for a feather of his own. Tally's mother gestured for her to return, and she complied swiftly. Warmed by the fluffy mysterious he scuffed leisurely through the tall grass toward Frigg waiting on the walkway. A quick tug on his coat turned him to Tally's flashing black eyes. She presented him with the feather and folded his fingers around it. He opened his mouth to object, but she shook her head and scampered back to her mother. After two blocks of silence, Jackie spoke.

"Mor, that Indian girl, Tally... she could see things like me."

Frigg warned Jackie that he didn't have enough information to conclude she had his ability, but she thought she was nice.

"Isn't there a zoo nearby? Maybe an ostrich lost the feather. Maybe it was from a different creature. Or maybe Jackie, maybe it made you think of Freya and little Tally's Thunder people..."

"Or maybe it was Okeanos riding through the sky looking for me," he added enthusiastically.

Amused she agreed, "Ja Jackie. Everything is possible.

He put it in a tall vase on the dresser while he got ready.

Saturday night was often jazz night with Larry and Nancy. All the women in the clubs shimmered in body-hugging cocktail dresses, including his mother. Their supple fabric capped her shoulders, clung to her full bosom and draped sensually over her rear before falling to the soft curve of her thighs. To discourage, the polite leers drawn to her assets, Jackie always mentioned brought her a big coat and advised "it might get chilly later." Frigg always conveniently forgot. In fine suits from Larry and a couple of his European companions, Jackie cut a mature figure. He strutted menacingly beside his mother as if she was a royal princess and he her body guard. Like his mother, Jackie the room females, young and attractive and not, single and not, atomized him with an intoxicating mist of adoration. He wished he knew how to dance, so he could find a reason to talk to them, to touch them. Jackie watched the men's feet when Nancy danced, but he wasn't ready to try it yet. He sat back and enjoyed the music. The sounds produced an amnesic effect on thoughts about his father or any worries he had. Larry, who played the piano, not only knew the musicians but also music, and through him he became a good listener. That's what he told Duke Ellington when he came to the table that night.

"That's one of the most important things Jackie, listening," Duke said.

His words were logical to Jackie because he perceived of music as an alternative world created by the musicians communicating.. If he wanted to hear what they were saying, he had to listen.

He was exhilarated by Duke Ellington's visit to the table, and he wanted to tell his mother when they got home, but she was not in the mood to talk. He left her making coffee and went to change for bed. A long chill ran through his body. A few moments later, he thought he heard Bill Edwards' voice. At the upstairs railing, he watched his mother greeting Edwards who had a face full of gin. The room sparked with an eerie current emanating from Bill as he stood there with his hat in his hand. Ever cordial, his mother invited him and struck up a conversation about the American Indians in the park. Jackie continued preparing for bed.

Edward's speech was so slurred, Frigg worried he might pass out. She focused on the coffee and decided, as soon as she gave him a cup, she would call his wife Phyllis to collect him. Bill was too restless to sit, and he slithered up beside her and groped her. She blanched.

"Mr. Edwards, sit down," she insisted sternly.

Walking toward her, Bill forced her into the counter corner by the sink. He pressed his soused, sweating weight against her. With her precious Staffordshire coffee pot in hand, she resisted. Then he closed in on her and fondled her breast with his whole hand. Instinctively, she doused him with the piping hot coffee. He sprang backwards and she placed her Staffordshire pot on its stand while Edward's hollered in pain. It summoned Jackie to the upper landing just in time for him to see Bill smack his mother. Raw animal instinct hurled his long, lean body over the banister and onto Bill who flung him to the ground. Frigg slapped at Bill with both hands. Jackie was momentarily dazed.

"You little shit," Bill said, kicked Jackie in the ribs and placed his foot at Jackie's head.

He turned it out of the way, but a nail Edward's heel tore into Jackie's neck. A geyser of blood shot into the air. Frigg fought to reach her son, but Bill crushed the tips of her fingers with such strength that the pain dropped her down on one knee. Jackie then heard his mother's wincing demands for Bill to let her go and her feet sliding and kicking across the linoleum. Edwards dragged her toward the stairs. The thud of her feet reverberated in Jackie's ears as her voice grew dimmer. With all her strength she yanked herself free. Bill walloped her, and she flew backwards into the staircase. All was silent. Confusion scrunched up Bill's face; he knit his brow and leaned over her weaving and bobbing.

"Frigg? Frigg? What are you doing on the floor?" he asked as if he had come across her in a heap.

Jackie positioned his palm on the floor to raise himself up, but it slid out from under him and under the couch. His fingers made contact with the cold blade of the sword he had stashed there. Mustering his strength, he grasped it, and charged Bill. He stopped right in front of him.

"Get away from her. Get Away!"

"Who are you telling me to get out of my own house?"

Jackie ignored the intoxicated illogic and insisted he, "Get out! Now!"

He was keenly aware he was about to stab Bill Edwards. An odd groan came from his mother, and when he laid his eyes on her crumpled and motionless form on the stairs, passion obliterated forethought. He lunged at Edwards and positioned himself protectively in front of his mother. Edwards moved toward her, and he involuntarily shrieked and swung the blade. A full third of the metal disappeared into Edwards' clothes. He didn't want to hurt him, just get him out of the house. Pointing the blade directly at him, he backed him onto the porch and locked the door.

Blood spurted from the wound preventing him from rushing to his mother, but he managed to call an ambulance. The room spun and darkened and he passed out.

The whole time the doctors were stitching him up, he asked about his mother who they assured him is, "going to be fine." An intern offered him a clean undershirt from his locker, and while he was putting it on, a detective entered the room. He explained that Edwards had been in an auto accident right in front of the Vik house and was in surgery.

"Doctors say he's been stabbed. You know about that?"

"Tada!" a nurse interrupted stepping in with Frigg, "fine."

Jackie embraced her. The detective tipped his hat and introduced himself.

"I was just asking your son…"

"He is only sixteen," Frigg announced firmly, and turned to Jackie. "We have to wait for Larry and the attorney."

"Attorney? Mor what's wrong?"

"What's wrong is Mr. Edwards might not make it, so..."

"So the boy should talk to his lawyer, right?" Larry asked dismissing the detective.

Rehashing the event brought up words such as "justifiable deadly force" that made Jackie's knees knock. He hesitated each time before he spoke, but he was still not "sure" of anything. The night seemed like a bad dream and the present was a hazy blur. By the time they left, it was Sunday. Frigg had Larry drop them off at the church around the corner from their house so they could "pray Mr. Edwards recovers." Before they went in, Jackie popped his color to hide the bandage on his neck, and Frigg kissed his cheek. "My son the Viking. Far would be so proud of you Jackie. You are going to Vallhalla for sure. "

He was sure her lightheartedness at serious times was a characteristic his father must have appreciated as much as he did. Still, anxiety bristled in all the hair on his arms and legs with the possibility he may have killed Bill Edwards. The detective's statement that he, "Might not make it," kept going around his head.

TOP was hanging out on the Vik's porch watching the police and firemen process Edwards' car. They launched a babble of questions at Jackie and Frigg when they returned. Seamus' was the only one Jackie heard clearly.

"Was it you that killed Bill Edwards Jackie?"

Difficult Departures

He handed him the newspaper.

The New Yorker Newspaper

THE NEWS FOR TODAY   MONDAY SEPTEMBER 25, 1944   ONLY THREE CENTS

PHARMACIST, WILLIAM P. EDWARDS ATTACKED BY WILD SWORDSMAN AND KILLED IN EARLY MORNING CRASH

By Francis F. Dwyer

New York City—William Edwards (37), owner of Edward's Drugstore in Chelsea, New York was crushed behind the steering wheel of his automobile in a head-on-collision with a tree just after 1:00 a.m. yesterday, Sunday, September 24. According to eye-witnesses, Mr. Edwards had a difficult time opening his car and may have been intoxicated. Once inside, the car accelerated and "he did not seem to have control." The vehicle overturned and skidded into a tree. The auto was so badly smashed; firemen had to remove the passenger door to extricate his body. He was rushed by ambulance to St. Vincent's hospital where he underwent several hours of surgery. At that time, doctors discovered Mr. Edwards was suffering from wounds they feel could only have been caused by "a very large blade or sword." Two other victims were seen at the hospital and one self identified as the attacker. Details of the circumstances are not known at this time. The suspect has not been arrested, but the incident is under investigation. Mr. Edwards passed away Sunday night.

189

Jackie was pale with guilt and remorse, but when his mother reached across the table, her wrists raw and reddened from battling Edwards, vanquished those feelings.

"You did what you had to do. We have to wait and see what the detective says. "

In the days that followed, as the attorney advised, Jackie kept to himself. He tried listening to music, reading, fiddling and carving, but nothing diminished his anxiety until he engaged in physical work, gardening. His klarsyn alerted him to a person visiting, and he went to the front door, but there was no one there or in the street. He waited. Nothing. Back in the yard, he felt it again, and then he saw movement between the slats of the tall, wooden fence. He peered through and saw the Passama-quoddy girl he had not seen for years, Tally. She had come to the city to play guitar at the White Horse Tavern nearby the Vik's. She chanced a visit. Since she had never met Edwards, he saw no reason not to visit with her, and he took her on a quick tour. In his room, she noticed the feather. He offered it to her.

"No. You keep it. This one also fell that day."

She pulled her long braid from under her sweater and shoed him an eighteen-inch feather like his tied into her hair.

"Oh, how pretty."

She blushed in response studying the framed illustration of Norse Goddess whose fair locks hung around her bare shoulders and breasts. He imagined Tally's naked body to be similar giving rise to his manhood..

"Freya?" she read from the label on the frame.

"She is the goddess who can fly with the cape made of…"

"Feathers. I remember."

"Yes," "Let's go to the workshop," he suggested picking up her guitar and escorting her hurriedly from the bedroom. "I'll get my fiddle and we can play together."

They strummed and bowed themselves into a symbiotic dimension where they remained for hours before it was time for her gig at the White Horse. She thought he should join her on stage, but claiming notice was "too short," he declined. There was a palpable energy around her when he hugged her goodbye and she slipped out the garden gate.

Over the next few days, his nerves refused to let him rest. He didn't know how much longer he could tolerate being confined to his house. Finally, word came from Detective Forest.

"The autopsy revealed Bill Edwards died in consequence of injuries suffered in the accident," Frigg read to him.

The wounds Jackie had inflicted on him were serious but not life threatening. His death was not on his hands, a fact he later came to regret to the core of his soul. He believed if he had aimed more carefully the first time and thrust Edwards through "his disgusting, vile, gin-drenched heart," his mother would still be alive.

A deliciously homey aroma filled the house from top to bottom from Frigg's eplekake. Jackie's favorite. It lured him from the workroom to the kitchen where he parked himself at the table. Holding his fork upright, he waited patiently for his mother to serve him a jumbo portion with a cup of coffee. As soon as she put it in front of him, he dug right in. She sat across from him collecting her reward, the vociferous grunts of appreciation he made.

"Ah gutten min," she sighed and added, "I love you."

"I love this eplekake," he grunted and then added loudly, "And you. I love you too Mor."

"I know Jackie," she echoed with a hand to her head.

He jumped up, untied her apron and folded it.

"Go and close your eyes. I will wash the dishes?"

"You don't have to. . ."

"I want to."

He crossed his arms and blocked her way to the sink. She laughed.

"You win. God natt Jackie."

"God natt mor."

The next morning, he awakened to what sounded like waves breaking on the side of the ship. Shaking his head to clear the disorientation that sometimes settled on him from switching his land and sea legs didn't help. Inhaling deeply, he would either get a noseful of his stuffy quarters or the wonderful prelude of aromas that played in the air before breakfast on Ocean Avenue. The air had a distinctly salt-air-seaweed fragrance, and seagulls screeched. Through the narrow slots his eyelids had opened, he saw a shadow pass in the hall, and a strong wind blew. Suddenly panicked, he threw the covers back and put his feet on the rug.

"A rug. I am home. What the Hell?! Mor? Mor," he repeated, and then shouted, "Mor!" Fog hung visibly in the hallway. *I must be sleep walking.* Heading toward his mother's room, he pinched himself, "Ow!."

Thick ropes of grey mist snaked from the crack under her door. They morphed into a being who was unquestionably Njord, the Norse god of the sea.

What is this shit? Come on Jackie, wake up! Wake up!

He didn't. Fear pulsed through him. It was not fear of the unknown which fueled him with courage and allowed him to run blindly into a situation. It was the fear of the known, the kind that caused him to pause to brace himself for the unknown. Breathing was difficult and painful. With the unsteady legs of a man who had been in the water for hours, he waved his arms to clear away the apparition. It clung to his pajamas and dangled from him like Spanish moss. Njord ghosted into his mother's room ahead of him and united with a cloud over her was motionless body. The muscles of her face were completely relaxed. He dropped his cheek in front of her nose to check if she was breathing, but he couldn't tell. He kissed her cheek, and he saw her blink.

"Mor. Mor. I'll call the doctor."

With her fingertips, she beckoned weakly for him to sit on the bed next to her on his father's side of the bed. Chills ran up his arms and down his spine when she touched him. She offered him a faint smile before her head fell on his shoulder and then flopped loosely in the other direction, and he instinctively knew she was dying. Determined not to let her soul join Njord, he held her tightly, but no amount of pressure could restrain the essence of her being; it escaped in white vapors. A Viking ship bobbed up and down in the air currents beyond the window. Njord magically manifested again, this time by the window. When he reached out to Frigg, his father's face replaced his, and he led her to the ship. As soon as they were aboard, they waved at Jackie and the vessel vanished.

A big "No!" burst out of Jackie in an agonizing bellow. "Mor!"

He arranged the covers over her body, and he sat on the floor beside her bed. Pounding and a violent crash brought him to his feet. The bedroom door exploded open and two police officers assessed the situation.

"Jackie! Jackie!" his father called, and he turned around, "It's okay."

He had to summon all of his strength to raise his eyelids. When he did, his shipmate Bart came into view.

"What are you doin' here?"

"Working. Same as you."

"What?"

"Jackie we're on the ship."

"Smitty?"

"Yeah." He put a piece of ice on Jackie's lips and let him the drops drip into his mouth. "You got Malaria man, pretty bad. Your temperature was a hundred and six. The medic said he didn't know anyone could get one that high. Jackie. Jackie?"

He succumbed to the fever again, but by the time they steamed into New York, he was improving. The medic to arranged for him to go to the hospital, but he refused.

"No. No hospitals."

Ashore, Smitty called TOP to give them a heads up that they had docked and Jackie was, "going to the hospital to get checked out, but after that...."

"The place is ready whenever," Seamus told him.

After Frigg passed, Jackie let the house go. When he shipped out, TOP's women rallied together to get it back in order. The mailbox and the small basket next to it for over-sized pieces brimmed with envelopes.

"She sure must have known a lot of people," Michaela said. "Look at this. There's even one from California."

"Charlie said all the parents were here all the time. She had a knack for it, even during the war. The boys brag 'her parties made us forget about the war for a little while.' Even had a negro singer at a couple of them."

Michaela flung open the window in the living room and told Patty, "Look at the dust!"

The two women aired out the house and cleaned it as if they were expecting their "mother-in-laws" which took almost a week. At Hansen's market, they bought the staples Jackie would need to get through a few days without cooking, but they had to get canned milk because Jackie still used the ice chest. Michaela put her hands on her hips.

"It is a beautiful case Patty, but there are refrigerators. He's living in the dark ages over here. No wonder he can't find a girl to stay with him."

"I don't think Jackie Vik ever had a problem finding a girl, though I haven't seen him with anybody special lately."

"That's understandable. He's mourning." She held a pile of sympathy cards. "This is a fine how do ya do?" What do you think, Michaela, throw them out?"

"No don't get rid of them. Put them somewhere? One day he'll want to read them, be reminded how loved his mother was."

Patty opened a drawer and saw Mr. Vik's death certificate.

"Cause of death, a cerebral aneurysm," she read. "What's that?"

"I think it comes from hitting your head, or something. The brain gets flooded with blood. Is that what happened to her?"

"Not if you ask Charlie.

"I'm listening…"

Patty sidled up to Michaela to whisper, "Jackie told him Bill Edwards killed her."

"Killed? Oh stop. You gave me the willies."

They left the house was neat and tidy, but Jackie didn't see their handy work. Every splinter of the house reminded him of his mother. He couldn't bear to be there. The Vik and the Jacobson families were full of octogenarians and centenarians; no one had died as young as his mother had. She was alive when they got her to the hospital. And the question doctors were most interested in was whether she had ever hit her head. She had when Bill Edwards knocked her into the stairs.

Son of a bitch! He said every time he thought about that night.

In his mind, a ship's horn blasted the day he came home from her funeral. He tried unsuccessfully to stop it. Distance was the only method that worked. Aboard ship, he didn't hear it at all, and he thought it had stopped for good, but as soon as he stepped foot on the New York dock, it blared again. As soon as he the hospital verified the Malaria diagnosis, and told him "the worst was over," he went directly to the Union Hall. Rather than play checkers or shoot the breeze as he usually did, he collapsed in one of the hard, wooden chairs where he the last vestiges of his illness hijacked him. Unwilling to go home or to stay with anyone, he grabbed a cab and headed to the Soldiers', Sailors', Marines', Coast Guard and Airmen's Club in Midtown. Charlie raved about how nice it was. When the taxi pulled under the sprawling tree on Lexington Avenue, the perpetual light burning in honor of those serving in the military welcomed him to the cozy townhouse. Unlike a regular hotel, there was no bar or women to distract him from the one thing he needed most, a bed. He crawled in and became a willing hostage to the sweating peace and quiet of his recurrent fever.

IX
The Blue
Caribbean

IX
The Blue Caribbean

"Sea of life. Life on the sea. Among clouds and winds and oceans, nothing troubles me." Jackie Vik

uring his recuperation at the club, Jackie decided the only way he could return to his house was if, as Fana suggested, he was to *"faire un coup de torchon. Yeah, a fresh start. That's probably a good idea.* The morning he shipped out to Cuba, he dropped a carefully penned letter to Michaela including a proposal for her to design and renovate his house on Ocean Avenue.

She'll come up with something swell like she did with our window at The Dog. That gave her a ton o' other work, but those jobs are pretty far from Chelsea. He chuckled, *far from your darling Smitty. And don't think I don't know. I do.*

To entice her and sweeten the offer, he included a generous down payment, to cover initial costs and gave her carte blanche to "work your magic," but he wrote a few specific guidelines. His mother's room had to be "so unrecognizable, I'm gonna ask myself where I am. My old nursery, a half a flight up from her room would be a good guest room if you agree Michaela, but Leave the workshop." Barring Smitty, she was not to tell anyone.

With a chest full of contentment, he boarded the ship sailing to the beautiful blue Caribbean and south to Brazil. There the ship was loaded with so much coffee he told the men, "Man we're bringin' every blessed man woman and child in America a cuppa Joe for a solid month." The beans' powerful aroma permeated their jute sacks forming an inescapable cloud of nauseating vapors.

At least a ship is not a farm, he told himself again.

As the low, square, pastel skyline of Havana Harbor, the next stop, came into view, excitement mingled with in his bones. He always had a great time in Cuba, but he had reason to question what kind of trip this one would be. Frequent reports of demonstrations and violent confrontations between anti-government rebels and the military had resulted in dozens of deaths since the New Year. An attack had been executed on Batista's offices and bombs had gone off in markets, tourist hotels and nightclubs, four within twenty-four hours of the ships' arrival in port. A few greenhorns consulted with Bart, who they knew was close to the Jackie, the Bo'sun because word was the captain was not granting shore leave. Having the men come to him, puffed up his self-esteem, and in an octave below his usual speaking voice, he said, "I'll see what I can do," which meant finding Jackie. It was more of a challenge than he had anticipated because Jackie had been in and out of his fo'c'sle.

He was frantically retracing his steps to find his battered, dog-eared copy of *For Whom the Bell Tolls*; he took it with him everywhere for weeks. Nancy had become his informal literature tutor, though her blatantly flirtatious behavior suggested she saw him as a potential paramour, despite her relationship with

Larry whose friendship meant a lot to Jackie. He refused to acknowledge her advances as anything but play and learned a lot about Hemingway who they both enjoyed. She gassed on and on extolling his overall literary style, his handling of the war in particular and his themes "in the context of history."

Nancy's gonna flip out if I meet him.

It was common knowledge that Hemingway had a residence in Cuba, Finca Vigía and its whereabouts was no big mystery; his schedule and whereabouts were. No one knew when he was going to show up. As such an avid outdoorsman and drinker, he could be anywhere. Jackie was more optimistic this time because he had read in the paper that filming for *The Old Man and the Sea* was underway in Havana. In addition to the factual tidbit of information, he sensed he might see him this trip, a meeting he wanted yet feared due to his self-perceived inarticulateness, but he believed the author would be forgiving. He reformulated his thoughts about Hemingway's writing.

Easy to understand what you write. It seems real. The descriptions of the forest made me smell the pine. I could feel that air on my face. Oh and that guy, Robert in For Whom the Bell Tolls; he's so emotional, but he's still a real man, passionate, like me.

Nancy used the word "vicariousness," which he had to look up and still didn't quite understand. He told her, "Robert's an enviable man, but he's not a happy man, like me." Finally, he found the book in the first place he had looked, his bunk. He stuck a bookmark where he had underscored, "In the night he awoke and held her tight as though she were all of life and it was being taken away from him." The line reminded Jackie of his experience with his mother, and he was impressed by Hemingway having summed up his feelings so well, though they were not about a mother and son.

He put For *Whom the Bell Tolls* in his small bag as he had on his previous duties to Havana. Striding down the gangway, he heard his name and stopped. It was Bart. His question as to why he was going against captain's orders confounded Jackie, and then he launched a laugh into the sky.

"Don't tell me. Bixby and Rodriquez told you we couldn't go ashore." Bart was nodding the whole time. "No! You know better than to listen to those bozos. Get permission?!" He scoffed. They're screwin' with ya."

"Really?"

"Havana is right there man!"

Disappointed in his own gullibility, Bart hung his head. Yukking up the success of their good-natured ribbing, Bixby and Rodriquez clattered up in a clamor of yuks and guffaws clapping their hands while a bright red flush highlighted Bart's juvenile gullibility.

"All right. All right. You had your fun. Leave the kid alone."

They quizzed Jackie about sites.

"I don't know. I go anywhere. Why don't you ask a fille de joie. Anything I know about Havana, they taught me. If she can't come up with anything, you can do her for a few pesos."

"Fille de what?"

"Fille de jois. French for working-girls, Bart."

"Working girls? My mother said…,"

Bixby and Rodriquez roared with laughter until Jackie cut his eyes at them.

"Your mother only knows what she heard. I know a lot of them personally and," he emphasized, "They' are nice girls."

"Not all of them," Bixby interjected.

"The ones you know? I guess not." He punched Bart in the shoulder, "How's your leg? Can you keep up?"

"It's good," he said and did a little soft shoe.

"Get your camera and come on. Could be the last time we see this place in a long time."

"A long time? Why?"

"No way to know which way the revolutionary wind is going to blow. Let's go."

Bart asked if two of his pals might come along.

"Sure."

Before they took off, Jackie made it clear, he didn't want to spend all his free time with them, and he laid out the plan. He would take them to a few places he knew, and then it was every man for himself. From the harbor, they walked along the cobble stone streets awed by the elegant Colonial columns and sensual Baroque arches, even around *Sloppy Joe's*, one of the most famous tourist spots because it was frequented by famous people, had shredded beef sandwiches and Bacardi from the nearby factory.

"Walking in here is like walking into a liquor cabinet," Jackie remarked.

Sloppy Joe's walls were unusual because they were shelves stacked to the ceiling and held a neatly arranged contingent of booze bottles, the more select behind glass.

"All this wood is mahogany," Jackie informed them with a wave of his hand. "This too," he added rubbing his fingers across the bar top. "José," he said to the bartender who shook his hand with a big grin.

"Jackie amigo. Bienvenido."

"Sloppy Joes, quartos y ron por favor," he ordered haltingly in Spanish,

"You speak Spanish?" Bart asked Jackie with a note of admiration.

"Naw. Pick up a few words each time."

The sandwiches exceeded their expectations, and they gobbled them up with vigorous enjoyment.

"'Everything starts from Sloppy Joe's the greatest meeting place in the world,'" Jackie read from the sign in the front.

In the steamy, 82 degree weather, they wended their way along through the streets past cabarets and clubs and the occasional jineteras here and there. The sound of musical scales on a trumpet drew them around a corner to a small grove of palm trees. Beneath it was a crowd of onlookers a mini orchestra, a saxophonist, a bongo and conga player, a man on bass and two more men with percussion instruments. The drummers beat out a rhythm to which everyone gyrated. Clad in the simplest of colorful cotton dresses, the Cuban girls exuded an exciting sensuality as they danced into the circle followed by their men. Perspiration saturated their clothes and darkened the fabric on their bodies. Their black and olive skin shined in the soft, late afternoon sun. The men from the ship rocked from side to side to the music and bobbed their heads to the beat for two numbers, and then Jackie gave the signal to leave. He took one step and a caramel-colored girl in a frilly dress with bows in her black hair glided into his path and shimmied her bare shoulders and breasts in front of him.

"Baila conmigo," she said with a lick of her lips and a tug of his shirt.

"Lo siento. Gracias. No. No. No tengo tiempo," he said pointing to his watch.

Sassily, she snapped her skirt and moved out of his way.

"Wow she sure was pretty," Bart noted.

"Pretty spicy. Like to go around the world with her," he said glancing over his shoulder.

Jackie led his tour down the streets commenting along the way about a famous hotel, a cathedral and the Bacardi headquarters. Slightly off course, he stopped an old man.

"Favor señor. ¿Dónde está El Cristóbal Colon, Calle 12 esquina Calle 23?"

"Sí. No está lejos. Si caminas un poco más, tu lo veras," he answered in a smoky voice pointing his gnarled finger down the street.

"Gracias," he replied. "Just like I thought. It's not far fellas."

Bart squinted into the distance. Neither he nor the others saw it because they were not sure what it was; they continued to shadow Jackie. He stopped in front of a stone gateway.

"I call this the museum of death. The three arches up there, Faith, Hope and Charity."

They raised their heads to the massive crucifixion above Hope's arch and then passed under it into the cemetery. Before them lay miles of tombs and mausoleums shaded by beautiful trees. It was a small city of the dead within Havana whose streets bustled noisily around it. The streets were so long they had signs. The permanent residents were marble men and women, hundreds of them who stood, knelt and reclined in poses of dignity, prayer and grace. Farther inside, all was quiet. The statue of woman holding a cross in her right hand and a baby in her left arm was the recipient of an outpouring of attention. It was buried beneath a mound of flowers so high they had begun to tumble to the ground. It had drawn an impressive mass of visitors who prayed and backed away.

"Must be a dignitary of the church, or a queen," Bart guessed.

"It's a mother and her baby," Jackie said. "I think her name was Amelia. It's an old tragedy; there are so many." In a serious voiced laced with sadness he told it to them. "She was rich, beautiful, young and in love with a guy, José, the wrong guy as far as her father, was concerned. You know how it goes; no money. But real love, true love will make you run through a fire or do all kinds of crazy things. It is unstoppable and when it's forbidden...? So these two kids, thirteen or something, so they had time ran around and met secretly for years. Finally, the old man died, and Amelia married José. They have a baby and..."

"It dies," Bart said finishing his thought.

"Both. They both die, Amelia and the baby. Man, José goes off the deep end. He was a mess, but he watched the undertaker put them in the ground, Amelia with the baby in a space at her feet. Still, he can't accept their deaths. He believes they're asleep, so every day he comes thinking she is going to wake up. He's knocking on the tomb and talking to her. I don't know whose idea it was, but Amelia and the baby are dug up."

"Oh man. That is crazy," Bart said.

"When they open up the grave to prove to José that his wife Amelia is dead? The baby is not at her feet where they put it, but in her arms."

"Is that true?" one of the guys asks.

"The Cubans thinks so. They bury her again, and that poor bastard, José came everyday until he died. Girls who have trouble getting in the family way come here and pray to her, and they all end up with a kid. So now they think she is a saint."

The tombs were so interesting the men were reluctant to leave, but they stuck to their plan to have time to explore on their own. They did stop for postcards together; Jackie bought one for his mother.

"My mother will get a…" he stopped speaking remembering she was gone but got it for her anyway.

On the way back to the center, the men complained about the dense humidity and hypothesized that it might have had something to do with the baby ending up in its mother's arms. Before long, they heard the trumpets and drums again and saw the dancers under the palm grove near the harbor. The same girl, who had invited Jackie earlier, stepped out again. Limited time and the oppressive heat combined with the bad memory of the last time. The girl danced circles around him, and he tripped and fell and sprained his wrist. Even though he had practiced with Helen, he didn't want to repeat that event in front of Bart and the boys. The girl flashed her large dark eyes and big smile while she cast an even heavier net of seduction, coquettishly rotating her hips, and pushing her breasts up deliberately and unashamedly with her hands. Jackie zigged every time she zagged. Determined, she playfully slapped his chest with both palms. One of the trumpet players called out over the music.

Souvenir de Cuba

1957

"Olvídalo Luisa, me acuerdo de él, el Americano. No puede bailar!"

The words stopped Jackie in his tracks. He had heard them before, and he knew what they meant. All eyes turned to the musician who said them.

"Can't dance?!" Jackie repeated to him.

The man shrugged cockily, and announced to the others "Like the last time."

Pride and patriotism razed his fatigue, and puffed him up to his full height. The musicians laid down a beat. Jackie handed Bart his camera and his book and grabbed the petite, eager dancer by her wrist. Delight twinkled on her face as he manipulated her with swaggering virility. He placed one hand at his waist imitating the Argentine dancer in Helen's studio. He didn't count or think about whether his moves were right or wrong; he threw himself into the moment and danced. Holding Luisa's hand above her head, he led her though a spin. Round and round she went, her hair and fluffy skirt flaring out in circles of curls and color. He leaped in the air with his arms outstretched and landed a perfect half-split. A collective, "Ay," arose the impressed crowd.

"Go Jackie!" Bart and his pals shouted.

"Jackie! Jackie!" chanted the locals whose ranks had doubled with passersby and local merchants drawn to the merry commotion.

With masculine grace, Jackie undulated his body in tandem with Luisa's, then lifted her by her waist and flung her like a rag doll to his left side and then to his right. Around the heady atmosphere of the circle they strutted, their bodies were so close they almost touched. Jackie shimmied and shook his hips. He danced up high and he danced down low while the ships' horns blasted messages of arrival and maneuvers and the gulls cried overhead. He knew he was doing well, but he was grateful when the music stopped. Panting heavily with streams of sweat running into his eyes, he gestured that he was finished.

"Gracias," he repeated several times breathlessly.

"Gracias Jackie," Luisa said and raised her eyebrows in approval.

Over the exuberant hand clapping for his impromptu performance, the musician, who doubted him called out, "Amigo!" and gave Jackie a thumbs up. He returned the gesture and bowed. His magnetism drew the giddy Luisa toward him in a gust of pink, and he bent down and kissed her full on the mouth. She twirled away and the drummers beat their congas rapidly.

The onlookers stepped aside creating a path for Jackie, el Americano, who could dance. He passed through to the clearing and into their future memories. The musicians struck up another tune.

"Good timing. We got a couple hours. The ship is right there. See it?" They nodded. "Don't lose track of time. The captain doesn't wait for anyone."

Jackie sauntered down a side street and dashed into the first bar he saw. In the men's room, he wet his neckerchief and wiped some of the sweat off; he washed it out and combed his hair, so he would look more presentable. Dancing so vigorously overheated him and the air-conditioning gave him goose bumps. He put his camera around his neck and stepped out to find only one wobbly table; he stabilized it with his Hemingway book. He laid his damp neckerchief over his face and closed his eyes while a soft breeze blew a mélange of cocoanut water, pineapple and rum over him. It was relaxing; he hoped the fresh air would keep him awake. He couldn't risk falling asleep and missing the ship; although, the bartender must have thought he was napping because he brought his drink and set it on the table without a word.

His house on Ocean Avenue came to mind and concern that Michaela's interior designs might *girl the joint up too much* needled him until a person sat at the other chair.

"Is this your book?" asked a man in English.

"Not a book, my favorite, so don't get lost with it," Jackie warned the man from under his neckerchief.

"They have air-conditioning inside."

"The breeze feels better," Jackie said assuming the guy was trying to get rid of him, so he could have the table to himself.

"Yes, that it does."

"Have you read Hemingway?"

"I have. Right now, I'm rereading Fitzgerald, *The Great Gatsby*."

"Fitzgerald is swell, but I don't understand that fancy world he lives in. I prefer Jack London and Hemingway, you know? I relate to them more, men's stuff, simple men… you know men like me."

When he removed the dark cloth, the bright sun narrowed his eyes, and all he could see was a white haze. He blinked and blinked to focus. The tablemate had placed a couple of his own books on the table and a newspaper. He was older than Jackie thought he sounded, and he had soft twinkling eyes and a short white beard like Santa Claus. He read a line from Hemingway Jackie had underlined.

"'In the night he awoke and held her tight as though she were all of life and it was being taken away from him.'"

"Yeah. Isn't that something? '...as though she were all of life and it was being taken away from him.' I know he wasn't writing about his mother, but I experienced something like that when my mother died."

"Sorry you lost her."

"Thanks. Me too. What a gift to be able to sum up feelings like that. Hemingway has really lived, and he knows about history, psychology, men...life; he gives all..."

The bartender stepped out and greeted the man, "Ah, Bienvenido Papa."

His mouth fell open. Nancy had told Jackie that the name Hemingway went by in Cuba was Papa, that he preferred it. Shielding his eyes from the sun, he saw clearly that Hemingway was sitting in front of him, and his surly greeting made him wince. The author ordered Daiquiris, two, one for himself and one for Jackie. He stammered and apologized.

"Mr. Hemingway." He shook his hand. "Good to meet you. I didn't know that was you. I...the sun was in my face."

"Nor I you," he replied chuckling, putting him at ease and asking if he had had a chance to go fishing.

They talked so freely, Jackie forgot he was the famous author until it was time to leave. While he was summoning the moxie to ask him to sign his book, "Papa" offered.

Jackie flashed a thank you grin and hurried off. At the end of the street, he tripped and his camera hit him in the chest. From the corner of the short street, he focused. Hemingway lifted his head and smiled when he saw Jackie; he clicked.

The sweet, carmel fragrance of the rum, loaded in Havana, min-gled with the rich, coffee aroma and hung in a delicious cloud over the men at work on the deck. The breeze made the heat bearable, but the men wanted to go for a swim, a privilege the captain denied. One by one, Jackie checked in with them in their world on the forward deck just to keep the trip light. He knew just how to make each man laugh, and he did. The captain had already announced to the harbor he was leaving to the starboard and the ship gave two quick and three long horn blasts, but Jackie's klarsyn had kicked in. He didn't know why, but he had a strong feeling, that ranked 85% to him, that the captain was in danger meaning the ship was too. If he interfered with the captain's command, and was wrong, the consequences might be a fine or a demotion and absolutely becoming a laughing stock. If he was right, the men's lives were at risk. Five miles out, the percentage increased to 98%. Despite his mother's long-ago warning not to upset people if he didn't know something 100%, he had to say something.

"Captain we have a problem."

"What's up?"

The captain waited for Jackie to continue as long as his short patience would allow, and then he barked, "Spit it out Bo'sun!"

Jackie threw hesitation to the wind and blurted out, "I have a feeling..."

Captain Wheeler had often sailed with Jackie and heard of his sixth sense, and after thirty-five years at sea, more than twenty-six as a captain, he knew anything was possible.

"A feeling?"

"Like there is someone aboard, stowaways..."

The captain drew in a long, slow, deep breath, and then he casually picked up the microphone and gave the "all stop," command. Jackie piped all hands on deck and they carried out the "stem to stern" search. The dozen men disappeared into the belly of the ship almost as quickly as they had appeared. Jackie stood and scanned the deck. The captain came up behind him, handed him a gun, pulled a second side arm from his waist and, as an afterthought, asked if he knew how to use it. Jackie nodded. The captain pointed to a rumpled cover tarp on a lifeboat.

The men whipped it off; no unauthorized personnel were there or anywhere according to reports from below.

"Sorry Captain, I..."

Holding up his hand, he silenced Jackie and assured him, "Better safe than sorry."

Jackie piped the order to carry on which everyone did. A conversation in a foreign language he had not heard on this voyage was in the wind; it nagged him. *They are here. I know it. Someone is aboard this ship.* He shuffled his feet nervously casting his eyes about, and then to the spot where the captain unfailingly stood when they got underway. He was not there. "I knew it!" he yelled out loud and slapped his thigh. He checked with the Second Mate and the Helmsman who had seen Captain Wheeler go into his quarters but not come out. This time Jackie was 100% certain of his klarsyn. He sprang into action and gathered the men.

"You two are with me," he told the brawniest deck crew, Jason and Sylvester, and he asked the purser to bring the medical kit. "Everybody know what to do?"

They nodded and spread the word they were preparing for a mock fire drill. If the captain, as protocol demanded, emerged immediately to assess the damage, the plan was to forget about it and report a false alarm. If he did not, they would know Jackie was right. Jackie and Bigs ambled up to Captain Wheeler's quarters. The fire team met them there with their hoses charged. Jackie signaled and Bart set the three-minute operation into motion.

"Fire below! Fire below!" he announced over the intercom.

The alarm sounded. The captain's hatch did not move. The fire crew of a half dozen battered it down and swarmed inside. As Jackie suspected the occupants ran out and into the waiting Bigs who wrestled with them. Through the opening, the crew saw the captain unconscious on the floor with the medic attending to him. A shot rang out. Sylvester had lost his grip on his stowaway who had his back against the bulkhead and his arm around Bart's throat and a gun at his temple. He shouted for them to let his comrade go. Tears trickled down young, Bart's cheeks from beneath his glasses.

"Boats," he pleaded, "Come on Boats."

Jackie had learned enough French from Fana to be able to get his needs met, and he knew Jason spoke French; he hoped the stowaways did not. The expression of absolute terror on Bart forced Jackie to speak to him.

"Everything is fine," he said out loud, and then under his breath to Jason, « Avançons. »

When he inched forward with him, he knew he had chosen the right word.

"Right now you are a stowaway who attacked a ship captain. Pull that trigger and you are a murderer."

"Not a new title for me," he shot back with a smirk.

« Avançons, » Jackie said, and took another step forward with Jason. "So we give you your friend. Then what?" Way out here in the middle of the Caribbean, « Avançons. »

With the next step their diminishing distance became apparent to the stowaway and became agitated.

"Let him go. . .now !" he blared.

« Pousser lui dans sa main avec le pistolet,» Jackie said.

Jason shoved his stowaway roughly at the man's hand gun hand and he lost his grip. Bart ran to the crew. Jason picked up the other pistol, and Jackie drew the M 1911 the captain had given him earlier, and they pointed them directly at the intruders. Captain Wheeler stepped out. The right side of his face was red and bruised and his eye was swollen shut, but his voice remained steady. As if nothing had happened, he retrieved his gun and asked the men to identify themselves and give their country of origin, and they learned they were Andrei Ivanov and Boris Kovaleva from Russia. In order to sort the situation out, they had to stay put until the captain spoke with the Port Authorities in Havana and New York.

"Handsomely done," he said to Jackie with a hand on his shoulder.

"Thank you Captain Wheeler."

When he returned his pistol, he replied, "Thank you Jackie," and ordered "Mr. Ivanov and Kovaleva," placed in the brig. "Bo'sun this is going to take a while. I heard a few of the men want to swim..."

The men's' sweat-bathed faces sent them scrambling for trunks or to the side to strip down. Jackie hung back to recompose himself. The sun leaned to the west behind the palms and filled the great, fair-weather clouds with shades of orange. A sudden burst in the sky plummeted as if it were somehow a star in the daytime. Jackie closed his eyes and wished for *Love that is more than a love*. A cool breeze drew his gaze upward, but it was not a star. It was a wing as white and colossal as the one he had seen long ago in the park with Tally, and this time the golden wheel of a chariot was visible. Thinking he was hallucinating, he decided he had better cool off.

In his swim trunks, he nimbled up the thirty-five-foot steel masts with ease and reveled in the expansive bird's eye view. Diving from that height was exhilarating and as close to flying as he could get. With his arms flat against him, Jackie stiffened into a straight rod and cut, feet first, through the air. The rum and coffee odors, the vivid tropical colors, the blaring heat and the men's whoops all vanished in a whirring, whizzing whoosh when he entered the warm blue Caribbean. Like an arrow, he pierced the water into the cold dark depths. The immense weight of the entire ocean pressed on him from every angle crushing his chest and preventing his legs from moving. Panic set in.

Be cool Jackie. Get it together. You're okay, he thought a thousand times, and a wave of bliss washed over him though the water was colder and the light all but vanished. The crew's horseplay whoops were quite clear, so he assumed he had to be near the surface. His lungs pinched him for air, and the muscles in his throat throbbed as he continued hold his breath. He thought he was going to explode when he finally saw the surface. It was so far, he doubted he could make it. He felt one of the men push him upward, and his ability to kick his legs returned. The sky full of sun and the undulating horizon had never looked more glorious. He gasped mightily, coughed up water, gulped in air and then floated for a while. A Hymn from his mother's funeral came to him.

'O Love that wilt not let me go, I rest my weary soul in thee; I give thee back the life I owe, That in thine ocean depths its flow; May richer, fuller be.' Not just yet my friend.

"Jackie! Jackie!" hollered Bart in a tone that said, the captain was looking for him.

Usually he didn't wear his Bo'sun's pipe swimming, but he had it. He blew out the water and then a few notes, so they would see him. He had never felt more relaxed in his life and he wasn't ready to go, but an old warning ran through his head.

Better alone than in bad company unless your in the sea. Then it dawned on him. *Wait. If they're over there, who helped me?*

Mythical creatures came to mind, and he wondered who, or

what it was. He was not secure enough to dive under again until he heard the same soft tintinnabulation of bells he had heard on his thirteenth birthday and in Southhampton several years ago. When he peered below the surface, a bright spray of sun spotlighted a hand snatching at little fish. A closer look revealed it to be a mass of seaweed, and a yellow rose. It was on a woman's hair, the same way Billie Holiday used to wear her gardenias. He couldn't imagine how it stayed there in her loose hair flowing freely around her shapely shoulders. She caught one of the little fish and released it. After he went up for air, he ducked back under, but she was gone. Jackie laughed.

It's mirage, an illusion from lack of oxygen, the residual effect of the impact of the water, Dengue fever or the effect of sleeping alone for too long.

Climbing up the rope ladder, he paused to sneeze, and he saw her head rise from the water.

"Look! A mermaid," Bart cried out.

The men strained to see.

"Come on baby. Sing to me," one called.

"Probably a broad from one of those yachts. Wish I had seen her earlier."

"If there was a mermaid out there, do you think I would be here yammerin' with you?"

They let out a collective guffaw and continued their celebratory rollicking over the earlier spy drama which was the basis for their conversations all the way back to the United States.

X
Home,
Where the Heart is

X

Home, Where the Heart is

Whenever he shipped out, his mother hugged and kissed him tenderly and thanked him for visiting.

"Back home you go."

"Why do you always say that, 'back home' Mor?"

"Home is where the heart is, and gutten min yours is with the sea. You can not stay away too long or you will die, like a big fish."

The South American-Caribbean duty had been proof of that. His grief for her passing was stowed and his health restored by simply going "back home." Refreshed, he was ready to visit land. When the ship approached the port in the middle of steamy July, he was elated to see his personal welcome home sign. It could not be removed like the one that used to be draped around the tower for the troops returning from the Hell into which their orders had sent them, the front lines. There in the raw bowels of conflict gone mad, they hid, ate, and slept in gouged-out trenches in the mud, the stuff their mothers had tried to keep them out of when they were boys. They had been challenged physically and emotionally in all the ways their superiors told them courageous men could be in war. What was not mentioned in any sessions or manual was finding a buddy's limbs or a slaughtered toddler in the process of being eaten by maggots or how, as good Christians, they were supposed to restore themselves in God's favor after deliberately killing a fellow human. None of the men who went to war returned; their corpses, their shadows or the men they had become returned instead. The trajectory of Jackie's life had kept him from experiencing those horrors, and yet when he steamed into port after his first duty, the sign "Welcome Home," which was still there a year after 1945, brought tears to his eyes.

I have to ask TOP if that sign was there when they came back from Korea. Poor bastards. God love 'em, all the boys that fight for peace, but especially, Lucky Lou, Bird, Charlie and Wes. I wonder what happened to that old sign.

The gantry cranes stretched up three hundred feet in the air overhead and jut out over the quays. All around was a floating lattice of tugboats, ships and barges bobbing like empty boxes. It could have been a port anywhere except for the unique geometric skyline cutting high into the clouds and cresting over the Empire State Building.

That's my welcome home sign. Nobody's taking that one down...not ever. Impossible.

This time of year was usually hot, but Jackie didn't think the East Coast would rival the tropics. He was wrong. The heat penetrated the bricks and dark streets of the oven of New York which cooked the residents. He had to force his body through the waves to walk. Perspiration beaded on his brow and seeped through his shirt. Radios from cars and shops announced, "Record breaking heat wave. The temperature is 97.5 and expected to climb." His thoughts scrambled through the house to locate a fan, and then he remembered Michaela had moved everything. He would have to look for one.

The words "Vilkommen" jumped off the new mat in front of the door. TOP's girls, unbeknownst to him, had cleaned up in anticipation of his return. The pile of autumn leaves and mail he expected were absent. The porch was swept and furnished with two old wooden deck chairs, large potted plants on either side of the old ice chest and a large macramé wall hanging he had made and long-ago forgotten. The window in the door was no longer square but round and trimmed in brass like a porthole. Without its black and white tiles and carpet the floor's narrow boards lent a deck-quality to the room. Natural light poured in from the new skylights above on either side of a ceiling fan which he launched into action with a pull of the string.

What's this? A refrigerator?

Freshly used breakfast dishes on the counter seemed out of place until he remembered he had given Smitty permission to stay if he needed. He didn't want to invest the energy in thinking. He stuck his head in the freezer section because his blood was pumping through his veins so quickly he was afraid his eyeballs were going to pop out. Relieved, he checked to see if there was a beverage, and there was, milk, juice and beer, all cold. Michaela had selected objects and art with care, and the place looked great. One wall had been dedicated to his hi-fi and albums and a six-foot painting of the forest which, depending on the total cost, might have to be returned. He guessed what a few of the items cost and realized he may have used the words, "cost is no object" too liberally in his attempt to convince Michaela to take the project. The fossilized memory of the room's former layout placed his palm on a sideboard no longer there, and he dropped onto a piano. It was exactly what he wanted, though he hadn't put it on the list. He had only requested he not be able to identify his mother's room.

This must be someone else's house.

The box. He knew the box. It used to be downstairs. On it, Michaela had taped an index card with a question mark. She didn't know what to do with it or its contents, a sizeable stack of his photographs. Shuffling through them, he paused every now and again. There was Fana, the Christmas he met her; the World's Fair with his parents; Theo and the jazz musicians at the Five Spot; Minvenn and Vippers, the cows; his parents in national dress; Tally in her feather playing guitar; VJ Day festivities; his ex-girlfriends, Hilde, Helen, Margrete; Sally on the car in the middle of her girls flaunting the triangle, barely visible, and finally, the woman's spirit that appeared that same day. Although faint, he was positive she bore a striking resemblance to the nymph in the Caribbean.

By the table, he stumbled over a laundry basket brimming with the mail that had accumulated while he was away. The idea that senders would write again if it were important tempted him to incinerate what was guaranteed a tedious task, but responsibility and curiosity prevailed. After a few swigs of beer, he covered his eyes with one hand, reached in and pulled out whichever envelope he touched. The stream of pretty, sympathy cards was finally interrupted by a statement from the New York Telephone Company. They wanted $14.01 for the past months. And then, there at his new table bereft of molecules of the days gone by, he unwittingly pulled out a sizeable packet of the grief in the form of a letter addressed to his mother. The sender was in California, a Mrs. Thomas Bonhoeffer; he had never heard the name before. Small pink and large white envelopes waited inside. The first, from the lady herself, explained that her husband, the Honorable Reverend Thomas Bonhoeffer had passed away "a good decade ago now, but I have only recently found the wherewithal to clear his belongings out of the attic." Upon going through his clothes, which she was donating to charity, she came across the garment he was wearing the day of his passing. To her dismay, the pockets held the enclosed envelope addressed to Mrs. Vik which she surmised he was on his way to mail. Mrs. Bonhoeffer didn't see the need to violate her privacy and open it, only the need to send it as soon as possible, "though the message is arriving quite late and no longer be news," with apologies, she closed. The Reverend's envelope contained official correspondence detailing Paul Vik's last days, a letter he had begun to his mother and a V-Mail birthday card for Jackie.

BIRTHDAY GREETINGS
Jackie

No one can ever mean to me
What you do, you're so dear,
And though I may be far away
You seem so very near.
So Happy Birthday, always
And many of them, too,
That's what this special greeting
is fondly wishing you.

I love you,
Far

V-MAIL

PASADENA AREA STATION HOSPITAL
c/o Postmaster, California
OFFICE OF THE CHAPLAIN

June 16, 1947

Mrs. Paul Vik
361 Ocean Avenue
New York City, New York

Dear Mrs. Vik

This letter is being written to confirm the telegram in
which you were regretfully informed that your husband, Corporal Paul
Vik was presumed missing in the performance of his duty. I realize the
suspense you have endured, and now the finality to those hopes which
you have cherished for his safe return.

Due to the condition of your husband who was found alone,
without identification and gravely ill, May 9, 1945, near San Miguel,
Philippines, he was placed on a plane for Walter Reed Hospital. His
condition made it necessary to remove him from the hospital plane at
this base hospital. He regained consciousness, but he was unable to
identify himself due to the serious head injury he suffered. The
medical staff did all they could to make him comfortable. He fell into
a coma and passed away on December 12, 1945.

Corporal Vik's identity was revealed when his squad leader
was brought here for treatment and saw a photograph the hospital had
taken. He was glad to have accounted for him and stated he is a credit
to our country. Having discovered in his records that he was Lutheran,
we called upon a local minister to conduct the funeral services.

We the officers and men of this base, want you to know that
in this time of sorrow, we share your grief. It is especially
unfortunate the circumstances of his anonymity and condition did not
allow you the opportunity to reach his bedside before he passed away.

We hope that it will be a comfort to you to know that your
husband was given full military honors at the funeral. He now rests in
the Riverside National Cemetery with other of our deceased comrades.
Each man occupies and individual grave upon which a beautiful white
cross is placed which bears his name.

Most Sincerely,

Thomas Bonhoeffer

Thomas Bonhoeffer
Chaplain (Capt) USA

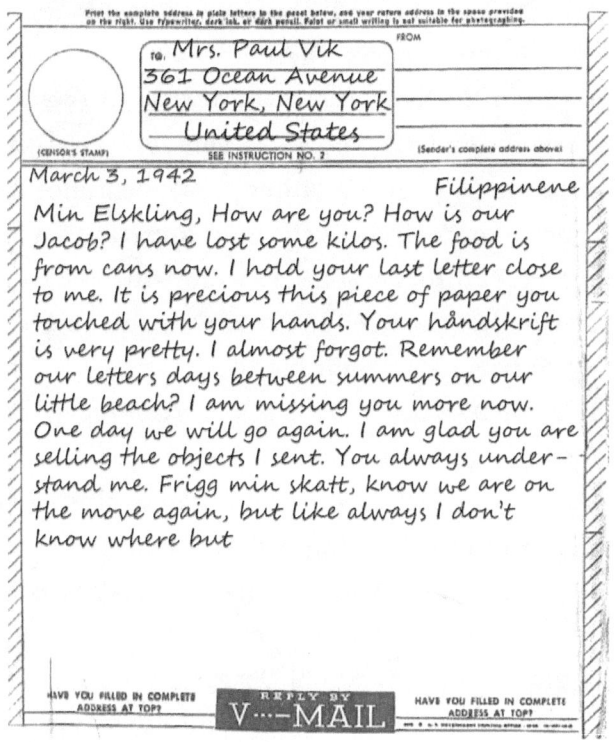

FROM

To. Mrs. Paul Vik
361 Ocean Avenue
New York, New York
United States

(CENSOR'S STAMP)   SEE INSTRUCTION NO. 2   (Sender's complete address above)

March 3, 1942   Filippinene

Min Elskling, How are you? How is our Jacob? I have lost some kilos. The food is from cans now. I hold your last letter close to me. It is precious this piece of paper you touched with your hands. Your håndskrift is very pretty. I almost forgot. Remember our letters days between summers on our little beach? I am missing you more now. One day we will go again. I am glad you are selling the objects I sent. You always under-stand me. Frigg min skatt, know we are on the move again, but like always I don't know where but

HAVE YOU FILLED IN COMPLETE ADDRESS AT TOP?   REPLY BY V --- MAIL   HAVE YOU FILLED IN COMPLETE ADDRESS AT TOP?

It stopped midsentence as if he was interrupted by someone, decided to continue later or thought he had to rewrite it without the Norwegian words for darling, treasure and the Philippines, "Elskling, skatt and Filippine," because it would not pass the censors. Jackie had no idea, but holding it, he could hear him and see him as clearly as if he was right there. Sweat from his thumb smudged a word, so he put it down.

I guess Mor told you Far. You did it. We won. The war is over.

A twisting in his chest pulled his hand up, and he realized he had not taken a breath for a few minutes. The pressure subsided as soon as he blurted out bawling. With the cry spent, he found solace in the firm belief that his parents were on their beach together. He looked at the wall, but the drawing was gone. He wrote a note to himself to ask where it was.

The tension in his hand broke the led tip of the pencil three times before he completed the short sentence, and he let out a scream. Jackie knew, after his father's disappearance his mother attended church more frequently and sometimes went just to speak with Reverend Jorgenson. He went with her from time to time, but now he felt the need to go for himself and to thank the family's church friends for their kindness.

Remember the Sabbath and keep it Holy, Mor used to say.

The full congregation imbued the nave with a cozy hue, and he was glad to be there. A sense of shame blushed over him when he caught himself leaning awkwardly to make eye contact with a pretty girl who acknowledged him but immediately bowed her head back over her hymnal. Before Jackie left, the minister let him know how much "Frigg is missed, and you too," and tears slid down his face. He invited him to stay.

"Usually we bring cookies, but I…"

"They are cookies, not the price of admission Jackie."

"Reverend Jorgensen, I had the house redecorated stem to stern, and I want to break it in. Next Saturday around noon . . . maybe you want to drop by?"

"It sounds wonderful. You can take this opportunity to invite your neighbors. I saw one or two at the coffee table."

After giving a few verbal invitations and taking a handful of cookies, Jackie ghosted out into the street. Socializing on his own was not as bad as he thought, but he dearly missed his mother, with whom he had always made the short walk home.

***

The following day at The Dog, the first thing Jackie noticed was the photograph of Marilyn Monroe. One of Charlie's military buddies had taken it in 1954 in Korea when she stopped by with Joe DiMaggio on their honeymoon. As far as pictures go, Jackie thought it was interesting, quintessential Marilyn in a skimpy, sequined-spangled dress unabashedly delighting in the troops ogling her. Charlie claimed to have gotten a few minutes of "one-on-one time," with her when he was back stage. His voice brimmed with genuine surprised when he said, "She wasn't what everyone expects, you know? She was really sweet. Looked right at me when I talked to her." Lost in the memory of lending her his jacket, he continued dreamily, "She was all covered in goose bumps, didn't expect Korea to be as cold as that. No one did." He sniffed the lining that, according to him, still smelled, ever so faintly, like her perfume and annoyed his wife Patty. To keep peace at home, he got rid of it as she requested, not by throwing it out but by stowing it at The Dog along with the photograph. Seamus framed it. Instead of simply hanging it, he nailed it to the wall "for safe keeping."

"See her scanning the crowd? She's looking for me," Jackie joked announcing his presence.

Cheers and congratulations cascaded down on Jackie in addition to the usual, "Hey. There he is, the savior of the ocean!" They patted his back and shook his hand adding, "You're in all the papers," and "A hero!" All the patrons assumed it was a special occasion and joined in when they belted out "He's a Jolly good Fellow." The walls trembled and glasses clunked. TOP asked so many questions all at once, Jackie was unable to answer.

"Aw, come on. I was just doing my job," he said.

"Jackie," Smitty said, "I have been out there with you and those deck apes. I mean they're all a bunch of nice guys, but you've got the brains. You saved the captain!"

They toasted again and TOP circulated the newspaper article about the stowaways among the curious. Jackie dismissed his actions as anything other that duty.

The New Yorker Newspaper

THE NEWS FOR TODAY   THURSDAY JULY 18, 1957   ONLY TWENTY-FIVE CENTS

BO'SUN JACKIE VIK SAVES CARGO SHIP CAPTAIN'S LIFE AND AIDS IN CAPTURE OF RUSSIAN SPIES IN HAVANA CUBA   By Harold Plume

Commies Taken into Custody at New York City Port Authority

New York July 22, 1957 - The FBI continues their successful roundup of Russian spies in New York. Thanks to the quick thinking of Jackie Vik, a Bo'sun in the United States Merchant Marine, they have arrested, the leaders of, what is believed to be, another Red spy ring.

Shortly after the SS Albert Le Roi embarked from Havana, Cuba full of cargo, Mr. Vik, a mariner for over a decade, reported to Captain John J. Wheeler that he "had a feeling" there were stowaways on board.

An initial search came up empty, but the Bo'sun's feeling persisted and he later observed the captain was not where he should have been. Concluding that he may be in danger, Vik with the Second Mate, Ian Olson, crew members Jason, Sylvester, and Bart Walter and an M1911 service pistol, they found and rescued Captain Wheeler. Vik said, "It was team work." The captain, who suffered life-threatening injuries, was the only one harmed.

The two stowaways' identities have not been confirmed but they claim to be Vladik Kovaleva and Andrei Ivanov of Russia. They were held in the brig until the ship arrived in port. Presently, it is not known if they are part of the espionage ring, the "Mocase" whose director, Rudolf Ivanovich Abel, was arrested last month in New York.

Kovaleva and Ivanov had in their possession microfilm with classified documents regarding the location of atomic warheads and missiles in Cuba, blueprints of official buildings in the United States, and dozens of aerial photographs of major U. S. cities. The alleged spies were not repatriated to their country but taken to FBI Headquarters. First Mate Ian Olsen, speaking on behalf of the captain said, "No doubt. Jackie Vik is a hero."

"We're here drinking and Jackie's out there single-handedly fighting the Commies."

The bar responded excitedly. Jackie tucked himself in the corner by the window and when the din died down Seamus leaned near to gossip.

"Big news Jackie. Smitty's smitten," he beamed looking right at him.

"Oh yeah. That's great Smitty. She's a good woman."

Smitty confirmed that he and Michaela were together.

"Yeah they went away for a weekend and…"

"Jesus Seamus. You're like an old washer wife for crying out loud.," Smitty complained.

"What's the problem? You're gonna tell him yourself anyway." Seamus poured another round, and held up his hand. "Don't want to drink all the profits, so this is a twofer cuz … well lads--," he said while his eyes burst with sparkles, for "Shannon's at it again."

"No! Really? The way you two are going, you'll have cheap help around here forever."

"That's the plan. If they're going to work for college tuition, they might as well do it here, right. Rye and Case already come in and sweep up. Remember how we used to do?"

"Girl or a boy this time? What do you want?" Smitty asked.

"I don' really care. Another girl would be good for little Doon. Six brothers. Can you imagine?"

"How did you manage that, only one girl. And she is a real cutie. Gotta be tough. No wait; I take it back. No one will ever bother her."

They all laughed and toasted Seamus. Out of the corner of his eye, Jackie saw Charlie sulking by the window, and assumed he had cycled into a dark mood as each of TOP did from time to time, and it was best to leave him alone. Above the din of the bar, the waitresses were jabbering about their lives, but he heard the name "Helen," and tuned in. "What a dream come true. I wish I could quit and go dance in *West Side Story* on Broadway." *Broadway? I thought the play was in Philadelphia.* It occurred to him that she might have lied to eliminate his expressed desire to see her again. Chances of him going to Philly were slim and she new it. Or perhaps she wanted to split on good terms, and be free. Charlie, clearly two sheets to the wind, joined Jackie and Smitty in the corner.

"Round of drinks Seamus. We'll drink to Bird's new girl."

"Don't start Charlie. I'll throw you out."

"You threatening me Seamus?"

"No. Promising."

Charlie sucked his teeth and tugged Jackie to the dining room door. In the booths, he saw a few diners.

"That's her."

"Who?"

"Bird's girl," he said under his breath grinning as if he were a misbehaving schoolboy.

"Oh yeah?" He strained to see. I thought you guys were puttin' me on."

Curiosity lured Jackie into the restaurant. The crowd had gone and the only sound was the big clock on the wall ticking. It was 3:00 pm. Bird's girl was probably gone, though there was one girl, barely visible, her head bent over a book. Returning to the bar, he saw the reader studying him.

"What are you reading there?"

"It's quite high-brow and intellectual," she replied sweetly, and held the cover up for him to see, "*The Hundred and One Dalmatians.* I..." she stopped and cocked her head inquisitively

Her face stirred the image of the young girl who had long-ago struck a white-triangle-revealing pose atop Mr. Jameson's car.

Is it possible? Is she little redheaded Sally? He thought and asked, "Sally, right?"

She nodded. "And you're Jackie, right?"

"Yeah. Jackie, Jackie Vik."

"May I?" he asked gesturing to the opposite banquette.

The coincidence inspired them to give an abbreviated summary of the fifteen years that had passed stating their occupations, marital status and where they lived. Jackie told Sally that after high school he had signed up with the Merchant Marine, inherited Vik's Woods and is working on changing his bachelor status. Sally's shared her story which involved her family's relocation to Larchmont in 1943 which she didn't like because it was far from the city. "Single," she said holding up her empty ring finger, "but maybe not for long and happily in town again since graduating and getting a position at Saint Vincent's Hospital.

"Used to be the Foundling Hospital," she clarified. "Where do you live now?"

"Where I took your picture…on the car?"

"You mean where you kissed me in the snow?"

"Yeah, remember that"

"Every girl remembers her first kiss," she tittered.

He couldn't figure out why TOP had made fun of her. She was a vision of femininity, her pale complexion flawless. Her red hair, which was longer than he remembered; now a rich auburn, it gave her delicate features a peach-kissed glow. From what he could see, she had a nice figure. Maybe they found the pairing odd; the degree of attractiveness off balance, though if he did, he could not share their perspective. Bird was as angular and gangly as ever, but his acne pockmarks had filled in. He was not a man who received many double takes from girls, but TOP found him a great guy, loyal, responsible and thoughtful. Over the years, a couple of girls had been won over by his deep, soothing voice and lean "Frank Sinatra build." Having grown up largely in the bookstore, he was very well read. Combined with the buildings his father had left him, he was a good catch. But was Bird dating her? Jackie was burning to know. Bird walked in. He was wearing a spiffy new suit and good shoes.

"Bird. Hi. Nurse Sally lived near me back in the day."

"I know?" Bird said visibly unsettled by Jackie's friendly attitude forward his girl.

"We're going to see *Designing Women*, with Lauren Bacall,"

"And Gregory Peck."

"Yeah, sure, sounds great."

"We have to go," Bird insisted holding out his arm out to her.

Jackie rose when she did. While she gathered her things, he heard the clang of metal several times. Bird reached behind the banquette and retrieved a crutch, the permanent, long, pole type with a fitting for the user's arm. Her head dropped a little as they moved toward the exit, and the sound of the crutch hitting the floor accompanied the heavy drag of her leg clasped in a metal brace. It pulled at Jackie's his heart.

A sympathetic "Sally," shot out a little louder than he intended.

Faint shame kept her eyes ahead of her when she paused and asked, "Yes Jackie?"

"It was good to see you again."

"You too Jackie."

Sally and Bird stepped into the sun, and Jackie slammed through to the bar inadvertently knocking Charlie in the head.

"Good. I should knock you out…"

"We're just having a little fun."

Charlie rubbed his head while his body swayed.

"Seamus, whiskey," Jackie ordered and barked at Charlie, — What is with you?"

The negative energy radiating between the two men kept their friends at bay, but Seamus brought Jackie his drink and leaned over the bar to whisper.

"Don't start nothing. He's been out of sorts for a couple of days now."

"What's going on?"

Seamus shrugged, "Beats me, but that is his last drink."

Charlie picked up two soupspoons and clunked them together, "This is Bird's girl. He laughed soundlessly with his mouth hanging open.

"You're drunk. Knock it off Charlie. That a polio brace, you know--like the president had. You make fun of him too?"

Jackie gulped his shot and decked Charlie. The spoons flew out of his hands. He rammed Jackie into the wall with his head. Immediately, Seamus grumbled in dismay. Smitty and Wes cleared the tables and chairs out of their path. Jackie and Charlie threw their arms around each other's necks and shoulders preparing to battle. Forehead to forehead, they exchanged words. Charlie was so plowed he wasn't able to maintain control over his volume, so some of his words were very loud and they came out of the side of his mouth.

"Let me buy you a cup of coffee Charlie. . ." Jackie offered trying to avoid the fight.

"Ha. After what you did!"

He had no idea what Charlie was talking about. They struggled and resisted and twisted, and finally they both went down on the floor. Seamus called out nervously.

"Jesus, Mary and Joseph. Open the screen door Wes. I don't want it busted. It's brand new."

Very casually, Wes opened it, and the pair rolled and their shoes kicked against the floor on their way into the small patch of yard that Seamus maintained in the back. Wes closed the door behind them. At one time or another, the men had all paired off to sort out their differences. Because they were all friends, no one took sides in the encounters which never amounted to more than harmless roughhousing. TOP, minus Charlie and Jackie, sat in the calm harbor of late afternoon at the bar exchanging banter and watching the ships bobbing in the water. Occasional thuds from the men slamming into the building punctuated the quiet. Lucky Lou came back from the men's room just as a big thud shook the building.

"What'd I miss?"

"Jackie and Charlie are sorting something out," Wes said.

"Break that screen, you're going to pay for it!" Seamus shouted loudly enough for the pugilists to hear outside.

They let each other go, and strutted in different directions; Jackie stared at Charlie as he ran his hands over his head.

"I will never forgive you," he barked.

"For what Charlie?"

"This is all your fault?"

He ran forward and smashed Jackie against the wall and pinned him there.

"Christ. Charlie. Stop. You're going to make me hurt you!"

He managed to get a foot onto Charlie's chest and shove him on the ground where he yelped in pain and held his ribs. Jackie got down next to him.

"Sorry man. Are you all right?"

"Get away from me."

"No problem," he said and sprang to his feet.

Charlie shouted between his winces, "Long time ago—my old man told me—you knew, and..." he held up his hand to stop Jackie from interrupting, "a few days ago—he told me again," he roared in pain. "You knew—you knew about him and Violet. That's why he left us, left my mother. He said, 'If a kid knows—everybody knows. Jackie must have heard something from someone.' He figured Mom would be a laughing stock if everyone knew he was running around on her but if he left...People would be sympathetic."

Jackie was dumbfounded. Charlie managed to sit up, but he had said all he could for the moment. Images Jackie had seen all those years ago ghosted through his mind: the hotel room; Mr. Muller naked with the pin-up girl in high heels; the silver cigarette case and the woman of the same name showing up, Violet. His words were soft and sincere.

"Charlie, I swear to you man, no one told me anything. If I said a name, it was..."

"Violet? How many Violets you met? If you had ..."

Charlie's eyes were lost in his swollen red flesh. Jackie helped him to his feet while he panted as he continued in booze lilted sentences.

"Oh he sent money, took good care of us, but she refused to divorce him. She loved the son-of-a-bitch. 'He'll be back,' she must have said it a million times." And you know what? He was," he hollered and grabbed Jackie by the shirt.

"He left that whore. My old man's coming back, Jackie."

"That's swell..."

"She's dead Jackie," he said and hung his mouth open crying silently.

He retched. Jackie leaned Charlie against the wall, so he wouldn't fall. He reached into his shirt, pulled out his Bo'sun's pipe and blew long and hard sounding the alarm for TOP to come and help.

"Take it easy, Charlie."

"The flu. The fucking flu. Can you believe it?" he yelled and retched again.

TOP filed out of the new screen door and by chance lined up side by side elated with beer and comradery. They saw Charlie down on one knee spilling bile out of his mouth and Jackie wiping away a tear.

"Charlie's mother died."

TOP delivered a heartfelt chorus of masculine sympathy, and then Seamus clapped his hands.

"Okay lads. Let's go. Lucky Lou set up the cot in the office. Smitty I'll give you a few towels to clean him up but out here. And watch out for the new door."

Wes followed the others inside, so he could call Patty and let her know everything was all right, but Charlie would be late. Jackie saw him about to keel over, and he helped him to the grass. Smitty came out with a pitcher of water and the damp towels and went back for glasses, but Charlie sipped straight from the pitcher. A breeze blew and a falling feather caught Jackie's eye. He looked up and saw the tip of the enormous wing flapping through the low, grey layers of clouds. He stared so intently, Charlie squinted at the sky and nursed his pitcher of water.

"What are you looking at?"

"A wing," he admitted assuming Charlie was too far gone to

believe the truth.

He rubbed his eyes, "Whoa. Jackie! Jackie! What is that?"

He repeated pivoting in a circle. Jackie wasn't sure if Charlie saw what he did or if he had been influenced by the power of his suggestion. He had seen other men drink so much they lost hold of the collective illusion of reality

"It's a wing, must be a hundred feet, right? Let's just keep that between us."

Charlie put his finger up to his lips, "Shhhh. I love you man," he declared and threw himself at Jackie and kissed his cheek.

TOP had rounded up a change of clothes. While they were undressing him and cleaning him up in the yard, he broke down in another bout of besotted, bereaved crying.

"I saw the angels coming for me. Jackie saved my life," he turned to the others, "Ask him. He saw them. Ask him!"

Jackie shrugged to dismiss the claim as drunken ramblings.

"Jackie! Jackie," he hollered though he was right by him.

"Yeah Charlie."

"I feel like shit man."

"You're probably going to feel like that for a while," he admitted and leaned his head against the wall, "but—you won't feel that way forever."

TOP, as it once was, was crumbling. He and Smitty were hanging out on the porch, swanning through the afternoon as old friends and seamen do, alternately reminiscing, sitting quietly and sharing their lives. Smitty was fighting back tears.

"Spill it Smitty!"

"Hey Man. I asked Michaela to marry."

Jackie stared at him. "I'd congratulate you—if you know--if you wasn't already married." A huge paused followed and Jackie asked quite seriously, "You didn't do something to her....Did you?"

Smitty shook his head. ""Till death do us part. It was the only way Jackie."

Their eyes met and they burst out laughing together.

"Christ Smitty you really had me going there. So what then? She finally agreed to a divorce?"

"An annulment."

"That's good, right? So what's with the tears."

"Gina just keeps…An annulment is going to take years!"

"Years?!"

"And there's no guarantee. Says so right here."

He unfolded the petition and handed it to Jackie, and he leafed through the pages.

"Damn Smitty. It would take me years to fill this out. Sheesh. What are you going before Lord God Almighty himself? Tribunal? Respondent? Witnesses?"

"There is a judge."

Jackie read, "'When and how did you and the Respondent meet? Describe the circumstances of your courtship. Was there any pressure to marry on either party?' Easy enough to answer those: High school. Back of a convertible Buick and Yes my Gina's father, showed up at the Dog waving a gun around. I'll be a witness for you."

Through his grin, Smitty thanked him but asked him not to "get involved. She is just as devious as her father. If I don't write what she wants, then the next time I ship out, she is going to tell little Tony I was killed in the army in Korea."

"You weren't in either of them…"

"I don't want to argue with her."

"Broads, always trying to hold the ocean in their hands."

"The sea. I went to get away from Gina. It's the only thing I know. Gonna be hard to spend time with my son and be with Michaela."

Other than a sympathetic pat on the back, Jackie had no response, though he wished he could help him. They fell back into another silence, and after a little while Jackie clapped his hands.

"Come and work at Vik's Woods. Good-looking guy like you will bring in the ladies fixing up the house, and you know about woodworking."

The suggestion lured a smile onto Smitty's face.

"And I'm almost never here. You want to get away from Gina? You need a place for you and Michaela to get set up.?"

He stretched out his arms to indicate the house was open to him.

"Okay. Thanks Jackie."

Smitty's smile expanded to his ears, and he threw his arms around Jackie in a hearty, hug.

XI
The Wake

XI
The Wake

Together with TOP, Jackie had attended the many funerals illness and the war opportuned, but he had never been to a wake. His plan was to drop in, offer condolences and leave as quickly as possible to thwart the resurrection of the intense emotions he experienced at his mother's funeral, a bleak, exasperating event that darkened sunny days into nights for over a month.   Dozens of mourners paid their respects: relatives from upstate whom he knew well; those from Paul's family in Pennsylvania whom he had only met once; Fred and Nora; the party circle guests; neighbors, the employees from Vik's Woods and random people with whom she interacted. All gathered quietly in the shimmering candlelit melancholy of the sanctuary.

Frigg's casket was unique for it held someone he loved. Wishfully, he prayed her funeral was actually a dream. Then José, the Cuban husband, who insisted his wife, though buried, was alive, triggered an overwhelming panic. He had already seen her laid out in the coffin at the funeral home and touched her when he slipped objects along the satin lining, his father's violin and tools, a pot, mason jars, a book of matches and a sewing kit. Civility quelled his desire to yank the white shroud off, slam it open and check again. Certain, he had seen her cross into death right before his eyes calmed him, but pangs of doubt nagged him; he felt her presence. Telepathically he communicated the beauty of the church atmosphere and all the people who came. He heard her ask that he take care of the store and continue going back home, "to Okeanos, the sea and Njord, your father." He promised and played his fiddle for her, for her charming playfulness and life's devotion to his father him.

Her patient lessons had taught him how to sew on his own buttons and hem his pants; clip the bushes to encourage the growth of bigger flowers; tie his shoes; and bake Eplekake, which he served with the disclaimer that it was "not as good as Mor made it." He saw her hand the countless times it reached out when he lagged behind or unfolding with a wondrous thing for him, a monarch butterfly, a bird or a cookie. He felt her strong, skilled fingers gently place his own in dough to "feel the consistency" when he kneaded it or on his back to correct his posture so "you don't get an ache." She adored the fiddle. Its strings acted as those on a marionette when he or his father bowed pulling her into dance, even in death as she did ethereally incorporeally when he fiddled at her funeral. Fully aware he was suspending her there with his notes, he played and played well beyond the time allotted until the reverend mentioned "the cars are waiting."

Watching them lift her coffin clawed at his soul. He worried they would jostle it, disturb her body's final sleep. Soberly, he staggered as unsteadily as if he had drunk all night all the way to the grave where he jumped in on top of the coffin. A collective gasp sounded loudly among the mourners. He retrieved a carelessly discarded cigarette butt and shot it at them with such a disapproving and menacing glare they took a timid step back. Thankfully, Uncle Rolf, stepped forward to help him climb out. He, Charlie and Smitty flanked Jackie for the rest of the service. TOP was genuinely worried about Jackie. Upon learning his relatives had to get back upstate, they made sure one of them stayed on Ocean Avenue, "till he don't ghost 'round," Seamus suggested. That took two weeks.

He got back to the store, visited the Union Hall and put the entire house in order, except his other's bedroom. *If she comes back, I want her to find everything as she left it.* Eventually, passing grief, time and Michaela's redecorating opened it. His parents' furniture was gone, but he could clearly see the old bed and night table. From time to time, he heard Frigg call his name. At times, he spoke to her as he did while he was getting dressed for the wake. "Apparently Mor, Mrs. Muller, you know Charlie's Mother, will be on a table. That's what Seamus..." *Why would they put her on the table? I guess she will be in the coffin, but still, gives me the damn willies.*

In the shower, he considered giving a last minute excuse to get out of it. The doorbell rang. He bolted downstairs in a towel.

Nancy, in dark glasses, greeted him with an armful of books.

"I see you were expecting me," she joked.

"Nope, but come in. Keep me company."

He raced up the stairs with Nancy behind him gawking at the new interior.

"The blue palette in the kitchen is stunning, and...Oh how divine, a canopy bed!" she shouted and stretched seductively on the spread.

He left the water running to sneak a peek at Nancy; she was adjusting her small, firm, plump breasts in her brassiere. His perception of her as his parents' friend ended after the first year he returned from sea duty. Larry had invited him to sit on the roof with him and "my friends, the two Davids, and of course, the ball and chain."

Nancy was there lounging on a chaise in a two-piece with her delectable peach hills and valleys simmering beneath the white-hot sun. Why the men hung obliviously over the roof's brick wall was a mystery. Traveling down her thigh, he arrived at a thin line of errant blonde hairs. He mopped his brow. *Who knew she had luscious grapefruits under those starchy blouses, all those buttons.*

"Jackie, make yourself comfortable," Larry called over and flung his arms out freely. Jackie took off his shirt and the Davids complimented him.

"Adonis lives and breathes,"

"Larry get your friend a chair."

"I got one," he replied and dropped himself in the one Nancy was patting next to her.

Erotic tension coursed through her fingertips applying oil on his broad shoulders, and involuntarily, his young, body responded, and he discretely dropped a towel on his lap. Seducing her was out of the question not only was she older, his parents' friend and a professor but she was with Larry in "some Bohemian relationship," is how he described it to TOP. To clarify, he related Larry and Nancy's behavior at an opening. "He was holding her but had an arm around a handsome model type guy. Ménage à trois came up with a couple, and Larry sort of pushed her away. Off she went. Larry didn't care; he was focused on the model-guy lifting his shirt and showing off his muscles. I guess he was hoping to catch an artist's eye, be immortalized."

"Were you in on that threesome with..." Smitty stopped and cut his eyes inquiringly to Jackie.

He slapped his chest and announced, "Hell no! Only one captain on the good ship Jackie." He took a swig of his drink. "Why?" and snapped his fingers. "Oh! You got the hots for Nancy."

Smitty chuckled at Jackie's ability to read him so easily, "Tits like that, isn't everyone?"

The Wake

"I guess but tits schmits; she's not just some broad. She's Nancy."

Literature brought them together when they happened into each other at openings and gatherings, but over the years, their interest escalated and they met deliberately in private. On one visit, Nancy, pointed out repeatedly that Larry would be "gone until tomorrow." The hint went unnoticed until he was at The Dog, and he shared how intellectually stimulating he found Nancy.

"Did you see her naked?" Lucky Lou asked excitedly.

"No Lou. We were talking about a book, this slim," he declared indicating an inch with his thumb and forefinger. "The Pearl. Took me ten minutes to run it down for her. Nancy says...," he imitates her tossing her hair back and fluttering her eyelashes, "'Yes, that's the sequence of events,' and then asks me like I'm a mind-reading genius, 'How do you think it would be different if Tennessee Williams had written it?' And then..."

"She took her blouse off?" Lucky Lou interjected.

"No," Jackie sighed slightly annoyed. "'Tennessee Williams? Ha. The fisherman would have been a hunky drunk with a sister he wanted to sleep with.' She busts up laughing, said I had 'a refreshing point of view,' and kissed me right o the smacker."

"So what are you doing here?" Seamus asked raising his eyebrows and slapped the bar with his cloth.

"What?"

"Larry threw him out," Smitty chimed in.

"He wasn't there," Charlie noted.

"Ah ha, so she did take off her..."

"No Lou. Nobody took their clothes off!" Jackie shouted." And shame on you guys. She was caught up in the moment, not coming on to me. Nancy's a classy uptown type."

"Right. That's why she's kissing you. No one up at the university would find out, right?" Smitty guessed.

TOP watched reality dawn on Jackie's face. He hit his forehead with his palm Ahead of the next visit, Nancy called to confirm, and he asked, "So, ah…um…Maybe I'll bring something. What's Larry drink, Rheingold?"

"Yes, but he won't be here."

He heard her smile, but he fretted over what he would say to her, an experienced, educated, upper class woman. All the lines he concocted sounded fatuous when he said them out loud. He resorted to the standards about hair, eyes and smile. On the bed, they explored their bodies over and under their clothes, but numerous anxieties prevented them from getting naked. He didn't share anything with TOP beyond a wry smile, and the confession that they were "Like I told you, we're friends, and I have to think about Larry." To himself, he theorized Nancy's close friendship with Frigg was an obstacle too, and that proved true shortly after his mother died. Their perfunctory fleshy romp escalated into a juicy giggle-laced nakedness and culminated in consummation.

Her skills in coquetry outshined those in lovemaking. Hers was devoid of the passion and drive girls usually unleashed when trying to climax or even creativity and variation. She didn't push back at his thrust. Missionary-style in bed was her preferred position. The sheer closeness of intimacy brought her pleasure, not climax. He had and he did with her. Their sexual connection boosted his ego because she lavished unbridled gratitude and appreciation on him. He really liked Nancy "as a friend," which, in order not to lead her on, is exactly what he said. Still she thanked him when he rolled off as if he had done her a favor. "You don't have to say that. You know you're my smartest girl Nancy," he assured her with a light pat on her thigh.

The Wake

After his mother died, he invited her to the house on Ocean Avenue where he was less anxious about Larry interrupting. He dove into a copy of Melville, because he didn't want to look into her eyes.

"Listen-----I wanted to ask you----Where does Larry think you are?"

"The library, I suppose. Our connection isn't what you think. I am happy with my studies and Larry is happy with---his artist fellows---you know?" she asked lifting her eyes to his face to see if her insinuation registered.

Jackie mulled over her comment. He had met almost every artist Larry represented. Without exception, all were men, young, toned men. "What are you saying? Larry's a fag?" he asked in disbelief.

"I guess I am a pretty good beard if you didn't know."

"Larry?"

"He has represented one or two clients who are incredibly gifted, your father for example. I'm positive nothing went on there."

"Ha. Far would have decked him. Well just to clarify he wasn't...God I don't want to think about that Nancy. I wish you hadn't told me."

Glimpses of Larry inviting him to take off his clothes, join him for a sauna or draping his arm around him brought his motive into question, but he refused to think Larry's feelings for him were anything but amicable.

"Would you like to go to Mrs. Muller's wake with me?"

"Oh Jackie you say the sweetest things," she giggled.

Her company would ease his nerves at the wake and dim the spotlight over his bachelor status in the presence of the couples and families at gatherings. TOP had their wives and their children around them. Bird was engaged to Sally. Lucky Lou was with a petite Irish girl he had recently met and that left Jackie as a third wheel with every member of The Only Pantheon.

Nancy's a beard for my unhappy aloneness.

Father Dolan, the expected throng of friends and neighbors from next door and Mrs. Muller's relatives from Finland and Ireland streamed onto the lawns and sidewalks. Every surface burgeoned with flower arrangement or was cluttered with dishes of food or scraps. The mirrors had been turned to face the wall, so "her soul would not get trapped in there," he overheard a girl say. Aunt Ilta was displayed in an open coffin on a table, just as Seamus said she would be. Jackie carefully avoided her. Charlie's footsteps weighed heavily under the gravity of sorrow for his mother and anger for his father who showed up with his pinup mistress Violet. He sat by the coffin beside Essi, his kid sister, and Aunt Rose, Violet's mother. He blocked them from approaching the table, but he let TOP pass. He raised his beblubbered face and his voice fluctuated with emotion.

"It's Smitty, and he put a tie on," he told Ilta, "You're a good guy Smitty dressing up. Go ahead and give her a kiss," and then jumped up and shouted at his father, "but not you! You stay over there."

"Stop that Charlie," Essi whispered tensely.

Jackie saw Smitty lean in and kiss Aunt Ilta's corpse. He cringed and hoped touching the corpse in anyway was not part of the traditions. Aunt Ilta's cousin Violet who had been carrying on with her husband walked up. Panting like a bull about to charge, Charlie snorted, clenched his teeth and shot daggers at her. He lowered his ear down to his mother's face in the coffin.

"What mother?" he asked softly. "Oh you..." deliberately he raised his voice. "You don't want that whore over here?"

The Wake

"She is still my cousin, I loved..."

"No. You don't get to use that word." He leaped up. "Dad! Get this bitch away from my mother," he yelled silencing the oddly boisterous funereal hubbub.

Violet bristled, stuck her chin in the air and stepped toward him. He jumped up with such force, the chair crashed to the floor. He pulled his old M 1911 service pistol from his belt, and shrill screams from the women around him. Father Dolan rushed over, placed himself between Violet and Charlie and eventually convinced him to give up the weapon to Jackie. The priest thought it was a good time for a few words that drew the mourners into a circle around the coffin. A woman said she had a poem to share. Jackie unintentionally tuned out until the end.

"...I would not have you sad for a day. But in summer just gather some flowers; And remember the place where I lay. And come in the shade of evening, When the sun paints the sky in the west. Stand for a few moments beside me, And remember only my best."

"That was lovely. Wasn't that lovely?" Father Dolan asked and held his head down to peer at Charlie over his eyeglasses. "Your mother would have..."

"Yes. She thought it was very good," he answered politely and waved Jackie over. .

"Holding up all right Charlie?"

He shrugged. Jackie flit his eyes around to avoid Aunt Ilta's corpse, but Seamus pushed up behind him.

"Essi."

"Seamus, thank you for coming."

"Sure." He leaned over the casket, closed his eyes and appeared to be communicating with Aunt Ilta before he kissed her cheek. "They did a nice job on her, they did."

Emotion welled up in Charlie, and dropped his arms around Seamus in an enveloping hug and then he moved him aside, "Let's give Jackie a chance."

Ilta didn't look particularly dead. Her salt and pepper hair was coiffed and lacquered; her lips and eyebrows made up, though he thought more heavily than she would have preferred. She never wore much "face paint" as she called it. Her rosary was wrapped around her fingers. At any moment, he expected her to open her eyes and tell him she had made whiskey pies.

"You boys can help yourself to a tiny sliver. Save some for your father."

She did always think of Mr. Muller. He spied him across the room with Violet. *Okay, so you're her husband and she's Ilta's cousin, but you don't show up together. Looks bad Mr. Muller. What's that word? Discreet, gotta be discreet.* Sympathy coursed through his heart and vanquished his squeamishness. He stroked her arm. As he had thousands times since he was a child, he planted a peck on her face. Her skin was cool and rubbery on his lips and he felt the little pat on the back she always gave him. Unbeknownst to him, the fringe on her shawl caught on his sleeve button. When he stepped away, the length of fabric stretched out behind him and raised Aunt Ilta's arm.

Essi saw it and cried out, "Mother!"

Gasps punctuated the din and she rushed smiling to the casket and saw the thread; she detached it with tender disappointment. Father Dolan shooed the astonished guests into the next room and unfolded a partition in front of Mrs. Muller suggesting, "Folks might want to have a private word." The atmosphere was festive, raucous with song, piano playing and big voices telling tales of Charlie and Essi's mother's kindness, generosity and legendary forgetfulness.

The Wake

"Jackie you're up."

The piano player. Blue, was a musician he had jammed with at The Five Spot, and the connection put him at ease. He began with a bit of light banter.

"Charlie's mother, Aunt Ilta...Ilta that's a Finnish name," applause drizzled. Choking back tears, he paused a second and continued. "Well I just kissed her. I guess for the last time." He shifted and scratched his head. "I'm not sure what to say. Lutherans don't usually..."

"Aw there's nothing to it, just say what you feel. We're all half in the bag anyway," Seamus noted to affirming laughter.

"Okay. . . Um Aunt Ilta was Finnish but Irish too..." a proud cheer erupted. "She made these whiskey pies. . ." elicited unbridled whoops, "really delicious," he shouted and waited for the noise to die down. "She loved us kids. I know she loved me cuz she was the only one of Mor's friends who stayed in the house while I was practicing...made awful screeching sounds with this violin. And she said? 'You're getting better;' that's what she always said. This song is her favorite. Lou or one of the boys gave you a handout, Swing Low Sweet Chariot. Sing out now, so she can hear you," then, he cut his eyes at the coffin on the table. "This is for you Aunt Ilta?"

They sang off key and loudly. Next Seamus was up, and he led everyone in *When Irish Eyes are Smiling* concluding with, "That's enough of that," pointed at Jackie and encouraged a round of applause.

"Me again?" he asked sheepishly walking back up."

"How about Stompin' at the Savoy?"

"We need a drummer for that Seamus. Gimme a second to figure something out with Blue." The brief consultation sent the pianist into a bag of sheet music while Jackie got everyone's attention with a long note on his Bo' sun's pipe "By the by, while you are all together, come by Saturday for my housewarming party. Same place on Ocean Avenue, but Michaela redid my whole place. It's incredible. Let's hear it for Michaela."

Above the light clapping she called, "Oh Go on Jackie," she called

"You're the best. So everybody come Saturday. Reverend Jorgenson will be there and Fana and Nancy and all of you, right?" Blue whispered in Jackie's ear, and he grinned. "Yeah. That's perfect." To the crowd he announced, "Me and Blue here are going to play *After You've Gone*."

"What time on Saturday?"

"Oh come on. You come any time."

"Actually, I also have something planned..."

"With Michaela..." he stopped and gave him a big Uncle Rolf hug. "She's a great girl. Smitty, you are like a brother to me. Listen. Whichever one of us goes first plans a big send off like this. for the other. Okay?"

"If we remember. We'll be pretty old."

"God I hope so Smitty."

"Nancy said to tell you she and Larry are coming Saturday, but she had to take off."

The two men danced until Smitty caught sight of Michaela who beckoned him nearer with a wiggle of her index finger and left Jackie alone. From his corner, the reveling mourners shrank and flipped upside down as if he was looking through the wrong end of a telescope. He packed up his fiddle and went outside where he stretched out on a cool sheet of moonlight. He squirmed and pressed his back into the ground to flatten the dry prickly, dry grass, and used his violin case as a pillow. Lovers' sweet titters and whispered nothings punctuated the silence. He always knew why he joined the Merchant Marines, but at that moment, he knew why he had stayed for so many years. Its threads of routine and purpose were woven tightly into the fabric of his existence that it was protected from loneliness. Ashore, loneliness lurked in bars, restaurants, movie theatres, streets, everywhere, even the eyes of female companions who slipped so easily beside him. Revisiting past relationships, he concluded all none would have worked. The sky provided an unlimited canvas for his imagination.

Heading for the horizon, we are heading for nowhere.

A raft rose up under him and to the exotic strains of a Didgeridoo glided him over the ocean. He heard splashing and "Jackie! It's Jackie!" The slam of an industrial throw-switch shot bands of phosphorescent green and blue as bright in a display that the Northern Lights would envy, and dozens of dolphins leaping and whistling came into view. Two appeared along side of him.

"Remember us?"

"From the Hudson, right?" Jackie confirmed excitedly.

They clapped and told him they would leave the lights on until he left and swifted off to catch up with the pod. Beneath the surface, lights illuminated Neptune's entire kingdom. Strangely, the sea lilies and brightly colored anemones, which he thought only lived at the lowest depths, flagged and somersaulted inches from his face. A sense of acute danger prevented him from touching the creatures, instead, he lifted a small, round rod from the sediment beneath the plants. The object whizzed from his hands and into the air with the force of a strong wind and knocked him backward. He held on with all his might as a fishing line whirred into each end of it. The lights went out. In the moonlight, the ocean surged over the world, including the lawn under the tree at the Mr. Muller's wake. His spirit wafted out of his body, and wings replaced his arms. They were as long and white and beautiful as Goddess Freya's cloak. He flew through the dense cottony pockets of Mammantus clouds.

Mammantus Clouds

He saw an area of the sky where eternity's rainbows and storms were lined up very neatly as far as the eye could see. The thin air belabored his breathing and his strength. Unable to ascend any higher, he caught a current to take him back, but the sea was flooding into the sky. On either side of his view corridor, mythological gods were talking loudly, and pointed at Jackie.

"Put—it—back!" he boomed.

Where the ocean ended and the sky began was no longer clear, and it dawned on Jackie that he had taken the horizon line. Hoping gravity would pull it into place, he dropped the rod which floated on the sea. He held his breath and dove into a stream of moonlight. There was no way to find the exact location where he discovered it.

"Jackie," cried one of the Hudson dolphins.

The other slipped under him and skimmed over the waves. As they approached the spot, the horizon rod heated up in his hand and with lightning speed the line unreeled from the ends. His wings were drenched, and he could barely raise them to fly. The dolphins communicated the problem to the gods in clicks. In the blink of an eye, he was in his body in a tree on the front lawn. He watched as two mermaids ebb out with the sea. Large scales they had shed shimmered silver and a throng of guests was collecting them. Seamus was doubled over with laughter at TOP's graceless efforts to deliver an unwieldy twenty-foot ladder. Warmth ran from Jackie's toes to his head as he reintegrated with his body. The tree bark bit his palm. It was dawn.

Right? Is that where I am? Is that ladder for me?

The sky whirlpooled around and all he could smell or taste was his rum-laced breath and the sweat pouring down his brow which he thought was because he was shaking so violently. He tried to fight the movement because it made him nauseous. He dedicated a second to hoping everyone had drunken barrels, so the night's antics, whatever they were, would be washed from memory. *Booze knocks you on your ass so hard, there isn't any energy to grieve. That's why they have these wakes. I don't even remember who died. Shit.* The fragrance of freshly brewed coffee kept him conscious. Those who had slept during the night were setting up the urn and cups on a table as the sun silhouetted the party-weary mourners into a ragged line of paper dolls.

"I don't think I have ever seen the dew shine so brightly," Jackie said from the ground to whoever was in earshot.

"It isn't dew. It's fish scales, see?"

His eyelids sanded halfway over his eyeballs and he saw a woman or, *a hallucination, that's what she is. Aching, chills, nausea. Too much booze. She can't be real. Logic says she can not be the girl in the seaweed in the Caribbean sea or a photograph I took twenty years ago,"* he said to convince himself he had not lost his mind.

The ground rumbled with Charlie's heavy footsteps. Apparently the mourners, the music, the food, nothing had dampened his grief. He was loud and bawling his eyes out.

"Jackie! Jackie," he shouted, "Oh my God," he knelt beside Jackie and embraced him more firmly than he ever had in his life, but Jackie was unable to respond.

"I can't believe this. I just can't believe it. You were one of Mom's favorites Jackie. Your speech touched my heart. Really man. I'm sorry I yelled..."

"Charlie," Patty called.

"Patty! Patty!" he replied and thundered after her.

The Wake

The girl was gone.

It would be so great if she was real, and she got coffee.

Jackie released himself into the painless arms of blackness.

XII

The Adirondacks

"Beautiful music is the art of the prophets that can calm the agitations of the soul; it is one of the most magnificent and delightful presents God has given us. "

Martin Luther

All the soul's invisible, dark passageways in which wrake and sorrow secret themselves had been thoroughly cleansed by tropical breezes, and he wanted to try to keep them that way. A wispy fog diffused the lights from cars, lamps and signs into giant stars that guided him along his way to Ocean Avenue. He stopped in front of his store, Vik's Woods. The angle at which the light hit the window didn't reflect him as well as it did the man nearby. What a lonely figure he cut in the buzzing red and yellow neon. They highlighted the lower depths of crevices on his worn skin. He thought he might know him, but he had stepped out of view into the shadows. When he was gone, Jackie leaned closer to see himself and got a harsh eyeful of truth. The reflection was his own. He leaned back and forth into the light to be certain, and squinted at himself. The longer he looked, the older he got, the uglier he made himself out to be, an ancient mariner, with no parents, no wife, no children and a house that didn't matter because his life was the sea. An enormous ball of insecurity rolled up inside of him as the cacophony of New York's revving, honking, wailing, laughing symphony soared to a deafening pitch. He covered his ears and hurried toward the left to Ocean Avenue. In the relative quiet, he could think more clearly, and he began to question the wisdom all the changes he had made. At that moment, he wanted nothing more than to throw himself into the cozy familiarity of the big overstuffed chair his father used to sit in, but the chair was gone. After thirty years of living with the previous lay out, he had been able to negotiate the stairs going up or going down and walk through the entire house in the pitch dark—"bollixed," as Seamus would say—to take a leak, get a glass of water or go back to bed, not anymore. The dramatic new set up challenged him even with the lights on.

Damn what does it mean if I am lost in the light? Going to take time to adjust I guess.

He had taken shore leave, so there would be lots of time to familiarize himself with the house, but it would take another thirty years for him to be as comfortable as he once was, and he did not want to do that alone. Cleaning out his jacket pockets he came across one of the mermaid scales wrapped inside a note. A phone number was written above the line, "Yes, I do like coffee," and it was signed, "Alida," with a heart. ♥ He had almost no memory of the night except for the girl he met at the end, and he hoped she was the author of the note. That was all he knew about her which meant he had to do something he loathed, use the phone

"I like to see a person when I'm talking to him. The eyes often say a lot more than the mouth," was what he told people. The truth was that speaking on the phone unsettled him because the weight of the receiver in his hand and the action of dialing reminded him of calling for help over his mother's breakdown and an ambulance after Mr. Edwards's assault. He did not use the phone unless it was absolutely necessary. Desire and impatience made it so. At the telephone table with the dedicated chair that Michaela bought, he sat and stared at the phone as if he dared it to give him a hard time. The seat was not designed for a man of his stature, and he could not get comfortable. He made a note, "Make a good-size manly chair," grabbed the receiver and returned it to the cradle. Except for coming up with what he was going to say to the owner of the number, who he hoped was Alida, he had no reason to procrastinate any longer, though he did pause to think about her phone number's Plaza exchange. Wes lived in that same Ritzy area whose girls entertained themselves with men like him but not with thoughts of marriage. He had dated a couple of those well-heeled girls. They adored him; their parents did not. He snatched up the phone and dialed anyway.

Brrrrrrring—Brrrrrrring—Brrrrrrring—Brrrrrrring.

He let it ring longer than usual because he didn't want to call again. As he was about to set the receiver back on the cradle the ethereal, blue resonance of a feminine, "Hello?" came through and scattered his anxiety. "In the middle of something at the moment," her time was limited, but she was "glad he called," and agreed to see him.

"Is later a possibility? I could pick you up around…"

"No!" she snapped. "No I um…Why don't we meet…"

"Oh, I see," he lied assuming, the reason was he was not the type of man her family would cotton to.

Bird's Books was the appointed meeting place, and he was particularly pleased that she knew it. He heard Bird and Sally in the storeroom chatting and laughing and he didn't want to bother them, so he located two copies of *Prometheus Bound*. In their brief conversation, she brought up the title as one they could like read together. Discovering it in the theatre section gave rise to unwelcome suspicions that Alida, like Helen, was in love with the theater. As he had a thousand times before in his life, he rang up his purchase himself, placed the books in a bag and the money in the register. Absent-mindedly, he sat the package on a table freeing his hands to browse. A case of nerves pattered his leather soles up the stairs to the old stacks where he and Bird used to hide their French risqué girl cards. He paced up and down the narrow aisles until a browser expressed mild annoyance, so he went downstairs, parked himself in a chair and alternately leafed through the book and checked for her out the window. A glare of golden yellow light sun burst onto the sidewalk with such intensity, Jackie had to look away. *What was that?* Curiosity leaned him forward, and Alida emerged from the light. He dashed back upstairs in order to execute the grand entrance he had envisioned, nonchalantly descending the stairs with jazz-player coolness. As soon as he heard the shop bell, he hastily tapped down the first few steps but caught himself and posed as if deeply engrossed in a random book he grabbed. Alida scanned the shop and saw his legs on the staircase. He felt her gaze travel up the creases of his trousers to his belt in surreptitious assessment, and an upbeat tempo thumped in his heart. Summoning all the control he had, he didn't move except to slide his finger to the end of the line he was, in reality not reading. He pretended not to see her and began his impressive entrance, but it was foiled by a penny underfoot that slid him clumsily to the bottom of the stairs and at her feet.

"Watch out for that last step. It's a doozy," she giggled.

Their eyes met and the spark of mutual attraction danced between them.

"It sure is," he said and dusted off his embarrassment. "I'm Jackie, Jackie Vik."

"So you told me."

She was very close to him and without averting her eyes from his; she lifted his pipe lanyard from his shirt and accidentally scratched him sending a tingle through his body.

"Such fine weaving," she said.

"Star knots. I made it myself," he said in a way that sounded like stammering in his head.

Her fingers ran down the ridges of the braid to the end, "A Bo' sun's pipe. I've never seen one like this. What are you reading?" she asked but bent her head to read the title, "*The Art and Science of Embalming.*"

"What?! No. I was…"

He dropped it on the table and picked up his earlier purchase.

"Bird!!," he called out and boasted to Alida, "I know the owner."

Through the stockroom curtains, he saw Bird and Sally, linked at the arms, saunter in the clumsy gait of new lovers blind to the world. They beamed and floated off on their amorous cloud.

"They're engaged," Jackie offered as an apology because he thought they should have greeted her. The heat steamed away his minor concern. Of more importance to him was finding a cool spot. The weatherman had threatened a heat wave, but Jackie not that the temperature would rise over one hundred and break the record set in 1936. Her Plaza exchange had encouraged him to slip on a blazer, so he was doubly hot. They agreed the best place to go was "the water," which they said in unison. He slung her oversized bag over his shoulder and they headed for the Staten Island Ferry where the air was less hot but not as cool as anticipated. Weather talk evolved into personal histories. He still wondered if she might have been the girl with the yellow rose whose photograph he had taken on his thirteenth birthday. When Alida said she had lived in the Village and went to the Little Red School house on Bleeker Street which was not far from Ocean Avenue, he thought it was possible. The problem was, at eight years his junior, she would have been in kindergarten when he was turning thirteen. He decided to forget it and enjoy her completely enchanting presence. She said she didn't have a fella, so he had a chance. He took off his jacket, and they cooled off in the warm breeze without saying much of anything.. On the return trip Alida thought it might be fun to find passages from *Prometheus Bound* and read them to each other.

"Like a rehearsal? Are you interested in acting?"

Alida shook her head as she examined the dual text pages in English and Greek. She showed it to him.

"Beautiful letters, don't you agree?"

The Adirondacks

ΩΚΕΑΝΟΣ.

ἥκω δολιχῆς τέρμα κελεύθου
διαμειψάμενος πρὸς σέ, Προμηθεῦ,
τὸν πτερυγωκῆ τόνδ' οἰωνὸν
γνώμῃ στομίων ἄτερ εὐθύνων
ταῖς σαῖς δὲ τύχαις, ἴσθι, συναλγῶ.
τό τε γάρ με, δοκῶ, συγγενὲς οὕτως
ἐσαναγκάζει, χωρίς τε γένους
οὐκ ἔστιν ὅτῳ μείζονα μοῖραν
νείμαιμ' ἢ σοί.
γνώσει δὲ τάδ' ὡς ἔτυμ', οὐδὲ μάτην
χαριτογλωσσεῖν ἔνι μοι· φέρε γὰρ
σήμαιν' ὅ τι χρή σοι συμπράσσειν·
οὐ γάρ ποτ' ἐρεῖς ὡς Ὠκεανοῦ
φίλος ἐστὶ βεβαιότερός σοι.

"I do. I wonder if it sounds that way too."

She read the English translation slowly and clearly.

"At the end of my long journey Prometheus, I come to you—having flown this swift-wingéd bird without giving commands; only by my will. Know that I suffer the pain of your misfortunes. That I believe us to be Kin must force me to feel this; because apart from all blood-ties, I know of no one for whom I would wish to do more than for you. You will know this truth, it is not in me at all to speak in vain with flattering language. Come give a sign of what I must do to help you and you will never say you have a truer friend than Okeanos."

"Okeanos.?

"Yes. The ocean.

"I know. My mother says that's my home."

"Is it?

"It is. So you are not reading this because you are performing it, are you?"

"No. Because it's beautiful."

The ferry pulled into port and Jackie rattled an ostentatious monologue about the skyscrapers and the city as if she was a tourist, and then he caught himself and laughed.

"What a big know-it-all, huh?"

"I enjoyed it. You know so much. I will never see the harbor the same way."

He kissed her gently on the lips just as the ferry sounded its horn and the flock of seagulls fluttered in a circle. Though he offered twice, she insisted on carrying her satchel herself as they ambled aimlessly through the sultry summer shadows of side streets where the intense heat muffled the usually sharp city sounds. When they happened to arrive in front of the White Horse Tavern, he automatically went in. They sat in the cross breeze created by the big metal fan blades on either side of the room, but he didn't think they could stay for long. Margrete, his former fiancée was there. Oblivious to him, she gabbed on and on with a man who Jackie surmised was her future husband by the ring on her left hand. Alida touched his heart when she reached for his hand and held it as gently as a schoolgirl. After showing her the Dylan Thomas chair, they sat. The men's room door took him back to an odd night there when he was sixteen.

A petite woman entered while he was combing his hair. She was older, in her forties he guessed. Her lips were full and covered in creamy red, her eyebrows heavily drawn over pale face make up that gave her the appearance of a mime. She leaned seductively, pulled out a cigarette and jutted her chin up as a way to ask for a light. Though he didn't smoke, he patted his pockets anyway. She tossed the cigarette on the floor and strode toward him with deliberate, salacious steps. All at once, he wanted to run and he wanted to stay. He did not move. She hoisted her skirt up revealing her mound of blond hair. No matter where he ticked his eyes they tocked back to her hand. He twisted away toward the sink and heard her shoes step one and step two and then felt her hand on his back. The spell of eroticism overcame him, and he sank his fingers into her fleshy ass and onto his waist while their lips mutually licked and lapped and sucked each other. When he deposited her weight on the sink, he saw himself in the mirror kissing her, a stranger, a woman who he really did not want to kiss. His giant spirit of resistance awakened and pulled him away from the siren. He felt incredibly empowered by having tamed his primitive instincts.

"The ladies room is next door," he told her abruptly.

"Than you?" Alida said bringing Jackie back to the Tavern.

He apologized for drifting off and blamed the heat. The entertainment began. A banjo, guitar duo played folk music followed by a man who read a poem with great passion, but which, they whispered, they didn't really understand. A girl stepped up to the microphone with her guitar. As she was getting situated, she flung her hair over her shoulder, and he saw the big feather; it was Tally. The last time he had seen her was years ago when she came through the garden gate and played music with him in the woodshop; he couldn't believe she still had the feather and she didn't look any older, not even one day. Her song was pretty and powerful and well received. Applause showered over her and lasted until she rejoined her table. A high-pitch laugh soared over the bar blather and he knew it was Nancy. He saw her at the front with Larry.

What are the chances?

With the excuse that he was "suffocating," he led Alida out

the side exit before he had been spotted. Opening the door of the club was no different from opening the oven after his mother had been baking all day; unbearable heat blew at their faces. A passerby mentioned it was over 101 degrees, which was extraordinarily; he was melting in front of her eyes. He understood better than ever why his parents went to the Adirondacks each year, and he brought their cabin up to Alida. Disappointment came across her face. And he rushed out another sentence.

"You are welcome to come. I didn't ask because we just met and…What about your parents?"

Alida told him she was on her own and staying in a residence for women in town. After he placed Alida's satchel next to his fiddle on the back seat, she snoozled up next to him in his big, fat, 1954 Chrysler Imperial Newport, and they headed for the mountains. The scent of the cool woods and the water poured in the open windows, and for fun he carried her over the threshold in his arms. Had she not been with him, he might have fallen apart. His parents stared at him from his mother's hand embroidered dish towels and the wooden furniture his father had crafted and adorned and every grain of the wood his father had lovingly used to construct it. In relaying the history of the place and its objects, Jackie elevated Frigg and Paul from the status of dead and gone parents to the foundation of his life; he missed them less. The bullfrogs repeated their jug-o'-rum, jug-o'-rum, jug-o'-rum while Jackie and Alida stayed up sharing their thoughts. At some point during the night the stars dusted cooling sparkles throughout the room and they floated into the deep slumber of mythological gods in love.

The mountain songbirds' symphony brought Jackie into the fresh white summer light of a new day with joy in his heart and it burst into a grin when he saw Alida gathering wild flowers in the meadow. Her flimsy frock, which he recognized as one of his mother's, fluttered angelically in the breeze. It snagged on thorns when they went berry picking. Alida felt awful for having taken the dress without asking, but her own was so warm she couldn't bear to put it on again.

"If I move the hem up, those rips will be gone," she said with sincerity scintillating in her eyes.

He lifted her face and explained softly that his mother was "not likely to show up, and even if she was here she would want you to wear it. Besides, it's only a dress. some fabric. Your comfort is worth more than that."

Still, to prevent further damage and walk more easily, Alida created a pair of baggy shorts by pulling the hem through her legs and tying it to the front. He admired her ingenuity.

"Let's count all the animals we see," she suggested in her charmingly ebullient manner.

He didn't want to spoil her fun, so he kept his doubts of the number exceeding two to himself. By noon, they had seen leashes of sleek red foxes and white-tail deer and a waddling brown sow with her two cubs in the lake. The mother bear lumbered toward Alida and Jackie pulled her back.

"It's okay," she whispered.

The animal stretched out at her feet and she rubbed her furry back. Jackie was dumbfounded.

"Everyone likes a massage, right?"

The bear rejoined her young, and within plain sight of them, Jackie and Alida sat eating berries and watching the gulls. They glided and whipped scraps out of the air which were being chucked by a pair of friends. Alida pointed to an unusually large white bird with black markings whose wingspan was triple the gulls. It dove not at the scraps but at the gulls.

"If it wasn't white, I would guess he is an eagle," she said.

The boys tossed more scraps and a gull alighted directly in front of them. They laughed in the boisterous cracked voices of adolescents.

"I used to do that when I was a kid," he said.

No sooner had the words come out of his mouth when he heard a gull squawk in absolute terror because the boy grabbed him by the legs and was swinging him around.

"No! Stop!"

"Hurry Jackie," she urged and then screamed in the high shrill anguished voice of a mother whose child had been taken.

Alida charged down the hill behind him holding her hat. The captor held tightly to the bird's leg with one hand and guarded his face against it's frenetically flapping wings. Down from the sky shot the large white bird that latched his talons onto the boy's hands, and he cried out in pain. The gull escaped, but the giant bird continued its assault. Alida caught up to Jackie.

"Serves him right," she said.

"I don't know. That bird could blind him, maybe kill him."

"Do something!" the boy begged his friend.

Blood was spurting into the air from the bird's pecking and clawing.. His friend yelled at it to no avail, so he swung at it furiously with a big baseball bat-sized piece of driftwood.

"Don't!" Jackie bellowed and started after him again.

The boy swung. His friend and the bird fell. Bloodied, angry and crying the boy lifted the limp bird and smashed it violently against the ground. Then he turned and attacked his friend for not having helped him more quickly.

Jackie carried the bird to where she was screaming, "Barbarians. They are barbarians!"

"Oh my God. How could he do that, Alida?"

He cradled the warm bird in his arms and tears ran through the lines on his wind-parched cheeks. The screech of gulls circled overhead while he felt the fading beat of its heart. The bird opened one eye and squirmed in agony. Jackie placed his hand on the bird's neck to snap it.

"Wait!" Alida said and dropped to her knees beside him, "Please. Give him a chance."

They named him Hero and carried him back to the cabin. Jackie cleared out a wooden trunk and lined it with a blanket for the bird. Alida hovered like a nervous mother over a sick child.

"Gently, gently," she urged him.

Though relatively certain he would be burying Hero shortly, he laid him on the table. Every few minutes during their dinner, Alida peeked in to see if he had regained consciousness. To remove her anxiety and have her attention to himself, Jackie suggested an after dinner dip. The air was still and it bathed them liquid clouds when they waded into the lake. Since the ferry ride, he had stolen innumerable kisses that had failed to incite any visible response. Persistence finally paid off the blue hour's bewitching light. Alida returned a peck with enticing nonchalance. There was a second, a third, a forth and oh the fifth which almost evolved into lovemaking, but Alida broke free and ran to the privacy of the Chrysler. Oblivious to all else, they got under one another and rocked the car so much it began to roll toward the water. Not until a moment after the climactic conclusion did they realized something other than their amorous acrobatics had been moving it, and it was rolling down to the lake. Disentangling their limbs was not as easy as entangling them, but with a good bit of laughter, they managed, and he jammed on the break. She had slipped on her dress and helped him into his shirt with tender affection. Just as he was about to kiss her again, playful spontaneity shot her out of the car. He sprang pantsless after her and enjoyed letting himself flop freely. He lost sight of her.

"Catch me if you can," she called.

Jackie did the sensible thing and put on his pants and shoes before offering his backside to the mosquitoes, and then he secured the car. From the corner of his eye, he saw Alida pop out from behind a tree A chill went down his spine when he heard the soft tintinnabulation of bells he had heard over the years. They sounded as though they were coming from the meadow behind the house. There sat Alida; her large satchel was beside her and she was playing a Celtic harp. He retrieved his fiddle and they filled the night with a magnificent duet.

The heatwave came and went but Alida and Jackie remained at the cabin. In a matter of days, they had bonded completely. Cooking in the kitchen, she took breaks and sat on his lap with an arm slung around his neck and coquettishly offered him a tasty bit of this or that from the table. They finished one another's sentences, and on occasion, shared a simple glance that would send them into sputtering laughter over some secret they shared. Their bodies and their psyches were in touch; this was their way. He was filled with a never before known joy. He envisioned, eating and laughing and living with her on Ocean Avenue in a cozy web spun from the invisible strands of contented love and humdrum monotony for all eternity.

"Jackie," Alida's voice sang utterly elated to see Hero's golden eye peer over the edge of the trunk. "See? He is all right."

The bird's head wobbled weakly on his shoulders and he toppled back over. They placed two small dishes, one of water and one of fish in the corner.

"Aren't animals marvelous?" she asked followed by an unexpected suggestion, words he long-dreaded, "I would love to have a farm full of all sorts of creatures," she gushed.

But the word "farm" didn't bring "the stench of muck" to Jackie's lips but a line of boasts about Uncle Rolf's farm and his good friends the cows, Minvenn and Vippers. When he heard himself talking, he knew he had fallen for her, the girl who wanted to save a bird.

"I want to pick him up," she announced.

She abandoned vanity, placed a thick glass punchbowl on her head, and swaddled her arms in towels in order to risk doing so. He burst out laughing at how charmingly ridiculous she looked.

So this is my love that is more than a love.

He advised against trying to handle the giant bird.

"Everyone is going to be on Ocean Avenue for my house-warming party—maybe—well" he paused sheepishly, "I was wondering if I could tell them it was---our engagement party?"

Hero broke the mini-spell by squawking and winging around the small kitchen. Alida and Jackie ducked when he flew over their heads. She opened the screen door and Jackie waved a towel to guide him toward freedom. Their team effort worked perfectly. Hero winged awkwardly into the open air, circled the house screeching thanks for a few minutes and vanished into his celestial home. Jackie was happy for Hero and happy for Alida. She would have been crushed if he had not recovered, but his chaotic departure prevented Alida from responding to the matter of the engagement party. He was not even certain she had heard him. She bubbled on and on about how they had saved Hero, how much salmon he had eaten and then she sighed the contented sigh of a girl who had experienced communion with nature. He wanted to ask again, but the timing was off, so he just kissed her. On the dark shores of sleep, while they were releasing their spirits to the sandman, she broke the silence.

"An engagement party? Did I hear you right?" she asked as if she had just heard him.

"Yes, I..."

She interrupted him with a long kiss and said, "I love it. I love your idea Jackie."

He jumped out of bed and rummaged around in three dresser drawers while she leaned on her elbow in bewildered amusement.

"Here it is!"

"It's wood," she remarked examining the ring he slipped on her finger.

"Yes. My father made it for my mother in Norway when they were kids, and when he had the money, he bought her..."

"This one is perfect Jackie."

The Adirondacks

✳✳✳

The new skylights in the Vik house on Ocean Avenue aerated the chaos of vivacious merrymaking of their party that rivaled those of their parents in pre-war days. The platoon of children had been assigned a room upstairs with the eldest in charge, though the grown-ups took turns looking in on them. Musicians were warming up and Michaela and Smitty were calling out directions for where to place extra chairs, glasses and newly arrived flowers. All of the guests who had been to Jackie's house prior to the renovations issued compliments and sighs of approval over how well Michaela had transformed it, except for Fana. The color was wrong, the skylights too small and "ridiculous for New York" and the sofa was facing the wrong way; nothing was right.

Larry told her, "Shush Fana, you know you are jaloux."

Smitty rang a bell and got everyone's attention in order to introduce Captain Wheeler whom Jackie had saved the previous week.

"A few of the ships are going to sound their horns around two o'clock for Jackie," he announced.

Eager to hear his account of the spy capture, an excited group gathered around him. After politely declining a half a dozen times, he obliged. A ruckus broke out in the upstairs room and Wes and Seamus ran up together, but it was his son and Smitty's who had gotten into a scrap because one insisted this was a wake and not a housewarming party, that "there was no such thing." Seamus wanted to know where the lad got the idea that it was a wake, and he said, "the body." He explained that it belonged to a man who had had too much to drink.

To which Seamus' son said, "I told you my father looks like that all the time."

"Not all the time," he clarified.

They reengaged the children.

"Why didn't you tell him, it's a coma?"

"They don't know what that is. Besides, did you smell that? Diaper change, probably one of mine. I'll send Shannon up."

In front of the house, Jackie and Alida scanned the area for a parking space. There were cars in every spot on the street; all the driveways were doubled up and so were a couple of the lawns.

"It's possible you are going to meet everyone I know or ever met today. I never realized how many friends I have, how much love. I am a lucky man. Lucky! And they are going to love you," he said and he smooched her cheek.

He knew of a dusty parking space in the rear of the building by the garden, but he continued to look because he didn't think it would make a good impression on her. In the end, he concluded her fondness for nature might actually make the garden spot preferable and pulled into the slim space by the fence. The strains of *For He's a Jolly Good Fellow* poured into the yard, for Bird had announced he and Sally had set a date and they were all, of course, invited.

"That's TOP," he said.

The ground and building vibrated. The windows rattled. Blindly, he reached behind his back for her hand but didn't feel it. He looked over his shoulder and saw Alida had turned into the female apparition he had seen on his thirteenth birthday Flakes of brick were raining down on them from the widening jagged cracks in the ceiling. The ships horns blew. The house was crumbling in front of him.

"Alida!" Jackie shrieked over the sound of his heart pounding in his chest.

He thought he was going to pass out. As if oblivious to what Jackie assumed an earthquake, the party continued and Fana clapped to get everyone's attention.

"He moved," she announced from behind the screen concealing the body lying on a cot in front of the window, and then added, "Encore. Encore," to Theo. assuming the music was awakening him.

Frigg's words came to him, "*The line between reality and fantasy is easily blurred. You might step into a fantasy too quickly. It is another world, you know? It can take your soul.*

A violent rush of air blasted over the house on Ocean Avenue, and through the windows, he saw the women run up the stairs to the children on the landing. He heard Alida call his name, but she sounded far away. The strong wind was coming from the enormous wings he had seen almost his entire life. They belonged to a pure white horse hovering high above the treetops attached to a golden chariot. Alida's hair was all he could see of her.

"Oh no," he said softly. *What's happening?*

Theo's strong, dark fingers attacked the piano, and he executed an exuberant and scintillating cadenza while Fana, Smitty and Charlie observed Jackie's body for signs of consciousness. A boy, no more than four, sat next to Theo on the bench and added to his composition by leaning his elbow on the keys. He gave him childish, little grin of apology and gazed at him with wondering eyes.

"Hello," he said in a strong British accent while Theo was playing.

"Asta, you made it," Smitty declared and threw his arms in the air in welcome. "Who is this?" he asked placing his arm on the boys head.

"Jackie," she answered, her eyes twinkling.

She removed him from the bench.

Theo stopped playing.

"This is Asta and..." Smitty announced, paused and added and her son, "Jackie."

Fana and Nancy exchanged a catty glance, ran their eyes up and down the beautiful Asta.

Alida dropped a rope ladder to Jackie, but he didn't grab it; he stepped back and immediately tore his way through the dense cotton in his brain.

Is this chariot real? Alida? Last week? I saw TOP go into the house. If it's cracking to Hell because of an earthquake, why didn't they run out?

A fog, exactly like the one he had seen when his mother's spirit left, ghosted in the air hindering his ability to see. With some hesitation, he grabbed the lower rung of the ladder, swinging in the wind. He had a firm grip. In front of his eyes, it morphed into Njord, the Norse god of the sea.

"Jackie my son," he exclaimed. "It's time. Come, come home, home to Okeanos where you belong."

Encircled by the guests, Asta's son shook his head of curls and pointed his thumb to his chest.

"I am Jackie. Jackie the Viking," he announced

His cuteness ignited a blaze of laughter throughout the room. Muttering floated from behind the screen, and Nancy and Fana hurried to his body with the little boy in their wake. They could see he had moved his arm, but he was not conscious.

At the top rung, Jackie listened.

"Aww. Mummy, I think the man has a tummy ache," he cooed and stroked Jackie's cheek.

Alida hung on the rope ladder and reached for his hand, and so did the little boy. When they touched him, the sensation of immeasurable joy surged through his veins. The revelers repaired to the outdoors to allow Asta a moment with Jackie.

"Oh mon Dieu!" Fana whispered.

They were all mesmerized by a blanket of heavy Mammantus clouds that rolled across the sky just above the roofs and crouched near the ground. Inside, Jackie's grip on the boy's fingers loosened and fell by his side.

People with Wings Publishers
Proudly Presents
Winchinchala

Author of Paranormal, Historical Fiction brimming with Action, Lust, Culture, Mystery, Myth & Love

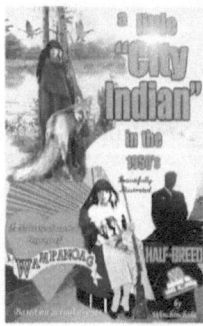

★★★★★ **WINCHINCHALA IS THE COMPLETE NOVELIST OF OUR TIMES.**

"Winchinchala is the complete novelist of our times. Her novel, THE LIFE & LOVES OF MARINER JACKIE VIK is a heart wrenching dreamlike fantasy with love, action and adventure written in dramatic yet simple tones. I highly recommend this book to anyone who likes to read!" S.Tarnowski, Florence, Italy

★★★★★ A LITTLE CITY INDIAN IN THE 1950'S IS SURE TO BE AN EPIDEMIC

"This is the most engaging book I have read in a long, long time.Winchinchala plays hardball with the human psyche, and just when you think you have run the gamut of all possible human emotions, bang zoom, ...and aother kidney punch sends you careening into the next chapter. Get a good HMO and get a copy of A LITTLE CITY INDIAN IN THE 1950'S." David Howland, Linguist, Tokyo, Japan

★★★★★ AN EXTRAORDINARILY INSIGHTFUL & INSPIRING ARTIST.

"Her vast and unique life experience comes through in her vivid, engaging writing with wisdom, humor and thought-provoking vibrancy. Her characters aren't carbon copies of her, but they do tell her own realizations, struggles and successes, give her characters gravity, authenticity. The reader gets genuinely involved in her stories; she writes books that entertain, teach and challenge." Lazlo Gardony, Professor of Piano / Sunnyside recording artist.

The Life & Loves of Mariner Jackie Vik

www.ingramcontent.com/pod-product-compliance
Lightning Source LLC
Chambersburg PA
CBHW020646030726
47498CB00002B/383